DEPARTURE DAY

ALSO BY MIKE BARON

DEPARTURE DAY

BIKER

BOOK 11

MIKE BARON

WOLFPACK
PUBLISHING
— EST 2013 —

Departure Day
Paperback Edition
Copyright © 2025 Mike Baron

Wolfpack Publishing
1707 E. Diana Street
Tampa, FL 33610

www.wolfpackpublishing.com

Paperback ISBN 979-8-89567-781-0
Ebook ISBN 979-8-89567-780-3
LCCN 2025944589

DEPARTURE DAY

CHAPTER ONE
BAKER

ON A COLD TUESDAY IN APRIL, JOSH PRATT PARKED his twelve-year-old Chrysler in Steve Fleiss's lot three blocks off the capitol square. Fleiss's office was on the second floor. Josh clomped up the stairs in boots with wet soles. Fleiss's receptionist Martha looked up.

"You look like you're ready for a dogsled race."

Josh shrugged out of his parka, hung it on a hook and wiped his boots on the hemp mat. "It's brisk."

"Go right in, Josh."

Josh knocked and entered the lawyer's office. Fleiss was on the phone. He held up a finger.

"I don't know what to tell you, Harmon, it would probably be more expensive to sue them than the damages are worth."

In his sixties, Fleiss's once-full head of curly black hair had turned gray and been cut to the texture of a threadbare sweater. A framed picture of a much younger Fleiss with Senator Bill Proxmire occupied his trophy wall along with pictures of Fleiss with Tom Jones, Aaron Rogers, and Al

Reichenberger. His law degrees from Tulane and University of Wisconsin. Certificates of Appreciation from the Red Cross, the Boy Scouts, and Shriner's Children Hospitals.

Fleiss said, "Let me know what you decide."

He hung up. Josh sat facing Fleiss. The window behind him looked out on East Mifflin. It was a cold dreary day. The window shrouded in a fine mist.

"You want coffee?" Fleiss said.

"Sure."

Fleiss went to a sideboard holding a Keurig. He popped in a cartridge. "Got a summons I want you to deliver."

"Okay."

Fleiss paid two-fifty per summons and only called on Josh when the recipient might react badly. He handed Josh his black coffee, sat, and slid a white envelope across the desk. Arthur Baker, 244 Groome Road, Madison.

"Baker launched a crowd funder to finance his movie. Raised two mil. Movie was supposed to be finished in August 2022. Patrons got together for a class action suit."

"What was the movie?"

"*Hunga Munga*. A cut-rate slasher movie."

"Has he ever done a movie?"

"Yes, he directed one called the *The Hodag*. Something about a monster. He's one of those cut-rate horror directors who grinds out shit, and it gets picked up by some streaming service. *The Hodag* was his biggest hit."

"What's it about?"

Fleiss laughed. "Teenagers on a camp-out get picked off by a monster."

Josh pulled out his phone and looked it up. "Two stars." He scrolled.

"'A mercenary-for-hire accepts a mission from a billionaire to capture a dangerous creature that could possibly help cure a terminal illness.' No camp."

"Well, he's more original than I thought."

"What's the last movie you saw?"

"*Oppenheimer*. At home on a streaming service. He's no Christopher Nolan."

"ANYTHING I SHOULD KNOW?"

"Baker's a martial artist, trained with Gene LeBell."

"Really."

"Yeah. You know who that is?"

"The Godfather of Grappling. I have his book."

Fleiss's intercom buzzed. "Your ten o'clock is here."

"Thank you, Martha. Wait 'til Josh leaves."

Josh put the envelope in his jacket pocket. He wore a blue sports jacket over a white shirt and gray Wrangler slacks. He left the office, holding the door for a middle-aged woman cradling a Pomeranian. She smiled sweetly. "Thank you."

Josh shrugged into his parka.

"Is it the monster guy?" Martha said.

"Even a man who is pure at heart," Josh said.

Groome Road was on the far east side of town, just south of the interstate before it turned into farmland. The streets had been plowed. Dirty slush filled the gutters. Snow hills bloomed in every parking lot. People took bets on which pile of snow would last the longest. West Towne held the record because they had the biggest parking lots and better bulldozers. Its last remnants disappeared on June 12th last year. Josh drove by Olbrich Gardens with its Buddhist temple. Ray had mentioned having the wedding reception there. Josh wanted an old-fashioned biker wedding. Ray said her parents would disown her if she agreed.

He turned on the radio. At this hour on a Tuesday, WORT was playing Dizzy Gillespie in an Afro/Cuban groove. "Manteca." Josh knew it from hanging out with Bobby Hines, grandson of jazz great Earl Hines. Bobby was a former member of the Jugan MC. Josh pulled over in a strip mall and consulted his map of Madison. He had a phone. Ray had bought it and programmed it for him. She showed him how to use the navigation app, but he was stubborn. He'd always used maps. He found Groome Road, memorized the landmarks and pulled back into traffic.

Baker lived in a fifties one-story tract house with a one-car garage on a street that hadn't changed in over half a century. A couple houses had TV antennae. Number 244 was a beige wood frame with green trim that needed paint. The driveway had been shoveled. A flagstone path ran from the street to the front door. Josh parked at the curb and got out. He left the down coat in the car. The sun had come out, and the snow was beginning to melt. An old Nissan pickup sat in the driveway. The garage was open. A nineties Harley Fat Boy sat in the garage surrounded by gear. A workbench. One of those multi-drawer red rolling chests. Air pumps, wrenches, woodworking equipment. A patched denim vest hung on the wall. Devil Dogs. Josh had never heard of the Devil Dogs. There were a lot of gangs he didn't know. The fact that his guy was a biker was both encouraging and discouraging.

As he headed toward the house, a dog exploded from inside, leaping up against the living room window. A rottweiler. Josh hoped it was friendly. His parka and jacket were the only articles of clothing he wore that weren't covered with dog hair.

The door opened before he could knock. Baker was six-five, glared at him from an XXXL Badgers hoodie, five-day stubble on his road-grader chin.

"Fuck you want?"

Josh held out the envelope. Baker looked at it.

"Fuck is it?"

"A summons."

"Fuck that."

Baker tried to shut the door, but Josh got his foot in. When Baker burst toward him, Josh ducked, grabbed the rim of Baker's front pocket in his right hand and thrust the envelope in with his left. He stepped back quickly and took a picture. Baker stuck his hand in his pocket and pulled the envelope out. Josh snapped that too. Baker tossed the envelope to the stoop and grinned.

"Now we got a problem."

"Hey, I'm a big Gene LeBell fan."

Baker checked himself. "How do you know about that?"

"The lawyer told me. Steve Fleiss."

"You train?"

"Zhong Yi Kung Fu on East Wash."

"I know where it is. I was thinking of stopping by."

"If you do, tell Nelson I said hi. Nelson Ferreira. He's the sensei."

Baker picked up the envelope and waved it. "Fuck izzis?"

"Your investors. Class action suit. They want to know where the movie is."

Baker seemed to deflate. "Aw shit. Come on in. You want a cup of coffee?"

Josh followed him into the house. The rottweiler followed, sniffing Josh's hand.

"That's Igor. He's a big pussycat."

"I have a dog."

The living room was straight out of the sixties with a shag rug and a cloth sofa. The only modern touch was the big flat-screen on the wall. Framed posters of grade Z horror movies hung on the wall. *The Hodag*, with a hairy beast bared its fangs. *The Beast of Bray Road*, some kind of werewolf. They all said, "An Arthur Baker Production." A framed picture of a much younger Baker in the sand with three other boy soldiers wearing camo and sunglasses, one of them giving Baker rabbit ears. A photo of a much younger Baker with the Devil Dogs wearing their colors in front of a roadhouse. A photo of a much younger Baker in a boxing ring facing an opponent.

"You were Army?"

"Yes sir."

Baker went into the kitchen. "Come on in here and make it yourself."

The refrigerator was olive green. An old microwave on the counter. At least the coffee came from an old-fashioned maker. Josh took half a cup and followed Baker back into the living room.

"Fuck's your name?"

"Josh Pratt."

"Well Josh, I have reasons, but no excuses. I've been going through a lot of shit. My mother's in hospice, and I'm having trouble making the bills. I had everything lined up. Then my lead disappeared. They found him in Milwaukee dead from an overdose. Down by the tracks."

"Jesus. What'd he take?"

"Fentanyl. I don't think he knew it was fentanyl. He'd been a junkie for years. He was perfect for the part, though. Everybody else just drifted away when the money dried up. I spent it on my mom and some other shit. I have no excuse. I'm a miserable human being. I've been thinking of blowing my brains out."

Josh held up a hand. "Whoa. Too much information. Are you religious?"

"Not so's you'd notice."

"I know a pastor that can help."

"Help what? My depression? Is he a psychiatrist?"

Josh waved a hand in dismissal. "Never mind."

Baker slapped the envelope in his hand. "What do I do with this?"

"Get a lawyer."

"I don't got the money."

"Anything you can sell?"

"My dad's comic collection. I don't know if they're worth anything."

"Depends on the title and condition. How far back does it go?"

"He started collecting in the sixties. I wouldn't know where to start."

Josh pulled out a pen and pad and wrote nostomania.com "Start there."

"Thanks, man. How do you know that?"

"I know the guy in charge from the Union Terrace."

"Cool. Sorry I got upset."

Josh stood. "You had a good reason."

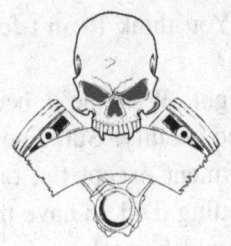

CHAPTER TWO
SURPRISE!

JOSH PHONED RAY FROM THE CAR. "WHAT ARE YOU doing?"

"I'm cleaning my stove. What are you doing?"

"I'm bored and horny. Are you home?"

"Come on by! But you'll have to take me to dinner."

"Deal."

An hour later Josh pulled up in front of Ray's condo on Lake Monona and took the elevator to the third floor. The instant she opened the door, he had a hard-on like a steel girder. That perfume she wore. He picked up her, carried her into the bedroom, and threw her on the bed as she fumbled with his belt and pants.

As they lay side by side in the afterglow, Josh stared at the ceiling, at the combo light and fan he'd installed last summer. Ray snuggled into him.

"You ever think about children?"

A wave of fear rippled through Josh. Commitment. Family. Diapers. He practiced his square breathing. "Well, we are getting married."

"That's right. What's the matter, big boy? Did I scare you?" She pulled away. "You think I can't feel what you're thinking?"

Well, there it is, Josh thought. What he'd been avoiding since childhood. Responsibility. Sure, he'd upped his game in every department except the one that mattered most to God. Begetting. Did he have the income to support a family? Would he make a good father? How would it change him? He saw how it had changed others. Some for the better, some for the worse. Was this not his ultimate responsibility as a man and a Christian? To have children and preserve Western civilization? Yeah, Western civilization. Having kids was no guarantee of love, hope, and progress. Just look at those Muzzies. He'd tangled with them before. They'd killed his friend and client, Polly Furst.

Could he live without Ray? No. He'd already wasted too much time getting to this point. Did that mean they had to immediately procreate? No.

Ray swung her legs out aloofly. She could do that. He grabbed her arm.

"Okay."

"Okay what?"

"Okay, I'll have a kid with you!"

She paused, softened, turned toward him. "Do you mean it?"

"If that's what it takes. But what will Idaho say?"

Ray rolled her eyes. "Idaho!"

Idaho Mongoose had starred in Ray's production of *Drunk Octopus Wants to Fight*, a play about a bitter ex-cop who holds court every night in a bar complaining about life, breaking up the occasional bar fight, and preventing an armed robbery. Idaho Mongoose's real name was Ruby Witterstaeter.

"Awright, now we got that out of the way, let's fight about his name."

Ray raised an eyebrow. "Assume its gender, do you?"

"If it's a boy, we're raising him as a boy. If it's a girl, we're raising her like a girl."

"Agreed."

"Awright, now let's fight about the wedding."

Ray blew a raspberry. "My folks want to rent the Unitarian Meeting House and have an Episcopalian pastor do it."

"I'd like to invite some biker buddies."

"Like who?"

"Well Bobby Hines for starters. He can play the wedding march."

"Bobby's always welcome, but nobody wearing their colors. And no mob of Harleys in the parking lot."

"I'm with you on the colors, but how do you expect them to get to the church?"

Ray pursed her lips and blew air straight up her face so that her bangs fluffed. "Your friends should be there. I'll talk to the folks."

"Do your folks have a pastor in mind?"

"Flo Stanton."

"Would you object if we had a separate ceremony after? At some point? Not on the same day, but one with a Baptist pastor?"

"Joshhhh, you know I'm an atheist."

"I thought you were an agnostic."

"All right, I'm an agnostic."

"Well, you've already agreed to Flo."

"Oh, what the hell."

"So you wouldn't object."

She smiled. "If it makes you happy, I'll do it."

"It will be our secret."

"Where?"

"Bethel Baptist. It's between Madison and Mount Horeb. Pastor John Jacobs. You'll like him."

Ray's phone rang. She picked it up and went into another room. Josh could hear her talking but couldn't make out the words. Until she said, "You did what?" She began talking like a cop, muffled words delivered in a monotone.

She returned and made a growling noise, grimacing.

"What?"

"A pipe burst in the studio. There's three inches of water in the basement."

"Oh no."

"I have to get over there and see what's going on. Fuck. We're supposed to start rehearsals tomorrow for *The Snot-Nosed Punk of Yore*."

"I'm afraid to ask."

"A teenage slacker gets hit in the head with a baseball. When he wakes up, he thinks he's Shakespeare."

"Who wrote it?"

"Manfred Gribble. He's had a couple movies produced. Nothing you'd ever hear of."

"You ever hear of Arthur Baker?"

"Yeah. He's that grade Z monster director. Never met him."

"How do you know about him?"

"I heard him being interviews on WORT. *Isthmus* did a piece on him. I saw *The Hodag*. Mindless drivel.

Worst monster ever. Some guy in a lion suit with this bizarre head."

"You want me to come with you to the studio?"

"No, dear. Dinner will have to wait. Let's shoot for tomorrow."

"Okay."

Josh showered and got dressed. He kissed Ray and left, circling clockwise around Monona. He used to stick to the shore but now there were gangs on Waunona Way. He got on the Beltline and headed west, got off on Whitney, then west on Schroeder, out of town. All the open spaces were gone. When he'd bought his modest ranch-style house on Ptarmigan Road ten years ago it had been the only house on the street. Within a year, housing developers had descended on all sides, buying up property and building McMansions all over the place. They started a homeowners' association, which he didn't join, and threatened legal action over the 2000 Camaro resting on cinderblocks in his front yard.

Lawyer Daniel Bloom, who'd been murdered by a madman named Moon, had told him it was always better to have the cheapest house in a rich neighborhood than the most expensive house in a poor neighborhood.

Words to live by.

Since then, developers had colonized all the open space that once existed between the Four Corners 7-Eleven and Ptarmigan. There was a clear demarcation between the myriad apartment houses that sprang up and the plush-hooded White Oaks, with its pinkie-in-the-air red brick entrance.

By now, his property was worth a million dollars. Phil had made a standing offer. Phil, who'd been standoffish at the presence of biker riffraff, had come around when Josh helped him buy a gun and learn to shoot. They'd gone to a shooting range about twenty miles west, an old quarry on a winding country road. Wisconsin was filled with winding country roads, and they were all paved because the milk had to get to market. Josh could ride those roads all day, and he often had.

He passed the 7-Eleven, and there was a pinch of open land that belonged to the university, which would hopefully remain undeveloped. Josh grunted. Here he was, sneerin' at the rubes.

"Watch it, boy," he told himself.

He approached his house. The Camaro was long gone, and he'd reluctantly fixed his yard. Green grass. He didn't have to water much. Wisconsin was a wet state. Someone sat on his front stoop with a backpack. Some kid. Josh stopped in the driveway and got out. Fig started barking. She must have barked when the kid came, but if he'd been there long enough, she'd have gone back to sleep.

He walked up. Lanky kid, hair a little long but not freakish, wearing an old gym hoodie with the hood down revealing a smooth face. There was something familiar about him.

The kid stood. "Are you Josh Pratt?"

"Yes. Who are you?"

"I'm your son."

CHAPTER THREE
BURGER

JOSH LOOKED HIM OVER. "YOU LOOK HUNGRY. COME on in and tell me what this is about."

He unlocked the door. Fig was on him for a second before turning her attention to the newcomer. The boy crouched, ruffled her fur and let her lick him on the chin. It was love at first sight.

"Set your backpack there. You want to use the bathroom?"

"Yes please."

Josh pointed to the hall.

The kid was in there a long time. Josh heard the toilet flush, sounds of washing. He came out looking better.

"What's your name?"

"Dolan."

"What makes you think you're my son?"

"My mother told me before she died."

"Who was your mother?"

"Fiona Frawley."

Fiona. Fiona. The name bounced around Josh's

brain like a pinball. And there she was. A beautiful twenty-something he'd met at a bar in Milwaukee, back when he was a Bedouin. He was ashamed to admit that he couldn't remember the names of all the women with whom he'd slept, but he remembered her and was disgusted at the way he'd treated her.

"What happened?"

"She's dead. She died from an overdose of oxycontin and vodka."

Josh was sick to his stomach. "How old are you?"

"Seventeen."

"You hungry?"

"Yeah."

Josh went into the kitchen. Fig followed, tail wagging. Dolan followed Fig.

"I could fry up some burgers."

"That would be great. Do you have anything to drink?"

Josh opened the fridge. "Orange juice, ginger ale, apple juice."

"Ginger ale, please."

Josh tossed him a can.

"What's the dog's name?"

"Fig."

"That's a funny name for a dog."

"I named her after a girlfriend I had."

Silence yawned.

"Have you had a lot of girlfriends?"

Josh's stomach churned. "How'd you find me?"

"My mom said you were a biker, but she lost touch with you years ago."

"She never told me she was pregnant."

"She said she was afraid to. She knew what you'd say."

Josh's jaw clamped while he beat the burgers into shape.

"What did she think I would say?"

"You'd tell her to get an abortion."

Josh laid the burgers on a cutting board, pulled out a chair and sat at the linoleum kitchen table. "I'm not the same person that I was. I made a lot of mistakes in my life. I went to prison. I met a pastor named Mike Dorgan, and he brought me around to Jesus."

Dolan sat back, unreadable. He took a swig of ginger ale. "So, you're Christian now?"

"I try to be. I ain't gonna preach. You still haven't told me how you found me."

"I know a little bit about computers. You weren't that hard to find."

Damn. He'd paid Ninja thousands of dollars to wipe his name from the internet. But the internet was a living organism, especially now with artificial intelligence, and it kept creeping back.

"So you got my address off the internet?"

"Well no. I learned you lived in Madison from news stories. One of them mentioned that you worked for a lawyer named Fleiss, even though you didn't really need the money. Fleiss had your address in his business account."

"You cracked Steve Fleiss's computer?"

"Well, yeah."

"Where'd you get the computer?"

"Public library."

"Jesus."

Josh scratched his head. How was he going to explain this to Ray? More importantly, what was he going to do about it? He had no choice. Not if he were a good man. He never claimed to be a good man, but he tried to do the right thing. On the other hand, what if the kid were lying.

A wave of shame washed over him. Who would go to all this trouble if he weren't really Josh's son? Of course they would do a DNA test. Of course it would verify what Dolan said. From the moment he claimed he was Josh's son, he knew it was true. He'd been dreading a moment like this all his life. In recent years the dread had receded, consigned to a locked room where he kept his worst memories.

Josh saw himself in Dolan's face.

Josh grilled the burgers in a cast-iron pan, cut up some sourdough bread, put ketchup and pickles on the table. He put a burger on the bread. It was big. He set it in front of Dolan. Dolan added ketchup and pickles. By the time Josh sat down, Dolan had wolfed down most of the burger. He set it down. He wiped his hands.

Fig sat at Dolan's feet thumping her tail against the cabinet. Thump thump thump.

"Can I give her a piece of my hamburger?"

"Up to you. She's spoiled rotten."

Dolan tore off a chunk and handed it to the dog who took it delicately in her jaws.

"Sorry I don't have a side dish."

"This is fine, thanks. This is the best burger I've ever had."

"I got a guest bedroom , or you can sleep in the basement if you're more comfortable. Two bathrooms up here, half bath downstairs. You want to take a shower?"

"Yes please."

"Use the one down the hall."

Josh washed the dishes in the sink and put them in

the rack. He had a dishwasher he rarely used. It was easier to just wash them by hand. The dishwasher offended him. It used too much energy for too small a task. He heard the shower running in the guest bathroom.

Josh went through his closet, found some jeans and shirts he wasn't using, threw them in the guest bedroom. Dolan came out wearing his dirty rags. Josh pointed to the guest bedroom. "Put some clothes in there for you."

Dolan went in and changed.

"There's a TV in there. I got Netflix, Freevee, and Tubi."

"I'm bushed. I think I'll crash, if you don't mind."

"Knock yourself out."

Dolan went into the bedroom and shut the door. Josh went in his office, a third bedroom he'd converted, sat at his computer and brought up his email. Emails from his old Bedouin buddies. Hank from Denver:

"Brother, can you spot me a couple Cs? They're about to boot me out of my cheap ass apartment. It aint' much, but it's all I got."

Josh wrote back: "You have PayPal?"

Scam after scam stating that his order had gone through, 851.90 here, 2745.00 there, for services he'd never ordered. He could tell by the return addresses. Bullshit addresses. Young ladies in his neighborhood were dying to meet him. He was just treading water. He got up, stretched, went into his bedroom, brushed his teeth and got into bed. Where was Fig? The door was open several inches, no Fig. He knew where she was.

CHAPTER FOUR
SHAME AND PRIDE

JOSH GOT UP IN THE MIDDLE OF THE NIGHT AND WENT to the bathroom. He returned to bed. No Fig. He got up, carefully opened the door to the guest bedroom, and there she was sleeping next to Dolan on the bed. She looked up and happily wagged her tail. Dolan never woke.

Josh left the door open a crack in case Fig had to use the doggie door. He went back to sleep, waking at six, then padded into the kitchen, ground some beans and made coffee. He sat in the kitchen reading *The Story of Jazz* by Marshall Stearns.

"Edumacate yourself," Bobby told him. His grandfather Earl Hines was in the book, which began with a deep dive into voodoo. Josh wanted to ride down the river and visit New Orleans. He'd been putting it off. Come spring, he'd do it. He'd find someone to go with him. Bobby would do it.

Fig rushed in and sat, tail wagging. She wanted breakfast. Josh poured a cup of kibble in her bowl, added hot water and set it on a plastic stool. She wolfed it down and sat, tail wagging. She did it after every meal, and it never worked.

Josh pointed a finger. "You will get treats."

A toilet flushed. Josh made pancakes and bacon. Dolan came in wearing clean clothes.

"You want breakfast."

"Yes, thank you."

Josh set down a stack of pancakes and bacon. Dolan smeared it with butter and syrup and wolfed it down.

"When's the last time you ate? Before last night?"

"I don't remember."

"How'd you get here?"

"I took the bus. Then I took a bus to that park on the west side and walked."

"Where'd you walk from?"

"That big park. Bunch of bangers hanging around."

"Elver Park?"

"I forget."

"That's ten miles."

Dolan shrugged. "Whatever."

"You're welcome to stay as long as you want."

"Thank you, sir."

"Where'd you learn to be so polite?"

Shrug. "Watching Sherlock Holmes."

"Seriously?"

"Good day, sir. I said, GOOD DAY."

Josh laughed. "What Sherlock Holmes?"

"An old BBC series. Jeremy Brett. I just thought it was cool."

"Got any plans?"

"I need to get a job."

Josh grunted, pleased. He felt pretty lucky. When he was seventeen, he didn't know shit. He lived in a foster home, unwanted, unloved. The couple who took him in did it for the money. They had two kids of their own whom they loved and spoiled. Josh slept on a cot in the basement. He inherited every household chore from washing the dishes to mowing the lawn.

When their son Aaron, two years his senior, an inch taller and twenty pounds heavier, started pushing him around, tripping him, and giving him noogies, he fought back. He threw Aaron to the ground and kicked him in the nuts.

On to the next foster home.

When he turned eighteen, he was out on his ass. He spent two weeks living on the streets in Milwaukee until one day he heard a roar. That highway sound. Twelve choppers rolled down Pax Street, backing up to the curb in front of Frank's Tavern. Josh stared at the bikes for a half hour before a biker came out to light a cig. Cupped his hands, scratched a match and puffed. Josh did his best to appear nonchalant. The man came over. His colors said Bedouins, Milwaukee. Mean Pete, Sergeant at Arms. He looked Josh up and down.

"You like?"

"Yeah," Josh said, looking him in the eyes.

"How old are you?"

"Eighteen."

"Come inside, I'll buy you a beer."

The Bedouins were the family he never had. His father had abandoned him at a truck stop when he was fifteen.

"Can you ride a bike?" Josh asked Dolan.

"If I had one."

"I mean a bicycle."

"I can ride."

"Okay, I got a bike for you. I'll look around. See if I can find you a job. You good with computers, huh?"

"I built my own computer when I was fifteen. I had a part-time job at Pete's Pizza. I delivered pizzas by bike. That's how I bought the parts. If this were the eighteenth century, I'd be married with four kids working a plot of land."

"There's a UbreakIfix at West Towne. They always need help. We'll drive over. They open at nine."

"Sounds good."

"I'm getting married. I'll introduce you to Ray this week."

"Seriously?"

"Yeah." Josh saw the thought hang in the air.

"Why didn't you marry my mother?"

Shame, sorrow, regret.

"Didn't you love her?"

"I was incapable of love. It took me a long time to grow up. I couldn't even say the word love until I was in my thirties."

"Why not?"

"My father abandoned me when I was fifteen."

"Jesus."

"Don't feel sorry for me, and I won't feel sorry for you. You want to check out that computer shop?"

"Let me do the dishes first."

Josh nodded, filled with shame and pride.

CHAPTER FIVE
UNFINISHED BUSINESS

THEY DROVE TO WEST TOWNE, MADISON'S LARGEST shopping center, anchored by a Sears at one end and a Target at the other. Sunglass booths, electronics, game shops, athletic wear, Nikes, Skechers, bicycles, a juice stand, a smoothie store, Dave and Buster's, Victoria's Secret, Barnes & Noble, Hallmark, Nordstrom. Westfield's Comics faced the west and had an outside entrance.

It was much warmer than yesterday, and they passed a half dozen bikers going every which way. It happened every spring. The bikers couldn't wait to hit the road, even if it was just to the corner grocery store.

They went inside. At this hour, there were no teen hooligans, just regular shoppers and old people getting their paces in. UbreakIfix was just off the food court. Popper's Tea, China Experience, Sarku Japan, Fancy Roll Plus, Gyros Express. At this hour, the many tables were mostly deserted. They walked through the food court smelling the sushi, chicken, and coffee. Inside UbreakIfix, John Murphy was dealing with a customer while another waited. The man at the counter was old and querulous. He wore rumpled gray trousers and a down-filled jacket.

"I hate doing anything online. I'm not alone. Ask anyone my age! You hit the wrong button and all of a sudden, you're dealing with the Chinese or someone trying to sell you a miracle device that will fix everything. Or cryptocurrency! I don't even know what it is!"

"I hear you, sir. We'll get this straightened out as soon as possible."

"Then there are the utilities. Every month. Enroll in auto pay! No late fees, no worries. With auto pay, payments post to your Xcel account on the due date! Investment company, same thing. Only it's not just the investment company. It's thirty-six different mutual funds. They all want me to go paperless. For my convenience! I can barely remember what I had for breakfast! I'd write checks out of force of habit. And then one day the bank tells me I'm overdrawn!"

"I hear ya. I hear ya."

"Then my granddaughter says I need an X account. So she signs me up. I forget about it. So, she comes over to the house Sunday night with her folks for dinner, a nice lasagna I cooked myself, and she says, 'Grandpa, are you using your X account?' And I say, 'No, dear. I forgot all about it.'"

"'Well, you ought to at least look! You've got to stay active. You could reach lots of people that way.'"

Murphy had a resigned expression.

"So she logs on to my page and hands it to me. 'See, Grampa? You've got lots of messages!' And I start scrolling down. And I see all these super buff queers, buck naked, waving their dicks around! So, I scroll down past that! Same thing! Dick after dick! Like flagpoles!"

"Mr. Bludhorn..."

The geezer looked around, saw the woman behind him, as well Josh and Dolan. "Awww, don't mind me. I'm just an old fart. I forgot to take my Prevagen."

"I understand."

"And it's not just Prevagen! It's fourteen other multi-vitamins and supplements. Without 'em I'd be talking in tongues! And drooling!"

"Mr. Bluhdorn, I'll call you as soon as we get it fixed." Just a hint of impatience. Once again, the old man looked around. He started.

"Sorry, sorry," he mumbled. Murphy winked at Josh.

Murphy gave the man a ticket. "We'll let you know as soon as it's ready."

Bludhorn turned to a middle-aged woman carrying a laptop. "I'm just an old fart with too much time on his hands."

He walked out. Josh mimed wiping his brow and throwing the sweat aside. Murphy turned to the woman.

"What can I do for you?"

"It's just so slow. It takes forever to download anything."

"Pretty sure it's a malware problem. Shouldn't take long to fix it. May be done tomorrow."

She thanked him, took her ticket and left. Murphy placed his hands on the counter.

"What's up?"

"You looking for a tech whiz?"

"I'm always looking. You know that. Who's this?"

"This is Dolan. He's looking for a job."

"How old are you, Dolan?"

"Seventeen."

"I can vouch for that."

"Can you fix phones?"

"I think so. I've fixed my friends' phones. Even one a friend dropped in a fountain. And I built my own computer out of parts I ordered online when I was fifteen."

Murphy handed Dolan Bludhorn's phone. "Go on in back. Feel free to grab a drink from the fridge. The situation is a bit messy. He claims he never signed up for Uber or even downloaded the app, but now they keep calling him several times a day. He doesn't know much about internet, and he stopped receiving his emails three days ago."

"Yes, sir."

Dolan went to the back.

"Where'd you find him?"

"He turned up on my doorstep."

"Huh?"

"He's my son."

Murphy grinned, not knowing what to say. "I didn't know you had a son."

"Neither did I."

"Is he telling the truth?"

"What do you think, Murph? Does he look like me?"

"He kinda does."

"Now I have to explain to my fiancée that he'll be living with me for a while."

"Ouch."

"Yeah, well I stayed over at her place a couple times while Mongoose slept on the sofa."

"Mongoose?"

"Idaho Mongoose. Don't make me explain. Hey, I gotta talk to him, and then I'm outta your hair."

"Long as you don't start rambling."

Josh stepped into the work area where Dolan sat at a long wooden counter covered with hardware, hard drives, thumb drives, keyboards, screens. Two curving screens sat at an angle as numbers marched left to right, and an inset video in the corner of the right screen showed a man in front of a stock exchange.

"You good?"

"I'm good."

"Okay. You call me when you want to come home."

"You don't have to go to all this trouble. I coulda ridden the bike."

"Yeah. I'll show you that bike later. If this works out, you can ride the bike, weather permitting."

"Say listen. I gotta go back to Milwaukee one of these days and clear some things out of the apartment."

"Did you notify the landlord?"

"The landlord's not going anywhere near that place."

"Why not?"

"You ever hear of Tren de Aragua?"

"Venezuelan gang. Are they in the apartment?"

"That's one of the reasons I left. My mother, she got the oxy from them. The only reason they left me alone was because my mother was a customer."

"Do the police know?"

"I had to tell 'em just so I could get Mom to an undertaker, which I can barely afford. I got a bunch of stuff back there I hate to leave behind."

"You don't think they already broke in and took everything?"

"It's not something they'd want. Baseball glove, some cards. They probably took the bat."

"Okay. I'll go with you."

"You don't have to do that."

"Sure I do." Josh pulled out his phone. "Smile."

Dolan smiled. Josh took a picture. "Call me when you're done."

CHAPTER SIX
THE HOITY TOITY

JOHN MURPHY PHONED JOSH AT FOUR. "HE'S HIRED."

"Really?"

"Yes. He's got the knack, and he's got the attitude. I'll give him a ride home."

"John, you don't have to do that."

"Forget about it. You have no idea what a relief it is to me to find a responsible young man who knows what he's doing."

"He may turn into a werewolf."

"I'll take that chance."

Josh phoned Ray. "Whatcha doing?"

"We have the flooding under control. I can get out of here if you like."

"I'm on the way."

A fist clenched Josh's heart as he drove to the east side. He had no idea how Ray would take the news, but it was his policy to tell people things they needed to hear as soon as possible. Josh parked in front of Ray's theater on Wilson Street at five p.m. Inside, volunteers were mopping up the last of the damage and prepping the stage, a foot above the floor. A man in carpenter coveralls was fastening home plate to green astroturf. Ray sat in the first row with a phone to her ear. She said something, pulled the phone away and said, "Joe! Joe! Move the plate back a foot."

"There won't be any room for the catcher!"

Ray stood and looked right. "Benny, how about you and Lamar trade roles."

Benny blinked. He weighed three hundred pounds. Lamar, sitting next to him with a script in his lap, weighed one twenty.

"What about my line? I've been working on it all week."

"I'll give you a new line."

"What's the line?"

"Oh shit!"

"That's the line? 'Oh shit?'"

Ray pursed her lips. "How about, 'The dog barks but the caravan moves on?'"

"All right."

She saw Josh standing at the back and held up a finger. She stepped onstage and repositioned home plate to her taste. She clapped her hands. "Where's Mongoose?"

"Here I am," said the diminutive thespian brushing by Josh.

"Okay. You're in charge. I'll see you all tomorrow." She slapped palms with Mongoose as they passed, went to Josh, and put her arms around him.

"Where we going?"

"How about the Hoity Toity?"

"That's all the way in Middleton!"

"What else you got to do?"

"You sold me, you silver-tongued devil. Then your place?"

"I thought we'd go to your place."

A frown creased her forehead. "Why would you want to drive thirty miles? What's wrong with your place?"

"I got someone staying there."

"Who?"

"I'll tell you at dinner."

"Uh oh."

"It's nothing bad."

"You're being awful mysterious."

"I'm a man of mystery."

They drove to the Hoity Toity, a long, low, brick and wood prairie-style restaurant near the UW golf course.

"How's it going?" Josh said.

"We're on schedule, and we've sold three hundred tickets."

"Who's playing the snot-nosed punk?"

"Three guesses."

"Mongoose!"

"Right the first time."

"You ever think about casting a boy for boy parts?"

"This is Madison, love. Not dinner theater in Fond du Lac. The people love her. She won a Jerry for *Drunk Octopus Wants to Fight*."

"Well, I gotta admit, it was highly entertaining. Did you write this new one too?"

"Guilty."

A young man with a swoop of glistening black hair greeted them inside the door, tats creeping out from the sleeves of his white shirt. "Two for dinner?"

"Yes, please," Josh said.

The host led them into the dining room, booths upholstered in dark brown leather. They slid in opposite one another. The host handed them the menus. "Grace will be your waitperson. She'll be with you in a second and tell you about our specials."

The host departed. Josh looked at the laminated menu.

"All right," Ray said. "Who's staying at your house."

The waitress approached. Pretty girl in a Hoity Toity shirt, tatted arms, pierced nose. "Hi! I'm Grace. Can I get you a drink?"

"I'd like a shot of Buffalo Trace and a Mutiny IPA."

"I'll have a vodka tonic."

Grace smiled. "Excellent."

Ray gave him the gimlet eye. "Talk."

"Got home yesterday, and there was a seventeen-year-old kid waiting on my stoop with a backpack. Said he's my son."

"What?"

"Named his mother. I remembered her. It was a long time ago. I had no idea she was pregnant. She never contacted me."

"Your son?"

Josh pulled out his phone and showed Ray the picture. "You tell me."

She took the phone from him, looked from the screen to Josh and back again. "I don't believe this."

"I do. That's who's back at my place."

Ray shut her eyes and took a deep breath. When she opened them, she smiled. "Okay. I believe it. What are you going to do?"

"I already got him a job. He's a good kid. He's

fixing phones at UbreakIfix. He took the bus from Milwaukee."

"Where's the mother?"

"She died last week from an overdose of oxycontin and vodka."

"Jesus. How did he find out about you?"

"His mother told him. He went online and found enough shit about me to give him an idea who I was. I don't know how he got my address. Maybe from an article in the Cap Times from years ago when that biker game came to my door."

"Oh my god. Why did they come to your door?"

"They had a beef. The cops came and straightened them out."

"What kind of beef?"

"I was a bouncer at a bar. They kept leaning on a client. I don't think they're around anymore. The Insane Assholes."

"I don't doubt it."

"That was their name. Insane Assholes MC."

"Honestly, Josh. You're too much. You're making this up."

"Babe, you know I'm far too literal to make this shit up."

"That's true."

Grace returned with their drinks. "May I tell you about our specials?"

"Sure."

"We have chili-Sichuan basted bass served on a bed of Honeycrisp apples, spiced almonds and Marcona butter. High-plains buffalo prime rib served on a bed of ancient grains with ugli fruit jam."

"Give us a moment," Josh said.

"Certainly."

She left.

"Let's go to your place."

"Tonight?"

"Why not? I'm going to meet him sooner or later. Let's just do it and get it over with. It's not going to freak him out, is it? Does he know you're going to get married?"

"I told him."

"Well let's just get it over with. From what you say, he sounds remarkably mature."

Josh took a deep breath. "You have a point."

"He can't expect you to change your life just because he showed up."

"Well, I am taking him in. He's my son."

"That's fine. You can introduce him to his future stepmom."

Josh breathed an immense sigh of relief. "I was hoping you'd say that."

"Why not phone him and let him know we're coming?"

"I don't know if he even has a phone."

Grace returned. Josh ordered the buffalo ribs. Ray ordered tuna.

"Perfect," Grace said. "Would you like refills?"

Josh looked at his glass. Empty. So was Ray's.

"Yes please."

CHAPTER SEVEN
CORNERED

THE EIGHT-STORY RED BRICK APARTMENT BUILDING AT 1128 W. Donna Drive on Milwaukee's upper west side had been built in 1958. Each floor held eight apartments, four on a side. The apartments on the west side looked out on a trash-filled vacant lot. A developer had bought the lot a quarter century ago when the neighborhood had hopes. Those hopes were gone. The neighborhood was dangerous. The old people who lived there were afraid to go out at night. They were afraid to go out during the day too. Back in the nineties, gangs infiltrated the neighborhood. The West Side Bluds. The Murder Crows.

Those days seemed innocent in retrospect.

Alfred Longchamps was a Gulf veteran. He had lived at 1128 W. Donna Drive for eighteen years. Fifth floor. He supplemented his Social Security by contributing articles to Jazz Online. On weekends, he played trumpet with the Irv Doncaster Quartet at Bishop's Café. Alfred had learned long ago he could get free records if he wrote about them, and he loved the music. He'd seen many of the greats. Miles Davis. Chick Corea. Herbie Hancock. He'd played with Jon Batiste and Eddie Barbash.

For the past three weeks, he'd been afraid to leave his apartment in the evening because a Venezuelan gang had moved in, occupying four abandoned apartments. The previous tenants fled in fear for their lives. The gang used the apartments to sell drugs, as shooting galleries, and for prostitution. They forced girls, mostly Latina, to work for them, rewarding them with drugs. Fentanyl-laced marijuana. Fentanyl-laced heroin. Fentanyl-laced cocaine.

The Frawleys had lived in the apartment across the hall. Dalton was unusually responsible and respectful for a boy his age, probably because he had to take care of his junkie mom. He could easily have slipped into the thug life. Thugs called to him on the street. They offered drugs and women. How Dolan had steered through that pack was a miracle. He kept his head down, never got angry, spoke when spoken to, offered no opening for them to attack.

A week ago, Alfred had been listening to Mingus on his headphones when someone pounded on his door. Dreading an encounter, he peeked through the eyehole and saw Dolan. He opened the door.

"Come in, Dolan. What's up?"

"Fiona's dead. She OD'd."

"Oh no."

"Yeah."

"You want to call the police?"

"What can they do? They don't come around here anymore. You called 'em, remember?"

"I did indeed." Alfred had called them several times when Tren de Aragua first moved in. They said they'd investigate. They never did. Gang members, some in their teens, roamed the halls with clubs and hatchets evicting those able to move. The only reason they hadn't booted him and Dolan was they'd both installed massive bars on their doors with iron stays, and they were on the fifth floor, the least desirable. The gang wanted the top floor for privacy and the view. They wanted the bottom floor for shooting up and prostitution. Alfred had no idea how many gang members lived there. At least a dozen. Their leader was a pale, slim young man, body covered with ink, shaved skull, and crazy eyes. Black skull tattoo staring from above his brow.

Dolan slumped on the sofa. Alfred gave him a Diet Coke. "I'm splitting."

"Where will you go?"

"Madison. My father lives there."

"Wait. What? What father?"

Dolan laughed. "Everybody has a father, Alfred. Even you."

Alfred laughed.

"My mother only told me last year. He doesn't know I'm alive. It was a one-night stand, but she followed his career. She told me she never contacted him out of pride. And disdain. He wasn't a very nice guy. So, I looked him up. He went to prison. It was over twenty years ago. He got out three years later. The governor pardoned him. I have no idea how he worked that. He became a private investigator. Normally a convicted felon can't get a license, but he can with a pardon. And since then, he's been on some kind of crusade to help people. There was a piece in the *Cap Times* how he stopped some jihadists from killing a bunch of people at a comic convention. He was helping some girl who put out a Muhammad comic. She wasn't too bright. They got her anyway. He spoke at her funeral. He's a Jesus freak now."

"Wow."

"I know, right? Who'da thunk it?"

"How you gonna get there?"

"Bus. Listen. These assholes are gonna take over our apartment as soon as they realize I'm gone."

"Shit."

"I know. I'm sorry, Alfred. If there's anything I can do to help, I will. I wish I had some money to help you get set up in a different place."

"I got some savings. I'll look around."

"Can I store some stuff with you? I don't want them to get it. They'll probably sell it."

"Of course. I got a whole room with nothing in it but records."

Dolan needed three trips to carry the cardboard boxes. He set them on the floor in the record room. "Those and those are my stuff. Mostly clothes, some books. The other two are Fiona's stuff. Mostly jewelry and a couple of hats she loved. I'll come get 'em if things work out with my dad."

"Leave them as long as you want."

"Thanks, Alfred. I'm gonna miss you."

"I'm gonna miss you too, kid."

They looked at one another. They embraced.

That was three days ago. Last night the gang smashed in the door to Dolan's apartment. Then they pounded on Alfred's door.

"Heyyyyyy…old man! We give you five days to get out of here! You leave now, no trouble. You stay, you got trouble." BAM BAM BAM. "You hear us? We know you're in there."

Alfred put on his studio headphones muting the sound. He went into the record room, shut the door, put on *Kind of Blue*, and plugged in the phones. He could still hear the thumping through his headphones. After a while it went away. Cautiously, he took off the phones. He went into the living room to check the damage. Cracks extended from around the door frame, but the bar had held. The gang had turned its attention elsewhere. It was only a matter of time before they returned.

Alfred did an inventory of his kitchen. He had enough food to last a week, but what happened if they cut off the water? Or the power? That would require them to have such knowledge, but even those morons could use a computer. If they spoke English and could read English. Obviously, some of them spoke English. At least enough to threaten the residents. Alfred had no idea how many original residents remained. Looking out his window he could see the thugs parading up and down the street, intimidating the dwindling citizens. He never thought he'd wish for the day when local gangs like the Murder Crows would return. He'd learned on the news that Black gangs in Chicago had gone to war with the Venezuelans, and many honest citizens were supporting them.

Fuck that shit. Alfred was a veteran. He didn't mince words. Why wouldn't the press call them what they were? Why all these euphemisms all the time? "Newcomers." "Dreamers." It made him want to throw up.

He had to do something. He couldn't stay locked up forever. He still had the Beretta M9 he'd been issued. He wished he still had his M16. But who would have imagined he'd ever need it again? At home? In Milwaukee? Alfred had an image of him going down in a blaze of glory, picking off a handful of Venezuelans before they wiped him out with superior firepower. *They* had M16s. Or at least AR-15s.

Who could he call? Not the police. They'd show up after the bloodbath. He knew a couple other vets from the local VFW. It was worth a call. He pulled out his phone. Wayne Garretson had served in Afghanistan. He and Wayne got along just fine. He called Wayne.

CHAPTER EIGHT
DOMESTIC BLISS

JOSH TURNED INTO HIS DRIVEWAY AT SEVEN THIRTY. TV light shone through the curtains in the living room. Fig sounded the alarm. Josh pulled into his garage, and they entered through the kitchen. Fig was at the door thumping and jumping.

"Are you waiting for a treat?" Josh said.

Fig immediately sat, on her best behavior. Josh opened a cupboard, pulled out a dental chew shaped like a bone and handed it to her. Tail wagging, she went into the living room and slithered under the table to chew undisturbed. Ray took Josh's arm as he went into the living room where Dolan slouched on the sofa, feet up on an ottoman watching a Chop Socky episode. He sprang to his feet.

"Oh, hi!"

"Dolan, this is my fiancée Ray."

She stepped up and gave him a hug. "Welcome to the family, Dolan."

Dolan was speechless. Because of Ray's beauty.

"Stick around. The revelations have just begun.

Ray and I have been together for four years. Ray's a theater director and dance instructor."

Dolan turned off the television. Ray looked from boy to man.

"Yup. He's your kid, all right. Josh tells me you have a job already."

"I hope so. Mr. Murphy liked what I did and told me to come back in the morning. I hope you don't mind. I checked out your system downstairs and got rid of a shitload of malware. Excuse me!"

"Don't worry about it. I'm no stranger to vulgarity. In fact, most of my productions are filled with shit fuck piss cunt cock crap. That's the way you do it. Lay 'em all out at once. Shit fuck piss cunt cock crap! Say it with me."

Josh and Dolan joined her. "Shit fuck piss cunt cock crap!"

"Okay. Now that that's out of the way, you and I will have time to get to know each other in the days to come. I'm going to go take a shower."

Ray went down the hall to Josh's bedroom.

"Say, bud," Josh said. "Maybe you ought to sleep in the basement tonight."

"I can do that. Hey, do you have a phone I can borrow?"

"You don't have a phone?"

"I know. How is it possible? I had a phone, but I had to give it up."

"What do you mean?"

"On my way out the door, two gangbangers confronted me, threatened me with a knife, took my phone and my wallet. They took the money and tossed it on the ground. At least I still got my wallet."

"Ouch. Okay. I got a phone for ya. Come on down."

Josh led the way into the basement where his computer sat on a long folding table, two curved screens angled at the single chair. There was a cot set up next to the wall with a pile of blankets. Josh crouched and entered the code to the big gun safe. He pulled it open. Dolan stared at the pistols on the shelves and the shotgun. Josh pulled out a drawer filled with boxes of ammo and four burner phones Ninja had left them. He handed one of the phones to Dolan.

"It's a burner. You have to activate it and then find the number. You know how to do that?"

"Yeah, I think so."

Josh closed the safe.

"What are you doing with all those guns?"

"Nothing. I'm not allowed to own guns. Keeping them for a friend."

"What friend?"

Josh stood. "A very good friend. Don't worry about the guns."

"I don't."

"You shoot?"

"No, I've never held a gun."

"Maybe I can get my friend to take you shooting. You okay down here? Need anything? That flat-screen on the wall gets all the streaming services. There's a fridge in the corner, but don't hesitate to use the kitchen. You okay down here?"

"Yeah. I'm good. Were those grenades?"

"They're fake grenades a friend got me. He's an FX guy in the movies."

"What do you do with them?"

"I don't know yet. But who's gonna turn down fake grenades?"

"I never dreamed I'd have someone like you in my life."

Josh grabbed Dolan and hugged him, then turned away embarrassed and went upstairs. Ray was waiting for him in the bedroom wearing a filmy blue negligee and an insidious perfume. Josh reverted to animal instincts as he tore off his clothes and made love to her. She'd told him when they first met that she had no intention of having children and wore an IUD. Their trust had grown strong. Brief glimpses of a maternal instinct emerged. With her cat Sid Vicious. With Fig. She loved them both and wasn't shy about showing it. Sid Vicious had stopped pissing on Josh's clothes when he visited and had even spent the night at his house when Ray couldn't get a cat sitter.

Ray sounded like a cat as they made love, growling, writhing, reaching around to grab his balls. It was an unspeakable pleasure, and sometimes he found himself thinking about it when he had nothing better to do. Just being a guy.

Ray lay on his chest, her hand rubbing his stubble.

"Want me to shave?"

"No. I like having a rough, tough biker guy."

"Much as it stymies your friends and family."

"My parents want us to come over for dinner next weekend."

Josh said a silent fuck. Not that he didn't like her parents. They were nice people. But they were college-educated Democrats and had little in common with him. Except for music. They loved jazz, and Josh had taken them to see Bobby Hines play piano at the Edgewater. Bobby's grandfather was Earl Hines, the great jazz pianist. Bobby was no slouch. Josh met him when a gang of random thugs drove Josh off the road and were about to attack him with baseball bats. They had nothing better to do. Bobby had been riding by on his Harley. He stopped, pulled to the side of the road and joined Josh. Just standing there silently. Bobby was six-four and weighed 280. None of it was fat. He'd been a member of the Jugan MC, which is how Josh met them in the first place.

Now most of the Jugan were on the run or doing federal stints for gun running. Only Bobby had escaped the prosecutor's wrath due to Steve Fleiss and Josh's testimony.

Ray gripped his chin. "Well? Speak! Is that all right with you?"

"Of course it is."

"It's like trying to drag a child to the dentist."

"I like your folks. As long as they don't bring up politics."

"They won't. We had a come-to-Jesus talk."

Josh laughed. "I'll bet they loved that."

"Jesus was never mentioned."

"He will be if Pastor John marries us."

"We're having two weddings."

"One for the bikers and one for the folks. You up for it?"

Ray rolled over and smiled at him. "Sure, why not. If it makes you happy."

"You make me happy."

Josh heard someone moving around in the kitchen.

"Let me go see what the boy's up to."

He got up, put on a shirt and pants and went into the kitchen where Dolan was staring into the refrigerator lights while Fig thumped. He pulled out a bottle of milk, saw Josh, poured himself a glass.

"Sir, I wonder if you could help me out."

"What do you need?"

"I just spoke with my neighbor in Milwaukee, Alfred. He's a veteran. Last night the gang broke into my old apartment, took everything that wasn't nailed down except for the mattresses, and is using it as a brothel. They tried to break into his apartment too, but he put up a bar. He's afraid they're going to come for him. Maybe tomorrow."

Josh ran a hand through his stubble. A fucking gang. Josh wasn't about to take on a gang. Not by himself. They'd have knives and guns. He needed help. He ran through his mental Rolodex.

"All right, but we're going to need some help. Let me make a few phone calls."

CHAPTER NINE

BLOOD IN THE WATER

THE ZHONG YI KUNG FU SCHOOL WAS IN A STRIP mall at 3361 East Washington Avenue. It had opened in 1990. Shifu Ferreira began studying judo when he was five years old in New York City, under his father. At age six, his family moved to Rio de Janeiro where he continued his studies. By the time he was ten, he wanted to try other martial arts. The school was open six days a week, including private lessons, youth shaolin, kickboxing, weapon sparring, and Lion Dance. Zhong Yi excelled at Lion Dance and participated in tournaments in China and Brazil.

At one p.m. on Friday afternoon, Nelson was teaching eager twelve-year-old Monica Hutchins the rudiments of kung fu as her doting father, who'd boxed Golden Gloves, watched from the sidelines. Nelson held up a ten-inch vinyl pad.

"Instep," he said.

Monica slammed her left instep. A satisfying report rang out.

"That's it, Monica. You just spin into it, like a baseball bat."

Monica bounced up and down, grinning. "Oh man, I can't tell you how long I've wanted to train!"

"You're twelve. It's a good time to start."

"She's been bugging me since she was six," Herman Hutchins said.

Nelson's phone rang. Normally, he wouldn't be teaching at this hour, but he made allowances for newcomers. He would have let the call go to voice-mail, but it was in the pocket of his black jacket. He fished it out and looked at the caller. He held up a finger.

"Monica, please forgive me. I have to take this. Herman, would you do the honors?"

Herman removed his shoes and came over grinning. Nelson handed him the pad. "You know what to do."

"Man, I think I'll sign up too!"

Nelson went into his office in the back, sank into his seat, springs groaning, and keyed the call. "Josh. What's up?"

"Are you sitting down?"

"Yes I am."

"I came home two nights ago, and there's this kid sitting on my stoop. Says he's my son. And you know what? He is. Long story. His mother and I had a one-night stand. I had no idea she was pregnant. She never told me. I don't know what I would have done. This was before I went to prison. His name is Dolan. He rode the bus from Milwaukee. Several nights ago, his mother died from a drug overdose."

"Oh no."

"Yeah. There's a lot more to it than that. Sorry to

bend your ear, but I have a bit of an emergency here. His apartment building's been taken over by a Venezuelan gang, and they're threatening his neighbor, who's a Gulf War veteran. The cops are useless. They won't even go there. I don't know how long he can hold out. Dolan asked if I could help. The only thing I'm good at is kicking ass, but I can't take on a whole gang by myself. I need some backup."

"I can't help you, Josh. This is a family business. I don't regret helping you before, but things have changed. I'm thinking of running for city council."

"The voters would love it."

"Some voters would love it. This is Madison. Never forget."

"I understand. Got any recommendations?"

Nelson laughed. "You might as well ask me what motorcycle I recommend. All the bad asses I know are serious people. Most of them have families. Am I the first person you called?"

"Yes."

Nelson could hear the embarrassment in his voice. "Don't worry about it. Y'know there are a couple guys here who might go with you, but you don't know them, and they don't know you. I can't advise them to do that. Where are the police?"

"Well, you know they gutted the budget in 2020, and a lot of cops quit, and those who are left don't want to stick their necks out for obvious reasons."

"What about your biker buddies?"

"I've sort of left that life behind, except for one or two."

"What about them?"

"I can think of one guy, but he plays piano for a living."

"So what?"

"So what indeed. I'll ask him."

"Look. If you just want to get him out of the building, get your buddy, go over there, and put on a show."

"These guys don't bluff. They're constantly trying to out macho one another. They're heedless. They don't give a shit. They'll shoot you dead. Then they'll go to prison and be big shots there. Many of them were in prison before they came here."

"You're in a tough situation, my friend. I wish I could offer more support. Doesn't this guy have any veteran friends?"

"That's a good idea. I'll ask Dolan."

"Bring him by sometime. I'd like to meet him."

"I'll do better than that. I'm going to sign him up. I think he'd dig it."

"Beautiful."

"Okay. Thanks for listening."

"Let's you and me get together for coffee or something."

"Next week. I'll bring Dolan."

"Okay. Good luck!"

"Thanks, Nelson."

Nelson put the phone away and sat in his office listening to Monica kicking the pad. Whap whap whap. It was a reassuring sound, one he'd known all his life. It wasn't that he was afraid, but Nelson was sixty-five years old. He had no doubt about his abilities. He worked out daily. But he'd worked hard to build up his business and his art, and he took great pride in its reputation and integrity. A proper martial arts instructor didn't go slumming for fights. Life was not a kung fu movie. He wasn't Count Dante. He rose, stretched, returned to the main room where students were trickling in for the evening classes.

He went up to Herman and Monica. "Monica, our session got cut a little short. Why don't you stay for the first class of the evening? If it's all right with you, Mr. Hutchins."

"Can I participate? And please. Call me Herman."

Nelson looked at Herman's designer jeans and Lacoste shirt. "Do you have any gym clothes?"

"Well yeah. I've been going to Ford's Gym. I'll get my sweats. They're in the car."

Moments later Nelson called the class to attention. They recited the pledge, and then Nelson turned it over to senior student Isaac Balfour. Nelson returned to his office, bothered by the notion that he should have gone with Josh.

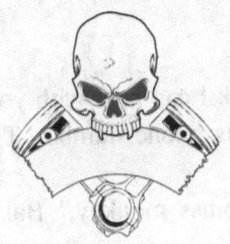

JOSH SET DOWN THE PHONE. DOLAN FROWNED.

"That didn't sound good."

"Yeah. Let me think."

He'd lost touch with his biker buddies. Most of them were too old anyway. A bulb went off. He went into his office and brought up Facebook. He searched for Arthur Baker. He found a *Hodag* page. He sent a message.

"Arthur, I need your help. Josh Pratt."

There was no reason for the biker horror movie maven to help him. Except, perhaps, as a cure for his depression. Josh recognized depression as he sometimes suffered from it himself. When that happened, he inevitably entered a downward spiral that ended with Pastor John throwing a bucket of water on him and shaking his finger.

"Gratitude, Josh. Attitude is everything. And the best attitude is gratitude. You have a roof over your head, a woman who loves you, and now a son who's not a criminal or a drug addict. Be grateful."

Josh slapped himself. He did it a lot. He had a message from *The Hodag*.

"What do you want?"

"Can we talk, Arthur? I think I can help with your lawsuit. Call me." He put in his phone number. The phone rang almost instantly.

"You have the balls of a brass monkey," Baker said.

"You never know until you ask."

"What do you want?"

"Arthur, my son knows a veteran who lives in an apartment building in Milwaukee. The building's been taken over by a Venezuelan gang. Last night they broke into my son's apartment and looted it. They tried to break into the veteran's, but his door held. However, that's not going to last. This gang won't stop until they evict or kill every legitimate tenant. They use the building to make drugs, sell drugs, as shooting galleries, and for prostitution. They recruit underage girls. They get 'em hooked on drugs."

"You want me to confront a Venezuelan gang?"

"You and me."

Baker barked. "What could go wrong? Are they armed?"

"Probably. But the moment they start shooting, that's when the police will take notice. They must know that."

"What if they're all hopped up on drugs and don't give a flying fuck?"

"It's occurred to me, but here's a man who served our country who's been locked in his apartment for days with no way out. They may have shut off his water and electricity too."

Silence.

"I must be out of my mind."

"I have ballistic vests."

"Can we shoot them?"

"No. I'm a convicted felon and you have enough trouble."

"Baseball bat?"

"Sure. I'm bringing a collapsible baton and a couple party favors."

"When?"

"I can be at your house in an hour."

"I must be out of my mind."

"Great. See you in an hour."

Dolan had stood in the office door the whole time. "Can I come?"

Josh thought about it. Dolan had vital inside knowledge of the building and neighborhood. "You can come, but you must stay in the car."

"I can fight."

"No doubt, but you must stay in the car. If you won't stay in the car, you can't come."

"All right."

"Dress warm."

Josh got his ballistic vests from the basement, put one on and slipped into a black leather jacket stitched together like Frankenstein. He'd got it from a thrift store for fifteen bucks. He put the collapsible baton in one of his camo cargo pants pockets. The pocket on his other leg bulged. He put on biker boots. Dolan sat in the garage sipping an orange juice, wearing leather boots, blue jeans, an REI insulated jacket, and a black watch cap. Fig sat with her snout on his thigh. They went out through the garage and headed toward the east side. They passed three chops in the parking lot of Monty's Blue Plate Diner, an institution across the street from the Barrymore, where Josh had seen the Shake Down Blues Band and Buddy Guy.

Baker came out the front door with a baseball bat. He got in the back seat and picked up the vest. "This for me?"

"Yup."

Baker took off his jacket and shrugged into the vest. He put his jacket back on.

As they drove east on the interstate, twelve bikers headed west, some with their old ladies. Dolan turned to watch them go.

"Thanks for doing this," Dolan said.

"Yeah, who you?"

"I'm Dolan. Josh is my father."

Baker thrust a ham-sized hand between the seats. "I got nothing better to do."

"Where's your club?" Josh said.

"The last time we rode together was ten years ago. The Devil Dogs were a bunch of blue-collar guys who just liked to get together and ride. Sometimes we'd get shit-faced and get into fights, but we didn't do drugs or prostitution or any of that shit. We had a bricklayer, two bike mechanics, some construction workers. Four vets. We all met in Afghanistan before Shit-for-Brains decided to bail. Fortunately, all of us had rotated stateside when that happened, or we'd all be dead. I thought about calling them, but this isn't their thing. Most are hard-working family men."

"You ever married?"

"Yeah, I was married to a brain-dead bitch. We had nothing in common. After about a year she turns to me and says, it's not working, is it? Then she held me up for ten thousand bucks to get out of my life. Haven't heard from her since."

"No kids?"

"None that I know of." Baker laughed. "Whoops!"

Josh and Dolan laughed.

"Dolan, call your friend and tell him we're on the way."

Dolan took out the phone Josh had given him and dialed.

"Alfred, it's Dolan."

He listened.

"We're coming to get you out of there."

Beat.

"My dad and a friend of his. Don't worry. They know what they're doing."

Beat.

"That doesn't matter. We'll be there in about an hour."

Josh held out his hand for the phone. "Mr. Longchamps? Josh Pratt. You know 'Shave and a Haircut?' That's how you'll know it's us. Pack whatever you need and be ready to go. Yes, sir."

He handed the phone back to Dolan.

"See you soon, Alf."

They passed Lake Mills. Traffic streamed by heading west. Josh turned on his CD player. John Cafferty and the Beaver Brown Band playing "On the Dark Side." Baker snapped his fingers and bopped in the back seat.

"I haven't heard that song in years."

"I got a lot of songs you haven't heard in years."

On the outskirts of Milwaukee, Dolan guided them to the apartment building. Down rubble-strewn streets with hobos sleeping in door fronts. Past boarded up businesses that had never rebounded from the BLM riots. The streets were lined with graffiti.

"Turn here. This is the street."

Donna Drive had once been a prosperous, middle-class neighborhood, home to German and Irish immigrants. But as they worked hard, prospered, and moved up and out, the area began its slow descent into chaos. Graffiti tagged most apartment buildings. Many of the cars on the curb were abandoned derelicts, covered with graffiti. WEST SIDE BLUDS. MURDER CROWS. SHRED HUSTL.

Most of the graffiti was old. Some of it was new. You could tell by the brighter colors. Josh wondered if the Venezuelans did graffiti.

And there it was. Spray painted in brake pad yellow with a bright red outline.

TREN DE ARAGUA.

Josh parked down the street a block on the other side. He and Baker got out. Josh leaned in. "Stay here. Lock the doors. If anything changes, like a fucking mob armed with AR-15s, call me."

"What if the police arrive?"

"If only." Josh shut the door. They headed across the street.

CHAPTER ELEVEN
EVAC

JOSH AND BAKER WALKED UP THE BLOCK. BAKER HELD the bat low next to his leg. Two bangers sat on the stoop, on concrete abutments opposite one another talking loudly to be heard over the boom box. A hot hatch cruised by blasting different rap, and the sounds mingled like shrapnel. The hot hatch slowed down in front of the building and someone in the shotgun seated shouted something at the bangers on the stoop who stood and fronted. The hot hatch chirped and roared away leaving its beats in the air like a trail of dog shit.

It wasn't until Josh and Baker reached the stoop that the two bangers noticed them. They were beneath notice. Until they started up the stoop. The two bangers stood at the top of the concrete steps blocking their way. One banger was built like a little dumpster, biceps bulging through cut off sleeves, shaved skull blue with inked lightning bolts. He held up his hand.

"Sigue moviéndote, motherfucker," he said.

Josh smiled. "Sorry. I don't speak monkey talk."

The other banger was taller, shaved skull, face covered with ink like a Dead Sea scroll.

"Fuck you want, white boys? You got no business here."

Josh grabbed him by the front of his pants and hurled him to the sidewalk. As fast as a snake flicking its tongue. The thick one's hand went into his kangaroo pocket but before he could whip out a knife Baker had grabbed him by the back of the head and hurled him to the sidewalk. Baker leaped down three steps and landed with both feet on the thick one's chest, causing him to wheeze like a collapsing air mattress. Ribs snapped.

Josh put the other in a chokehold and choked him out. They dragged the two bodies to a narrow alley between the apartment building and the next. Josh pulled plastic zip ties from his pocket. They slapped Gorilla Tape over their mouths, tied the bangers' hands behind their backs and lifted them into a dumpster. They dropped the lid.

Baker waved his hand in front of his face. "Whew!"

They entered the apartment building. The lobby was covered with graffiti. Half the mailboxes were pried open. Josh gestured toward the stairs. They entered the stairwell. Voices drifted down from above. Spanish. Raucous laughter. The smell of marijuana and some sweet liqueur. They ascended silently to the fifth floor. The party boys were on the top floor. Carefully, they opened the heavy metal door and stepped into the hall which smelled of garlic and empanadas. There was no one in the hall but rap blasted from an apartment midway down.

Josh stopped in front of Dolan's old apartment. He

turned toward the unit opposite. He rapped softly. "Shave and a haircut." No response. He rapped again, a little louder. The peephole darkened. Locks unsnapped and the door opened.

"Quickly," Alfred urged, shutting the door behind them and locking it. He struggled to lift the heavy wood bar he'd installed. Baker took it in one hand and dropped it in place. He held out his hand.

"Put 'er there, brother. I'm a Marine."

They shook.

"Thank you for coming."

"Okay," Josh said. "We're going to get out of here. Do you have your stuff ready?"

Alfred pointed to a duffel bag. "There it is."

"Okay, I'll take that. I'll go first, then you, then Arthur. This is Arthur Baker, by the way."

"I see the lights are still on."

"Yeah. These dumb fucks don't know how to turn off the electricity without doing it to the whole building. They were just waiting for me to starve to death or something."

"Art, grab Dolan's shit."

Alfred went into his record room. "Come on. I'll show you what he's got."

Art pointed at a duffel bag. "That's it."

Josh pointed to the pistol jammed in Alfred's belt. "What's that?"

"Nine mil Beretta."

"Well don't pull it unless they pull theirs. Ready?"

Baker gripped the four-by-four and lifted. He held it in both hands and tried a few swings. He leaned it against the wall and picked up his bat. Voices in the hall. Loud voices directly outside the door. Someone began kicking the door. Arthur put a finger to his lips and his hand on the knob. He winked. With exquisite timing, he ripped the door open, and a punk in a peacoat tumbled through and fell on his face. Arthur kicked him in the groin. He screamed and shrimped. Josh and Arthur stepped into the hall. Four bangers lunged, two with clubs, two with knives. Josh paused, thrusting out his chest as if inviting a blow. The blade hit carbon fiber, and Josh swept the banger's arm into a triangle lock and threw him down, stomping on his groin. Baker danced out of club range. It missed him by an inch. He swung his bat in a tight arc bringing it down on the guy's head.

The remaining banger ran for the door.

Josh grabbed Longchamps' suitcase and hustled him down the hall to the stairwell. Baker followed with the duffel bags over his shoulder. They banged into the stairwell and scrambled down the stairs. They'd done two flights when Josh held his hand up. Bangers boiled up from below. Josh reached into his left cargo pants pocket and pulled out a grenade. Baker's eyes bulged.

"Holy shit."

"They're fake. You guys ready?"

"Yeah, baby."

"Yes sir," Alfred said.

Josh pulled the pin and tossed the grenade. It bounced off the cinderblock and careened down two flights. Cries of terror. Cursing. People tripping over themselves to get out. Josh, Alfred, and Baker hustled down the steps, pushed open the door into the alley and ran out. The gang had gone into the lobby. Erratic thumps sounded from the dumpster.

Josh pointed toward the end of the alley. "Let's go."

They were twenty feet from the end when four thugs in hoodies blocked the way. Two of them held AR-15s. The other two held machetes. The youth in the Brewers hoodie raised the rifle to his shoulder and fired. He missed. Alfred pulled his pistol, took a shooter's stance and squeezed off three shots. The target collapsed. The others vamoosed. Josh led them out of the alley, around the block and back to where he'd left Dolan in the car. Dolan unlocked the doors, they piled in, Josh pulled a U-turn, and they headed south toward the interstate.

They traveled in silence until Delafield, where the Golden Arches beckoned. Josh pulled off and they went through the drive-through. Josh got four double cheeseburgers and four Cokes. They were back on the interstate within twenty minutes.

Baker whooped like a bronc buster. "I haven't had so much fun in years! Thanks for bringing me, bro!"

Josh smiled. "Turned out better than I hoped."

"Y'know," Alfred said, "I shot plenty in the Gulf, but I don't believe I ever hit anyone."

"You're gonna have to lose that gun," Josh said.

"I can just toss it."

"Not here. No rush. I'll get rid of it."

"Where am I gonna stay?"

"You can stay at my place tonight, brother," Baker said. "We'll find you a place in the morning."

"I don't have money for a hotel."

"You come with me, brother," Baker said. "You can stay as long as you like."

"I appreciate it. That fucking gang took over the building a block down. The Wayzata. I have friends there. One's a mom with two teenage daughters. She's scared shitless that gang is going to force them into prostitution. Another's a Vietnam veteran. Gus is seventy-nine years old. He doesn't have much time left."

Josh squeezed the bridge of his nose. "One thing at a time, Mr. Longchamps."

CHAPTER TWELVE
DESSERT

SUNDAY WAS DINNER WITH THE MCRANEYS. THEY lived in a two-story red brick colonial in University Heights, down the street from Frank Lloyd Wright's Airplane House. Their "WE BELIEVE" sign had quietly disappeared during the pandemic. Josh pulled into their driveway at six. Ray got out and opened the unlocked front door.

"We're here!"

Hal came out beaming, arms outstretched, enfolding his daughter. He was a tall, silver-haired patrician in distressed blue jeans and a gray and red UW hoodie. The house smelled of pot roast. "Your mother's in the kitchen."

Ray went into the kitchen. Hal shook Josh's hand. "How you doing, future son-in-law?"

"Keeping busy, sir."

"From what Ray says, your life is very exciting."

"Well, I wouldn't call it that eventful."

"Would you like a drink?"

"Yes, thank you."

Hal walked to a wet bar in the family room and held up a bottle of Buffalo Trace.

"That's good."

"Ice?"

"Yes, please."

Hal poured three fingers into two cut glass tumblers and added ice from the fridge. He handed a glass to Josh and sat in a recliner angled toward the big flat-screen TV on the wall. Josh sat on the sofa.

"We've reserved Saturday, June fourteenth for the wedding at the First Unitarian Church. You know where that is?"

"Yessir. It's famous. Frank Lloyd Wright."

"The church can handle four hundred guests. We're not planning to fill it, we have a list of about fifty, and you're free to invite as many of your friends as you like."

Josh did a quick mental calculation. He couldn't think of more than a dozen. Dolan, Heinz Calloway, Fleiss, Nelson, Bobby Hines, their girlfriends and wives, his neighbors Dave and Louise who introduced him to Ray. That was about it. Talk about a biker wedding was him just amusing himself at Ray's expense. He did get the sense that she wasn't as adamantly opposed as she pretended. Part of her yearned to get down and dirty. She had tattoos. Not as many as Josh, and none so visible. But still. He was planning on teaching her how to ride. He had a neat little 650 Hawk that was just her size. Dolan eyed it every time he went into the garage.

Baker. He should invite Baker. And maybe Longchamps.

"I'll put a list together."

Ray and Marianne walked into the family room beaming.

"Ray tells me you have a son."

"What?" Hal said.

Josh wanted to crawl into a hole. He had no reason to be ashamed. He'd done nothing wrong. Not in seventeen years.

"Yes sir. He showed up at my place a couple days ago. He's seventeen years old. I had no idea he existed. His mother never told me she was pregnant. I only saw her once."

Hal pressed his lips together. Not good. Not good at all.

Ray sat on the armrest and put her arm around her father. "He's a different person now, Dad. You know that. You know he went to prison."

"Right, right. And he found the Lord."

"Sir, it was a long time ago. He is my son, and he'll be staying with me until he decides what he wants to do."

"Which means he'll be staying with the two of you."

"Dad. I've met him. He's an outstanding young man. He's mature, wise even. Not some spoiled brat."

"All right, all right. When do we get to meet him?"

"We'll have you over for dinner."

"Come on, let's eat," Marianne said.

They went into the dining room, the walnut table covered with white linen, a floral bouquet in the center. Josh and Ray sat across from each other. Hal stood to carve the roast on the credenza. He loaded a plate with roast, green beans, and mashed potatoes and set in front of Josh. Josh was famished but controlled himself. He

wasn't used to being served first. Ray waited too. Marianne was next, then Hal filled his plate and sat at the
head of the table. A crazy Picasso-like painting of a
jazz musician wailing on a sax hung above the buffet.

Josh was about to fold his hands and lead them in a
prayer, but he caught himself just in time. Not the time
or the place. They liked him well enough. Enough to
have him for a son-in-law, but no Bible-thumping
please. He prayed silently. Hal filled their wineglasses
with burgundy, lastly his own. He raised the glass.

"To our wonderful daughter and her wonderful
fiancé. We welcome you into the family."

They clinked and sipped. Josh tried not to wolf.

"This roast is delicious," he said.

"Thank you. It's my mother's recipe."

Ray casually raised her foot beneath the table and
probed the inside of his thigh. Her shoe was off.

"Ray, sit up straight," Hal said. "You're
slouching."

She popped right up. "Sorry!"

"Sir," Josh said, "who will perform the
ceremony?"

"We have a good friend who's an Episcopal minis-
ter. Her name is Flo Stanton. She has agreed to
perform the ceremony."

"I was thinking of writing our wedding vows," Ray
said.

"Uh oh."

Ray laughed. "In fact, I've been thinking about
writing a play about us. Biker Bride."

"Who'll play the biker? Mongoose?"

"No, I'm actually thinking of having a male lead."

"Have you started writing this play?"

"No, but I'm making notes."

"Where's the dynamic, dear?" Marianne said.

"She's a wild free spirit. She has queer friends. He's a straight, blue-collar biker who loathes homosexuals."

"I don't loathe homosexuals."

"It's not you, Josh. It's inspired by you."

"Dear," Marianne said, "might I suggest that you find another project? At least until you've got a couple years under your belt."

"Good idea, Ray," Hal chimed in.

"Oh, I was just kidding. I was just teasing."

Josh nodded. "She was teasing."

Once again, her stockinged foot found its way onto his thigh.

"Sit up, Ray," Marianne said. "You're slouching."

Ray straightened right up. "Sorry about that. I keep thinking of the production we want to do of *The Hunchback of Notre Dame*."

"Will Mongoose play the hunchback?"

"No, I have someone in mind."

"Is it a man?" Hal said.

"As a matter of fact, it is. I'm also thinking about filming all our productions going forward, but I need someone who knows their way around a camera."

"I might have someone for you," Josh said.

"Oh really."

"Arthur Baker. If it's sleaze you want, he's your guy."

"I'd love to meet him."

"I'm thinking of inviting him to the wedding."

"Go ahead."

Marianne pushed back from the table. "I hope you left room for dessert."

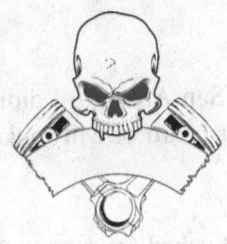

CHAPTER THIRTEEN
DRIVER'S LICENSE

Luis Alejandro leaned back in his BarcaLounger, stretching. He pushed the hood back off his head, which was inked like a wall. He'd had to remove some of the tattoos to make room for others. A gold crucifix hung around his neck next to a silver skull. He pushed forward, lowering the footrest, picked up a straw, and snorted a line off a dinner plate. He looked up at his lieutenant Delcey Rodriguez standing with his hand around the girl's arm. She could have been anywhere from fifteen to twenty. It was hard to tell. She'd led a hard life. Delcey had found her on the street tricking herself out in Germantown.

Luis wrangled another line and held the straw out to the girl. She knelt on the other side of the table and hoovered it up.

"What's your name, girl?"

"Amira."

"Where you from?"

"Guatemala."

"How long you been here?"

"Three weeks."

"How'd you get here?"

"They put me on a plane in San Antonio. I didn't know I was coming here. I never heard of Milwaukee before."

"Where'd you get that bruise?"

"A man used me, and when I asked for money, he hit me."

"That won't happen here. We'll protect you. We'll feed you. We'll make you feel real good. Would you like to join our team?"

She shrugged. She was a petite brunette, could not have weighed more than one hundred and ten pounds. Her skin was good. If she was shooting up, Luis couldn't see it.

"Why don't you take a shower and choose some nice new clothes. Delcey, show her the bathroom and the spare bedroom. When you get out, we'll get you something to eat."

"I'm not hungry."

"You must eat. No more blow until you eat."

Delcey pointed to the hall. "Bathroom is on the left. Bedroom is opposite."

They watched her go. Delcey collapsed on the sofa. They were on the tenth floor of the Wayzata Arms, a block down from Donna Drive. Luis had not yet figured out who had led the raid. They'd searched the old man's apartment for clues but came up empty. Gangster Disciples, most likely. They'd controlled the northwest side until recently, when six of their members were arrested in a massive SWAT operation, due to their infiltration of White Fish Bay. The gangs called it White Folks Bay. Luis was smart enough to know not to prey on the white folks in their own neighborhoods.

Luis was five-nine, weighed one hundred and fifty pounds, shaved skull covered with tats. He'd immigrated through the southern border four months ago and could not believe the ease with which it was done. It was before the recent election that everything changed. But by then, his group was comfortably ensconced in the Wayzata Arms, which they'd taken over from the ground up. There were thirty-six apartments, and they controlled eight of them. Two on the second floor as shooting galleries, three on the fourth floor as fuck pads, two more for the gang, and one on the tenth floor where Luis lived.

Delcey did another line. He switched to Spanish. "Oh yeah. I forgot."

"Forgot what?"

"We got footage from Donna Drive."

"What footage?"

"From the security cameras. Two bikers."

"Show me the footage."

Delcey brought it up on his phone. "I'll freeze it when they come in."

The view was blurry, and then it crystalized. Delcey sat next to Luis on the sofa. "Okay. Catch this." He zoomed in. The viejo came out followed by two men. Luis knew that look. That build. He'd lay money they were covered with ink.

Delcey zoomed in. The image improved.

"This guy. Right here. He's in charge."

A white man, maybe forty, light beard, shaved skull, prison build. That rolling gait.

Luis nodded. "Find out who he is."

"Yeah, I can do that. I know how to do that."

"Fuck's Manny?"

Manny was in charge of the crew at 1128 W. Donna Drive.

"I don't know, jefe. He said he'd be here."

Luis sighed. The burden of his office weighed heavily. At the age of twenty-four, he'd taken over the gang in Caracas. El Presidente announced his jihad against the gangs and forced them out. He and his top lieutenants took a freighter to Guatemala where they'd joined the endless caravan of refugees seeking the sweet life in the United States. It had taken them four months to make the trek, with time off for robbery, drug dealing, and human trafficking. By the time they arrived in Nuevo Laredo, they'd built up a nest egg.

They were surprised at the ease with which they crossed the border. The hospitality of the volunteers who fed them, housed them, and cheered them on their way. The indifference and depression of the border patrol. Their timing was good. Now the border was patrolled and ICE revamped. Agents swarmed major cities armed with warrants, scooping up illegals by the dozen, sending them via bus back to the southern border. In some cases, putting them on airplanes to South America.

Luis wasn't worried. He had six cops on his payroll. He had fourteen bangers who never slept. They patrolled the neighborhood looking for upscale johns. Rivians and Teslas and Mercedes and BMWs. While the pimps negotiated, his boys took pics of their license plates. He wanted to know who his clients were. No threats, no favors, but if he ever had the need, he could call on those clients to help him out.

Like at a deportation hearing.

He was more concerned with the *bichos* who'd

invaded 1128 and shot Hercule. Thank God for
Delcey. He'd worked at Docotor, the largest computer
repair company in Venezuela. He was adept at tracking
phones and cracking data centers. Bones too. Every
time the gang took over an apartment building, they
put someone in charge of security. He was in charge of
all the security centers. Some so old they hadn't been
staffed in years.

The 1128 crew had been so fucked up they hadn't
even looked for the vehicle. They just let the intruders
take the old guy and fly. At least they had the video.
Devil Dogs. Luis had searched for them on the net.
Ex-Marines. That was bad news. They had no chapter
in Wisconsin. It was just one guy. The other guy
looked like a biker but wore no colors. Where had they
come from? Why had they come?

Luis regretted he hadn't taken advantage of the
free-for-freeloaders driver's license. He hadn't wanted
to go on the record. He wondered if it was too late.

"Delcey, I want you to go the driver's license place
Monday and get a driver's license."

Delcey looked up alarmed. "Huh? Why should I
go? Why not send Roberto? You need me more than
him."

"Roberto's not smart enough to get a driver's
license. You got that fake birth certificate."

"I made that. Give me the right tools, and I'll make
you a driver's license. Just like the real thing."

They'd taken several driver's licenses from johns.
The johns never came back.

"We got to think about the future. Sooner or later,
someone's gonna want to know how we got in the
country. We got to find some relatives or something.
We got to get legit."

"We're never gonna get legit! We got records in Venezuela!"

"Why do you think they set us free, stupid? They don't want us back. Anybody asks, they'll deny we were ever there! Don't make me mad. Do as I say."

"Okay, boss. I'll give it a shot. But if they start to send off vibes, like they're calling the police or something, I'll leave."

"Understood. You're a smart boy, Delcey. See what you can do. We've got to get in front of these bikers in case they come back."

"Why would they come back?"

Luis shrugged. "Why did they come in the first place?"

CHAPTER FOURTEEN
JOYS OF PARENTHOOD

JOSH AND RAY GOT BACK TO HIS PLACE AT EIGHT. Dolan was in the basement watching TV. They heard a laugh track through the open basement door. Josh went downstairs, found Dolan stretched out on the sofa, feet up on a milk crate, Fig in his lap watching an old sitcom.

"What's that?" Josh asked.

Dolan turned. "Come on. It's *Seinfeld*, man! Don't tell me you've never heard of *Seinfeld*."

"I don't watch much TV."

"What do you watch?"

"Old movies. Boxing. The Pack. You doing okay?"

"Yeah. I had a turkey sandwich for dinner, fed Fig."

Fig looked at Josh and grinned, tongue lolling.

"She sleep with you?"

"Yeah. Is that okay?"

"Of course it is. What are you doing tomorrow?"

"UbreakIfix."

"Okay. I'll be gone most of the day, but I'll be

back by five. We'll go out to dinner. Want me to pick you up at the mall?"

"I'll have the bike."

"Fits in the back seat."

"Sure."

"Need anything?"

"No, sir. I'm good."

Josh turned to go.

"Josh?"

Josh turned. "What?"

Dolan pointed to a deer antler fragment on the wall.

"What's that?"

"We had a guy named Snake. We were on a club run in Minnesota, and Snake was in front. He struck a deer in such a way that the antler pierced his forehead and came out the top of his skull. We grabbed the deer which was thrashing about with Snake stuck to its head. I reached for my knife, wrestled the deer down and slit its throat. The rest of the gang hog piled on the deer as it went through its death throes. They decapitated the deer. The ambulance arrives. The EMTs are stunned by the blood and gore, not to mention the pierced biker. They sawed off the antler and took Snake to the hospital. He survived none the worse for it."

Dolan grinned quizzically. "Come on."

Josh made the Boy Scout symbol. "Swear to God."

He went upstairs. Ray sat on the living room sofa looking at her phone. "Oh, you won't believe this."

He sat next to her and looked at her phone. An email. "What?"

"A producer named Melvin Hyman wants to option *Kung Fu Musical*."

"How does he even know about it?"

"We taped it and put it up on the website. Wants to have a conference call this week!"

"That's great, babe! Good luck!"

"How's Dolan?"

"He's watching *Seinfeld*."

"Oh, I love that show. Did you watch?"

"I've never heard of it before."

"You are such a bumpkin. Have you seen *Citizen Kane*?"

"Never heard of it."

"*The Godfather*?"

"I've heard of it."

"*Star Wars*?"

"Yeah, I saw the first one. With the wookie."

"What's the last movie you saw?"

"*The Bikeriders*. I saw it at West Towne."

"Wow. You actually went to the theater. Why that one?"

"It was about the birth of biker gangs in the United States. It was really good."

"Stick with me, kid. I'll bring you up to speed. You've seen my DVD collection."

"You forced me to watch *Blazing Saddles*."

"You didn't laugh once."

"It wasn't funny."

"What about *Easy Rider*?"

"Saw it."

"What about *The Wild One*?"

"Never heard of it."

"God, you are such a bumpkin. I'll make a list of movies we can watch together. Do you like musicals?"

"I don't know. What's a musical?"

Ray rolled her eyes. "You know. Like *Singin' in the Rain*. Or *Cabaret*."

"Never heard of them."

"You led a deprived childhood."

"Yes, I did."

Ray put her hand to her mouth. "Oh. I'm so stupid sometimes. I'm sorry, Josh."

Josh laughed. "I don't care. I got over that a long time ago. It's funny. My old man showed up at my house a couple years ago, and he was an even bigger scumbag than I remembered."

"Yeah. Not too many people are serving life in prison for gassing a family at a motel. I've thought about writing a play about that, but I don't think you'd appreciate it."

"No. But I have thought about writing about my life. I would if I could."

"We can explore that later. Y'know, it's funny. Your dad was a scumbag murderer. And your son shows up, and he's practically an angel. I don't know too many kids his age who are as polite and respectful as he is. He seems pretty smart too."

"I'm thinking of asking Dolan to be my best man."

"Where is he going to school?"

"I never thought about that."

"Ask him his grade level. His record. That sort of thing."

"I will. It's all sorts of new to me."

"Well, it's only April. He should be in school."

"You're right. You're right. I'll have to ask around. Know anybody who can help?"

"You want west side parents with kids in school. Know any?"

Josh felt a headache coming on. "No."

"Well, you're a detective."

"Right. Right. I'll ask around."

"Where's my ring?"

"Working on it."

"I'm just razzing you." She stood and pulled him into the bedroom. "Wait here," she said.

Josh stripped and got into bed. He heard the water in the sink, and she returned wearing nothing but panties. She'd told him she had an IUD, and he had no reason to doubt her. Ray didn't lie. When he'd first met her, she was stressed about the environment and how people could even bring children into a world like this. Her outlook had changed over the years. She wasn't about to wave the American flag and pack a pistol, but she'd edged toward the middle.

After they made love, Josh went in the kitchen and brought back two glasses of V8. Ray put on a Lannie Flowers T-shirt, sat cross-legged on the bed and turned on the TV. *America's Got Talent*. A young man singing "New York, New York."

"You want to go someplace after the wedding?"

"You mean like a honeymoon?"

"Yeah."

Ray put a finger to his lips and put her hand on his. "This kid is really good."

When the kid finished, the crowd went crazy. The kid was assured a career.

"You're a good man, Josh Pratt. I'm lucky to have you."

"There was a time when I could have gone full psycho. I'm grateful to have gone to prison. I'm grateful to have met Pastor Dorgan. If I hadn't met him, I'd probably be dead by now."

"I'm lucky too."

"I get down on my knees and thank God every day that He came into my life."

"Let's not get sloppy."

"When I think of the things I've done…"

She put a hand on the back of his neck. "Stop. There's no point beating yourself up."

"I know. I know. You're right."

After the lights were out, he lay awake a long time thinking about the cruel things he'd done to women, to men, to animals. It made him sick to his stomach. He carried it with him like a hundred-pound weight. Not a day passed he didn't think about those things. The women he'd abused. The man whose arm he'd cut off with a chainsaw. He feared searching for them. He feared knowing what had become of them.

He could never write his story. He could never tell another person what he'd done. The shame crept up on him. Even knowing he'd been forgiven, he still carried that weight. He would carry it until the day he died. And if there was a heaven, if there was an afterlife, he would carry it there too.

CHAPTER FIFTEEN
ROAD KING

RAY SHOWERED, GRABBED AN APPLE, A BANANA, AND a fruit bar and called an Uber. She was halfway out the door when Josh stumbled into the living room.

"Where are you going? I could drive you."

"No need, baby. I'm meeting Mongoose for breakfast. I'll call you later."

"Have fun."

She blew him a kiss. "He's here." She left.

"As much fun as one can possibly have with Mongoose," Josh muttered.

He went into the kitchen and brewed coffee. Dolan came up.

"You happy in the basement?"

"Yeah. That's where the computers are."

"You want pancakes?"

"Sure."

"How'd you sleep?"

"Great. Hey, before you came home last night, I talked to Alfred. He's really worried about his friends down the street. They live in an apartment building called the Wayzata Arms a couple blocks away. They told him the gang has taken over the building, only there are a lot more of them than at my place."

Josh mixed the batter. He sensed his son's concern. He respected veterans. If he hadn't screwed his life up, he might have enlisted. The Bedouins had been his trial by fire. He was proud of what they taught him. How to fight. How to be a man. But ashamed of the things they'd done. The Bedouins were drunken brawlers, but they weren't evil like the Pagans. They dealt a little reefer, a little blow. They didn't traffic in guns or women. There were always women around. There was a certain type of woman who gravitated toward bikers. Most left disappointed. Some found life mates. It all depended on the biker. And the woman.

"I don't know what to tell you. There's just me and Baker."

"Don't you have a gang?"

"Not anymore. Tell your guys to call the Veterans Administration. There must be something they can do."

Dalton snorted. "They're worthless. Ask Alfred."

"What about the VFWs?"

"I asked Alfred about that, and he said most of the members at local VFWs were old and fat. They got some Vietnam vets in their seventies and eighties. Even the Gulf War vets are old. That was thirty-five years ago. Given Milwaukee's mayor, if they showed up to evict the bangers, the cops would probably arrest them. Everything's screwed up over there."

Josh pinched the bridge of his nose. "Call your buddy, get their names and phone numbers."

"Thanks, Josh!"

"Don't thank me. I don't know what I'm going to do. I have to think about it."

They sat down and ate the pancakes.

"I saw some ground buffalo in the freezer. You want me to make meatloaf?"

"Sure, if it's any good."

"I make a great meatloaf Mom always said. You have everything I need. Red onion, liquid smoke, and barbecue sauce."

"Sounds good already."

"I'll pick up some vegetables when I'm at the shop today. I saw a Sprouts there."

"Sounds good."

"What are you going to do?"

"I'm going to see Baker and your buddy, talk to them about the situation. I'm inviting them to my wedding."

"Am I invited?"

"You're my best man."

Dolan's mouth hung open. "You hardly know me!"

"Blood is thicker than water. You hardly know me, yet here you are."

Dolan laughed. "That's true."

"Were you in school?"

Dolan picked at his pancakes.

"School. Did you go to school?"

"I was a junior last year at North Division. I had to drop out when the gang came. They were dealing drugs to my mother. I just couldn't be there all the time."

"How were your grades?"

"C minus."

"Okay, we got to get you enrolled."

"Do I gotta? I already know enough about computers to work on them."

"Well sure, if you want to be a low-paid tradesman. Is that what you want to do?"

"I don't know what I want to do."

"Well, think about it. I think that's the most important thing someone your age should do. Think about where you want to go in life. I didn't, and I ended up in prison."

"Yeah but look at you now."

"Thanks to the grace of God. You don't want to follow my path, Dolan. I'll tell you what. We get you into school, you do well, I'll give you an allowance, and you can train in kung fu. You want to learn kung fu?"

"Who doesn't? Why do you ask?"

"I have a friend who runs a kung fu studio on the east side. Do you have a driver's license?"

"No."

"Hmmm. Ever drive?"

"A little. I'm only seventeen."

"Okay, we need a plan. I'll teach you how to drive. We can do it in the parking lot at West Towne. Once you master the fundamentals, we'll take it out to the country."

"That would be great. I'm so glad you're like a real guy, and not some drunken tattooed hoodlum."

Josh grinned and peeled off his sweatshirt. His arms were fully sleeved.

"I was thinking about getting a tattoo."

"Keep thinking. You ain't getting shit until you're an adult, and that's a year away. You want me to drop you off, or you want to ride the bike?"

"I'll ride the bike. Says it's gonna be in the sixties today."

"Okay. I gotta go across town and talk with Baker and Longchamps. Figure out what we're gonna do about his vet buddies."

"I think Arthur freaked them out. Everybody knows not to mess with bikers."

"Get your shit together, and I'll teach you how to ride."

"You have four bikes."

"They're like accordions. They multiply."

"You ride the big one. The Road King."

Josh smiled. "That's right."

"What all did you do to it?"

"I've been waiting all my life for someone to ask that question." Josh took a deep breath. "Engine: 88 with oil cooler. Changed the cams to S&S gear drives with .510 lift. Took out the fuel injection and replaced it with an S&S Super E, Yost Power Tube, S&S manifold, and Pingle High Flow petcock. S&S Tear Drop air cleaner cover with a K&N filter. Screaming Eagle Hi Performance ignition unit with a 6200 rpm rev limiter. Accell Super Coil, fire wire plug wires, and spiral wound metal core wires. Accell Platinum tip plugs. Five-speed tranny with Barnett Kevlar clutch, self-adjusting hydraulic chain tensioner. Screaming Eagle dualies. Progressive springs in front with higher viscosity, Progressives in back. Changed the rear swing arm bushings to 'STA BOW' nylon, high density. SBS semi-metallic disc brake pads, and the brake lines are stainless steel braids. Went to tubeless wheels."

"Wow. I don't know what that means."

"You'll learn. Imma take the bike. Don't drive my car."

"As if."

"You got any money?"

"Twenty bucks."

Josh pulled out his wallet. "Here's a C-note. For incidentals."

"Thanks, Josh."

"See ya back here around five. You need anything give me a call."

Josh put on a Badgers hoodie and a heavy black leather jacket with a horizontal orange stripe. He wore biker boots and carpenter's pants. He opened the garage door, worked the bike around nose first, rolled down to Ptarmigan, fingered the starter, and took off.

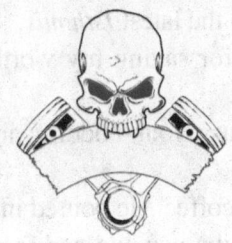

CHAPTER SIXTEEN
IDEA

JOSH BACKED UP TO THE CURB IN FRONT OF RAY'S theater at ten, got off, and went inside. Preparations continued for *The Snot-Nosed Punk of Yore*. Josh sat in the back row and phoned Baker.

"Yeah?"

"Mind if I stop by?"

"No, come on by."

"How's Alfred?"

"He's holding up. We're talking about his friends' situation."

"That's what I want to talk to you about."

"Come on by."

Josh left without seeing Ray. He took Williamson to Atwood, circling Lake Monona clockwise, then Cottage Grove Road to Groome Road. Baker's truck was in the driveway, garage door open. Josh parked on the street and rang the bell. The door opened.

"Come on in. You want coffee?"

"Sure."

He followed Baker into the kitchen where Longchamps sat flipping through the latest *Isthmus*.

"Hello, Josh. Thanks again for saving my worthless ass."

"No prob. I'm here to discuss your buddies and what we can do to help them."

Baker handed Josh a mug of coffee. He poured in a little cream and sipped. He pulled a pen and pad from his jacket and laid them on the table.

"I'd like you to write down their names, their contact info, and the address. Their apartment numbers too."

Alfred took the pen and pad. "Wayne Garretson and Daryl Briggs. They both live at the Wayzata Arms. Last I talked to Wayne, he was still getting in and out, but he has to walk by these fucking gangsters in the lobby every time. Maybe they're not in such a rush like they were at my place, 'cuz it's a bigger building, and they got all the apartments they need. But it's just a matter of time."

"What do Wayne and Daryl have to say about the situation?"

"They're not happy. Darryl shops for some single mothers who live there. They're afraid to come out of their apartments. Last time they did, one of those scumbags came up and ran his hand over her ass, told her how she could make some big money. She's got a three-year-old daughter."

"They tried the police?"

"Yeah, and a cop told him that while it was technically assault, it was just hearsay, and if the mother wanted to file a complaint she had to come down to the station. Everybody knows the cops are demoralized and understaffed, and the mayor ain't gonna do shit about it."

Josh pointed to the notepad. "Write."

Josh turned to Baker. "You still with the Devil Dogs?"

"Not in years. Not since I moved up here from Texas."

"I looked 'em up. Mostly Marines."

"That's right. God knows we could use 'em, but they're not looking to expand."

"You in touch with 'em?"

"Couple guys. We trade holiday greetings. Maybe get together twice a year. I gotta ride down there. They're not interested in riding up here."

"That's too bad. You've ridden around Wisconsin. You know what it's like."

"Yessir. Some of the most beautiful riding in the world."

"I could ride all day. All those winding little roads through valleys, the forests…"

"Hell, I'm ready."

"What I'm thinking, a dozen bikers were to pull up to that apartment building, those gangbangers would shit their pants."

"Maybe. You got to remember. They got guns and don't give a shit if they use them. They've all been in prison. They're not afraid of American prisons. They're afraid of going back to the shithole they came from."

"A shootout between a motorcycle club and a Venezuelan gang might attract the police."

"Yeah, but you don't want that kind of attention."

"Oh hey, that reminds me. You're both invited to

my wedding June fourteenth at the First Unitarian Church."

"Congratulations!" Alfred said. "If I'm still around."

"Why wouldn't you be?"

"Well, I can't stay here. Art was kind enough to take me in, but I've got to find a place for myself. I've got to make my own way."

"Got any money?"

"Some. I get a pension from the Army, and I've salted away a few bucks. I got an IRA."

"Got any family?"

"Got a son lives in Tennessee. We don't talk much. He went to Columbia, got a degree in psychology. He got hired by this big firm to head their DEI initiative. Couple months ago, they fired him."

"How come?"

"He was a straight white man."

Josh and Arthur laughed.

"So he thinks you're a white supremacist."

"You got it."

"Family is family," Baker said. "You should reach out."

"Maybe."

"You can stay here as long as you like. I got the room."

"That's very kind of you, Art." He looked at Josh. "Who's the lucky lady?"

Josh pulled out his phone, found a picture of Ray and showed it to them.

"Wow," Alfred said.

Baker whistled.

"Ray McRaney. She was a theater and dance

major. Runs a theater on the east side. We're an odd couple."

Baker smiled. "No matter how woke they are, they all love a big bad biker. Weren't you in a club?"

"The Bedouins."

"But not anymore."

"Nope."

"Why not?"

"The Bedouins broke up when we got in a fight with another club up by Rhinelander. It was a long time ago. Cops killed three. I went to prison. Found God. Got out, thanks to God's mercy, and decided to follow another path."

"But you still ride."

"Yup."

"What do you ride?"

"Modified Road King."

"What all'd you do to it?"

"You're the second person to ask me today. I should have handouts already."

"Well?"

Josh drew a deep breath. "Engine: 88 with oil cooler. Changed the cams to S&S gear drives with .510 lift. Took out the fuel injection and replaced it with an S&S Super E, Yost Power Tube, S&S manifold and Pingle High Flow petcock. S&S Tear Drop air cleaner cover with a K&N filter. Screaming Eagle Hi Performance ignition unit with a 6200 rpm rev limiter. Accell Super Coil, fire wire plug wires, and spiral wound metal core wires. Accell Platinum tip plugs. Five-speed tranny with Barnett Kevlar clutch, self-adjusting hydraulic chain tensioner. Screaming Eagle dualies. Progressive springs in front with higher viscosity, Progressives in back. Changed the rear swing arm bushings to 'STA BOW' nylon high density. SBS semi-metallic disc brake pads, and the brake lines are stainless steel braids. Went to tubeless wheels."

"You took out the fuel injection?"

"That's right."

"Let me show you my baby. I made a few mods."

Josh followed Baker into the garage. The Fat Boy's silver tank was emblazoned with a black skull and crossbones on one side and the silhouette of a were-wolf on the other.

Alfred appeared in the door holding a Tyranena IPA in his hand. "I got an idea."

Josh looked up. "What?"

"Have you thought about contacting a Christian motorcycle club?"

"Holy shit."

CHAPTER SEVENTEEN
PROTECTION FOR SALE

DARYL BRIGGS PEERED THROUGH HIS PEEPHOLE. Nobody in his field of vision. The hall was quiet. The odds were with him. The gang was not quiet. Not quiet by day, not quiet by night. They played loud salsa and partied. So far, his floor contained only regular tenants minus the two parties that had bugged out. The apartment beneath his was for entertaining customers. Loud music played, starting at one in the afternoon and went all night.

Even with his hearing loss from the war, Briggs couldn't sleep. He had a prescription for clonazepam for PTSS and used Flent's ear stopples. Sometimes he could sleep, mostly he didn't. He had been sleep-deprived since the gang moved in four months ago. He was ready to kill. He clutched his Colt .45, which he'd carried throughout his deployment in Afghanistan, in his right hand. He wore the kukri he'd brought home from Nepal on his belt. Cautiously, he undid the chain. Then the dead bolt. Slowly, he opened the door inward. He stuck his head out. The corridor was deserted. He'd just got off the phone with Wayne who was expecting him. Wayne lived on the fourth floor, while Daryl lived on the eighth. The odds of encountering bangers in the stairwell at this hour were about fifty-fifty. It was two o'clock in the afternoon. They didn't really get active until night. Usually around seven o'clock.

Daryl slipped out the door, shut it softly, and locked it. The once clean corridor carpet was now spotted with guasacaca, cigarette burns, and unidentifiable stains. The elevators were at the front of the building. The stairs were at the rear. He opened the door slowly. It shrieked like a burned cat. He had meant to oil it, but he kept forgetting. He gently shut the door and paused on the landing, cupping his ears. He wore hundred-dollar hearing aids. His friends told him they emitted an irritating whine, but he couldn't hear it. All he heard was normal sound amplified. The stairwell was quiet. Gun in hand, he descended the stairs pausing at each landing to listen. Someone screaming in Spanish on the sixth floor. Doors slamming. He hurried on down to the fourth, pulling the door open. This door squeaked less because Wayne had oiled it.

He walked quickly to Wayne's apartment. He knocked on the door. Seconds later it opened inward, and he slipped inside. Wayne was six feet tall, former Army Ranger, still lean and spry in his sixties. He'd be seventy next month. They'd talked about a birthday party, but no longer. Nothing that would attract attention. The gang was like the monsters in *A Quiet Place*. Any sound attracted them.

Wayne and Daryl sat on the sofa. Wayne picked up a bottle of rum from the living room table and poured a couple fingers into a red Solo cup, handing it to Daryl. He poured one for himself. They touched cups and drank.

"Salud," Daryl said.

"You hear from Alfred?"

"Yeah. He called this morning. Told me he'd called you. I didn't see that coming. His teenage neighbor. Whoda thunk it?"

"Yeah. And now they want to do the same for us, but the situation's a lot more complicated. Alfred's building only had maybe a dozen of those yellow-jackets. We got twice that many, and they're all armed."

"They were armed there too. Alfred tell you he shot one?"

"Oh yeah. I told him he shouldn't talk about it."

"It ain't like we're gonna tell anyone, and if we did, it was self-defense."

"I see you're packin'."

"I'd be a fool not to."

"They know you're armed?"

"No sir. I don't want to incite them."

"Same here." Wayne reached between the worn sofa cushions and pulled out a Ruger nine. "The only way they're gonna find out is the hard way. But I'd prefer to get the hell out of here, until somebody does something."

"Like the po-po? Fuggedaboudit." Daryl laughed. "If they were gonna do something, they would have moved already."

"Al says they're working on a plan."

"Who's working on a plan?"

"The two bikers who hauled him outta there."

"If a couple dozen bikers was to pull up in front of

the building, all these little shits would scatter like cockroaches."

Wayne put a finger to his lips. Daryl cupped his ears. Voices from the corridor. Spanish. Pounding on the door. Wayne jumped. He and Daryl looked at each other.

"Hey, viejos!" a man called through the door. "We are just here to make sure you are okay and whether you need anything! Open up!"

Daryl and Wayne were still.

Pounding. "We know you are in there, viejos! Do not fear us! We only want to help you! We are the new management, and we wish all our tenants to be happy!"

"Should we let them in?" Wayne half-whispered.

"The only reason to let them in is to teach them not to mess with us."

"If we start shooting, that'll bring the cops."

"If we start shooting, it'll be too late. We got to teach them they can't mess with us."

Wayne reached behind the sofa. He had to stretch. He pulled out an oak Louisville Slugger. "I had this since I was twelve years old. I played short-stop, and one year I hit four home runs."

Daryl put a hand on his kukri.

"Don't use that."

"What if they have guns?"

"Let me talk to them. Let me see if I can buy us some time."

Daryl went into the kitchen, opened the lower cupboard and seized a cast-iron skillet. Wayne waited until he was back in the room, standing on one side of the door.

More pounding. "Open up, you pendejos! This is the management! We know you're in there."

"We don't want any!" Wayne replied.

Pause. Furious pounding and kicking. "Now you got to open up. Don't worry! We only want to talk to you!"

"Talk through the door!"

"Listen, motherfuckers! Don't make me use an axe!"

"What do you want to talk about?"

"Building security! We provide it. You no longer have to worry about drunks and junkies trying to rob you."

Wayne peered through the peephole. He held up three fingers.

"I'll open the door on the chain, and we can talk that way."

"Hokay."

Gripping the baseball bat in his left hand, Wayne put the chain in the slot, unlocked the deadbolt and opened the door to its five-inch limit. The door exploded inward with the force of two powerful kicks. Three gang-bangers piled into the apartment. Daryl swung the cast-iron skillet in a short counterclockwise arc striking a wiry man with an inked head in the temple. The banger collapsed. Wayne swung the bat at the second intruder's knees, striking with a satisfying crack. The third banger reached for the pistol in the small of his back, but Daryl was on him with the skillet, sideways to the face. His nose exploded, and he dropped the gun.

The three bangers were *hors de combat*. Daryl grabbed the first one, dead to the world, and pulled him by his neck away from the door. He and Wayne grabbed the next by armpits and ankles and dragged him in. The one with the exploded nose scrabbled backward like a crab, got to his feet and booked, leaving his gun behind. Daryl picked it up. Taurus Judge, chambered for .410 shotgun rounds. The chain broke but the door was intact. They shut it and locked the dead bolt.

"Great," Wayne said. "Now what?"

Pumping from the adrenaline dump, Daryl looked at the thugs on the floor. "Got any zip ties?"

"I got nylon rope."

"Let's tie these bad boys up so they don't do anything stupid."

"One's got a wrenched knee, and the other has a concussion."

"You got to understand the thug life mindset. They'll keep going until you stop them. Maybe we can trade 'em for something."

"Like what? Fresh groceries?"

"Let me think on it. How you doin'? You ain't gonna collapse on me, are you?"

"I doubt it. But I will have a drink."

Wayne poured four fingers in both cups, handed one to Daryl. They touched cups and swallowed. Wayne went in the kitchen and returned with a roll of clothesline.

"Let me do it," Daryl said. "We learned how to do this in Afghanistan from our interpreter."

He tied both bangers hand and foot, hands behind them. He covered their mouths with duct tape.

"Well, I think we oughtta call Alfred and ask for some advice," Wayne said.

CHAPTER EIGHTEEN
A COMPLICATED SITUATION

JOSH SAT ACROSS FROM THE ADMINISTRATOR IN HER office at Vel Phillips Memorial High School, on the west side. He had worn clean blue jeans, a white shirt, and a blue sport jacket. Eugenia Hawkins sat behind her desk looking at Dolan's school records from his previous school. Mrs. Hawkins was in her sixties, curly hair cut short. She wore black-rimmed glasses and a burgundy turtle-neck sweater. She pursed her lips.

"He's coming into the academic year rather late."

"Yes, ma'am. He's had a difficult time. He's a remarkable boy. He grieves for his mother but has never been tempted to do drugs. How many other teenagers can say the same?"

"His circumstances are most unusual. And you were unaware you had a son until a week ago?"

"That is correct, ma'am. I make no secret of my past. I am ashamed of what I did, but I am no longer that man, praise Jesus."

Looking down, she pursed her lips. It was probably a mistake to bring Jesus into it.

"I looked at your record, Mr. Pratt. What, exactly, is atrocious assault?"

"A violent attack that is particularly heinous or cruel in nature."

"It doesn't say what you did."

"I cut a man's arm off with a chainsaw."

"I see. I am not unimpressed by your progress, Mr. Pratt. I consulted the school's attorney, and he said that considering your background, your behavior since getting out has been exemplary. He did say that you had been involved in several violent incidents over the years, but in each case, the police declined to press charges."

"I'm no saint."

"I'm aware of that. I'm also aware of several incidents when you saw ordinary citizens in danger, and you stepped in. That is certainly in keeping with the legend of the good Samaritan."

"Dolan has exceptional computer skills. He built his first computer when he was fifteen. I think he would do very well studying technology."

"Let's schedule an interview with Dolan. Let me look at my calendar." She turned to her computer and poked. "The earliest I can do is April twenty-fifth. It might be better if you waited until the start of the school year in the fall."

"He's been out of school too long already. I think a taste of academia, even if it's only for a week, will get his head back in the game. This is a kid who wants to learn."

"All right, why don't you bring him in? Say three thirty?"

Josh pulled a pen and pad from his jacket and wrote it down. "Thank you, ma'am. Dolan'll be happy when I tell him."

"I look forward to meeting him."

Josh went to the employee parking lot where he'd parked his bike. Sitting in the saddle, he turned his phone back on. Baker had called.

"Call me. We got a situation."

Josh called him back. "What's up?"

"I'd better let Alfred explain. They called him."

"What's up, Alf?"

"Y'know those two friends of mine living down the block?"

"Yeah?"

Alfred told him Wayne's version of events. "Let me give you Wayne's phone number. You gotta talk to him yourself."

"Can it wait until I get home?"

"How long will that be?"

"Half hour."

"I think so. I don't think they're in any immediate danger."

"They still got those two bangers tied up in their apartment?"

"Talk to Wayne."

"Will do."

Josh got on his bike and booked it, pulling into his driveway at four thirty. Fig greeted him with a fusil-lade of barks. He dumped a can of Purina True Instinct in the bowl and went into his office. He pulled out his phone. Alfred had forwarded Wayne's phone number.

"Hello."

"Wayne, it's Josh Pratt. We haven't met but…"

"I know who you are. You're the guy who got Alfred out of that building."

"That's right. And I'd like to do the same for you. But first, tell me what happened."

Wayne laid it out, no boasting, just matter of fact. "And now we got these two birds in the living room. One pissed his pants."

"Are the others bothering you?"

"Well yeah. About an hour after the incident, a whole bunch of them came by pounding on the door and shit, and Daryl told them that if they didn't back the fuck off, he was gonna start cutting parts off their buddies. Well, they didn't. They stepped it up. So Daryl took a wire cutter and snipped the pinky off the one. He wouldn't tell us his name, so we call him shitbird. We waited for a pause in the pounding, I jerked the door open, and he tossed the pinkie out. They went crazy. Then they went silent. That was about two hours ago."

"Shit. Maybe you shouldn't have done that."

"What have we got to lose? At this point, they have to kill us anyway to save face. They can't burn the building down 'cuz they're living here. We're checking our ammo."

"Is there a fire escape outside your window?"

"Yeah, we thought about that, but I'm seventy-two. I mean, I could probably do it, but it would take a while, and someone would notice, and then they'd all be waiting for us at the bottom."

"Fuck fuck fuck."

"They're gonna figure out how to cut our electricity and water any minute."

"All right. I was hoping we'd have more time to

prepare. Let me see what I can do, and I'll call you back."

Josh heard the garage door open and close. He'd given Dolan the code. Minutes later Dolan came in through the kitchen. Fig was all over him like jam on toast. Dolan got down on the floor, and it was a love fest. Josh stuck out his hand and boosted him to his feet.

"I was gonna pick you up."

"John had a doctor's appointment. He closed early."

"Just talked to Wayne."

"What's going on?"

"Well, the gang tried to force their way in, they opened the door, there were three thugs, they knocked two out of commission, and the third fled. Now they got two bangers tied up in the living room, and the whole gang is howling for their blood."

"Fuck! What are we gonna do?"

"You're not gonna do anything. I'm thinking. Shit."

Josh racked his brain. He had Baker. Maybe Baker had an idea. He called Baker.

"What?"

Josh laid it out for him.

"Shit."

"If we could show up with maybe ten, twelve bikers, that would do it. They don't want to start a war with a biker gang. We just need to get those two guys out of the building."

"Well, I might be able to get together ten bikers, but we're not in a club. They don't have colors."

"Do they look like bikers?"

Pause.

"Maybe six. Big guys who know how to handle themselves. The others are great guys, but they're not big guys. They're accountants, lawyers, insurance salesmen, that sort of thing. And it's going to take a while. May take weeks."

"Maybe we should talk to a lawyer."

"What if we were to just call the police and tell them two veterans are being held prisoner in that building?"

"Jesus, I'm dumb. Let's try that. I'll call you back."

Josh called Wayne.

"Yeah?"

"I got an idea. You're in District Three, right?"

"Yeah."

"You're not too far from the station. As soon as we get off the phone, you're going to call the station and tell them your situation. I'm going to call the station too. I'm going to tell them I got a tip from two veterans that a Venezuelan gang is holding two veterans hostage and threatening to kill them."

"You think that'll work?"

"It's worth a shot."

"Okay. I'm on it. Shit. There go the lights."

CHAPTER NINETEEN
FELONS

JOSH PHONED THE THIRD DISTRICT POLICE STATION.

"Third District," a woman answered. "Sergeant Helm speaking."

"Officer, my name is Josh Pratt. I live in Madison, but I have two friends, both veterans, who are being held hostage by a Venezuelan gang in your district."

"How so?"

"This gang has taken over an apartment building at 1225 Ridley Boulevard. The Wayzata Arms. The veterans' names are Wayne Garretson and Daryl Briggs. The gang has already tried to force their way into the apartment. My friends were able to repel the gang, while detaining two. Now the gang is raging up and down the corridors threatening to kill them. They tell me the gang is using the building to deal drugs and traffic women."

"We're aware of criminal activity at that address. What do you mean when you say your friends detained two gangbangers?"

"Three thugs forced their way into the apartment. You have to understand that. My friends want nothing more than to be left alone. They forced their way into the apartment, but Wayne and Daryl, being veterans, were able to overcome two, and are holding them as insurance in case the gang decides to burn down the building."

"Hang on just a minute."

Josh waited. He heard the desk sergeant talking to someone else. Five minutes later she came back on the line.

"We just received a call from Wayne Garretson verifying what you said. We're dispatching three cars to check out the situation."

"I don't know if that will be enough."

"Sir, we're experiencing a staffing shortage right now, and that's the best we can do. Is this a good number to reach you?"

"Yes, Officer. Thank you."

Josh called Wayne.

"Yeah, I just spoke to them. They're sending three cars."

"Hope that's enough."

"Well, I think when those cops show up, the bangers will just crawl back into the woodwork. We're packing now. Well, I'm packing. Daryl didn't bring anything."

"Where will you go?"

"I called the VFW yesterday, and they have a couple apartments on their second floor so we're going to go there."

"What VFW?"

"Post 41 on North Cleveland."

"Okay. Good deal. You want us to be there?"

"I don't think that's necessary."

"Call me when they get you out of the building."

"Will do. And thanks for helping."

Dolan stood in the doorway. "What's happening?"

"The police are sending three cars to get your friends out of the building."

"They're good guys. I met them when Alfred took me to the VFW."

"That's where they're headed. They have apartments they can use."

"I'm so relieved! Too bad it's not the gang that has to move."

"Things are fucked up in Milwaukee. It's one of the most segregated cities in America."

"I thought it was this great liberal bastion."

"So does Milwaukee. I got an appointment with you to see the admissions officer at Memorial High. April twenty-fifth. We're gonna try and get you into a class before the end of the year just to see how you fit in."

"Thanks, Josh. You want to show me how to drive?"

"What else I got to do?"

They took Mid Town to University Ridge Golf Course on the far west side. At this time of day there was little traffic. Josh turned onto the access road and pulled over to the side.

"Okay. First thing, hands on the wheel. Two hands at all times. Ten and two. Like this. See?"

"Yeah."

"Next, situational awareness at all times. You keep your eyes on the road except when you're checking your mirrors. See, you can switch stations here on the wheel, but I don't want you messing with the radio until you know how to drive. You ever drive an automatic?"

"I've never driven anything."

Josh turned off the engine. "All right. Let's switch places."

Dolan sat.

"Adjust your seat."

Dolan slid the seat forward a couple inches.

"Belt."

Dolan fastened his seat belt.

"Turn on the engine."

Dolan turned the key. The V8 rumbled to life. He put his hand on the shift lever and pulled it back to Drive. Very carefully he feathered the accelerator so that the big car pulled back onto the tarmac. They headed toward the clubhouse at twenty miles an hour. A Bronco came toward them.

"Eyes on the road, just stay on your side of the road."

They passed the Bronco. The parking lot and club-house appeared.

"Pull into the parking lot and park it in front of the clubhouse."

It took Dolan a couple forays to park the big car straight. Josh told him to turn it off. They went into the clubhouse. Technically it was for members only, but no one questioned them as they went through the restaurant out onto the veranda. It was cool, but not cold, and golfers were visible everywhere. A young man in a Bucky Badger shirt offered them two menus. They ordered cheeseburgers.

Dolan wolfed half, set it down, wiped his mouth, drank cola. "Do you play golf?"

Josh laughed. "Nope. I don't understand how

people can even watch a golf tournament on television. You?"

"No. I was never interested. I played some baseball in high school but that was about it. I also wrestled."

"You wrestled?"

"Yeah. At one hundred and thirty-five. Participated in one tournament at Sojourner Truth High School, won my first two matches, lost the third."

"That's good. Wrestling's underrated. I'll take you to Zhong Yi next week, introduce you to the shifu."

Josh ordered a beer. They sat in companionable silence. Dolan pulled out his phone and scrolled.

Young people, Josh thought. He was not a scroller. He checked his mail every time he returned to the house. That was enough. He could barely use his phone and his computer. It was a good thing Dolan showed up because the computer was heavy with malware, like a rowboat weighted down with barnacles. He could tell by the sloth-like speed everything ran. His mail took forever to appear and forever to send. He'd tried deleting huge blocks, but nothing seemed to help. The last time he had a good tune up was a year ago when Ninja breezed through.

"Can you tune up my computer?"

Dolan looked up. "Huh?"

"My computer. It's slower than a garbage truck. I think it's got malware."

"Which one?"

"The one in my office. Downstairs too."

"I already did the downstairs. There are some programs I can download. I'll do it when we get back."

"Groovy."

Josh's phone rang. He didn't recognize the number. "Josh Pratt."

"Mr. Pratt, it's Wayne Garretson."

"How'd it go?"

"Not so good. Me and Daryl are at the police station. We're under arrest for kidnapping."

CHAPTER TWENTY
CHRIST'S WARRIORS

"IS THIS YOUR ONE PHONE CALL?"

"Yeah."

"Why didn't you call a lawyer?"

"We don't know any lawyers."

"Okay. I got you covered. Don't talk to the police. Repeat. Don't talk to the police."

"Well, we told them what happened."

"That was stupid. Don't talk about it to anyone. Where are you?"

"We're at the Third District station."

"Okay. I'll see what I can do. Hopefully, I'll have you out tomorrow."

"How you gonna do that?"

"They gotta set bail, and I'll get you a lawyer."

"We don't have money for that."

"Don't worry about it. I'm sorry this happened to you. I'll see you Monday."

Dolan's forehead knitted with concern. "What's going on?"

"Alfred's vet buddies got arrested for detaining two of the thugs who broke into Wayne's apartment."

"What?!"

"I wish I could say I'm surprised, but they've been headed that way for a while. The police I mean. Now I gotta get 'em a lawyer."

"You got one?"

"I work for a criminal attorney. Finish your burger."

Josh called Fleiss, and it went straight to voice mail. "Steve, I got two vets arrested by the Milwaukee PD for kidnapping. They detained two Venezuelan gangbangers who broke into their apartment. They need a lawyer. Hopefully tomorrow. Give me a call."

Dolan stared over his burger. "Jeez."

"It's a crazy world."

"They broke into their apartment?"

"I know. You working Monday?"

"John said as long as I want."

"He paying you?"

"He pays me cash. Says legally, I'd have to fill out all these forms, and then he has to deal with his accountant who has to deal with the IRS, and it just kinda snowballs from there."

"How much?"

"He gives me a hundred and fifty bucks a day."

Josh shrugged. "Beats standing on a corner holding a sign."

"What are you gonna do tomorrow?"

"Imma go to church. Been a long time since I went, and I gotta talk to Pastor John. Want to come?"

Dolan wrinkled his nose. "I've never been to church."

"Won't hurt you. It's a pretty drive. Bring a book."

"Yeah. I was looking through your library there and found *Poe Must Die*. I've been reading it at the shop when I'm not working."

"That's a good book."

"It's crazy, man."

"You wanna go hear a band?"

"Sure!"

"Okay. The Ghost Particles are playing Staybridge. They start at eight."

"Great!"

"You hear much music?"

"No. I mean, only on the radio."

"You dig live music?"

"I've never seen any."

Josh checked his watch. It was already seven.

"You want dessert?"

"Sure."

Josh signaled the waitress. Dolan ordered a flan. Josh had another beer. It was seven thirty by the time they left, Josh feeling the slightest buzz, a mere echo of what he felt when he rode with the Bedouins. It was a miracle he hadn't killed himself. He clicked on the maps app on his phone.

"Staybridge Inn, Middleton."

"Take University Ridge Road to Mid-Town Road. Turn left on Mid-Town."

Hands on the wheel. Eyes on the road. Dolan turned on the radio. An old blues tune from WORT, the hippie-dippie radio station that was older than he. They arrived at the Inn shortly before eight and parked in the lot. Two chops occupied the next space over, one with JESUS IS LORD painted in black on the red tank. The buzz had gone away. The lounge was about half full as the Ghost Particles, five guys in their fifties and sixties who'd been in dozens of bands over the years, set up on the small stage.

Josh and Dolan grabbed a table in the back. A waitress came over, young lady smiling, purple hair, nose ring, inked arms.

"What can I get you?"

"Couple of root beers, please," Josh said.

Dolan stared at her ass as she walked to the bar.

"Wait persons wanted," Josh said. "Must be fully inked."

Dolan laughed. "I know, right?"

The two bikers at a table near the front were wearing their colors. CHRIST'S WARRIORS over a picture of Jesus wearing a crown of thorns. MILWAUKEE CHAPTER. For a moment Josh wondered if this was more than a coincidence. He'd been praying all his life but didn't believe in divine intervention. Man plans, God laughs. The band strummed a preliminary riff and burst into their first song.

"It's a drinkin' man's town, anyway you fall," the lead singer sang in a lugubrious alto. Josh looked around. The crowd took him at his word. The booze flowed. The band worked its way through "Save the Ashes," "All Gone Now," and "What Remains."

"What remains is what we lost. And every day we pay the cost."

"Jeez," Dolan said. "All these songs are about heartbreak and loss."

"So are the blues."

At the break, Josh walked over to the Warriors. The one closest, who looked like Lemmy Kilmister, looked at him dubiously.

"I'm a biker and a Christian," Josh said. "I saw your bikes."

The biker's patch said Paul. The other, who had a shaved skull and an earring, was Terry.

"Sit down," Paul said.

Josh sat.

"You interested in joining?"

"Sir, I appreciate the offer. How long you in town?"

"'Til Monday. We both have jobs in Milwaukee. What's your name?"

"Josh Pratt."

They bumped fists.

"You know about Tren de Aragua?"

"Oh yeah," Paul said. "Fuckin' cops are a joke."

"That's why I came over. I have a friend, a veteran, who was living in an apartment building the gang took over. A couple of night's ago they broke into my friend's apartment. They want the whole building to run drugs and women and God knows what else. Not your problem. Now he told me of another building the gang took over, and this one's even bigger, and there are elderly people and some veterans in that building, and they're scared shitless, and the police are worthless."

"What do you want from us?"

"You boys free Friday? I'd like to invite you over to my house for a barbecue. It's just me and my son Dolan there..." Josh gestured. Dolan waved. "And maybe my fiancée. I would like to develop a tactic for getting rid of these gangs without fatalities."

Paul looked at Terry, who raised his eyebrows.

"What's your church?"

"First Baptist Church of Mt. Horeb."

Paul and Terry looked at one another.

"We passed that yesterday," Terry said.

Josh signaled the waitress. "What are you drinking?"

Paul looked at his bottle "Tyranena IPA."

The waitress came over. "What can I get you?"

"Three more of these please."

"And three Jack Daniels," Paul said.

"Of course," the waitress said. She slinked away.

"You driving?" Paul said.

"I'm teaching my kid to drive." He stuck a thumb over his shoulder. "That's him."

"You ride?"

"Yup."

"What do you ride?"

"'99 Road King. Saw your bikes."

"Yeah," Paul said, "I'm looking at an Indian Chief."

"Great bike," Josh said. "I've ridden them."

The band filed back. Josh pulled out one of his business cards and wrote his address on the back. "Come by around two."

Paul glanced at it and stuck it inside his denim vest. Josh returned to Dolan. "Those guys are coming over for a barbecue Friday."

"Who are they?"

"Christ's Warriors. May be the answer to our problems."

THURSDAY MORNING JOSH RODE DOWNTOWN TO Fleiss's office. They got in Fleiss's Mercedes and hit the road. Josh told him what happened. Fleiss kept both hands on the wheel and didn't react. He waited until Josh finished.

"You've never met these men?"

"No. They were referred to me by another veteran who I hauled out of an apartment building down the street last Saturday. I don't see how the cops can charge them with kidnapping when these scumbags broke into their apartment."

"They can do whatever they want. But will it stick? Sounds bogus to me. I might be able to get them to drop the charges. The Milwaukee PD has enough bad publicity as it is."

"That guy you had me serve summons to. Arthur Baker."

"What about him?"

"He's an ex-biker. He helped me get the vet out of the Tren de Aragua stronghold on Saturday."

"Interesting."

"We're working up a plan to rescue more vets."

Fleiss held his hand up. "Stop. I don't want to know."

"Well, what's new with you?"

"I'm seeing someone."

"Seriously? That's great, Steve. Who?"

"Her name is Michelle. She's a court reporter."

"Getting married June fourteenth. Bring her to the wedding."

"Congratulations! Ray must be walking on air."

"She's treading the footlights. New play. *The Snot-Nosed Punk of Yore*."

"What's it about?"

"Kid gets hit in the head with a baseball, and when he wakes up, he thinks he's Shakespeare."

They rode in silence. They passed Lake Mills. Oconomowoc. Brookfield. Fleiss parked in the lot adjacent to the Third District station. Four cruisers were parked in front. The building was the three-story glass and curved-roof style that had permeated every community in America. It was an improvement over the soulless Soviet-style concrete blocks that had dominated the seventies. Josh wore clean jeans and a leather jacket. Fleiss wore a gray two-piece suit, white shirt, blue tie.

A counter stretched across the lobby, from a metal-detector walk-through to the wall. A half dozen people waited on wooden benches. The place smelled of cigarette smoke and Pine-Sol. There were two clerks on duty, with a black line marking the floor.

WAIT HERE FOR NEXT AVAILABLE CLERK.

A woman in her forties with short blond hair in a

bob wearing a blue police uniform waved them over. Her badge said Sgt. Betsy Wheeler.

"What can I do for you?"

Fleiss produced his driver's license. "I'm Steve Fleiss, an attorney, here to see my clients Wayne Garretson and Daryl Briggs."

She took the driver's license and made a copy. She handed his license back and looked at Josh. "Sir?"

"Josh Pratt. I'm a private investigator."

"You'll have to wait here, but Mr. Fleiss can go back. Both of you gentlemen have a seat. I'll call you when you can go back."

Josh and Fleiss sat on one of the wooden benches. They stared at their phones. A few moments later a beefy cop with a red face came out.

"Mr. Fleiss?"

Fleiss handed Josh his keys and cell phone and followed the cop back, pausing at the metal detector. The cop riffled through his briefcase. Josh checked his email. Costco chose him for a free thousand-dollar credit card. A young woman with enormous breasts wanted to be his friend. Paul from Christ's Warriors wrote, "Can we bring anything?"

"Beer," Josh wrote back.

Eugenia Hawkins wrote, "Confirming your appointment with Dolan for April 25."

"We'll be there," Josh wrote.

Josh watched people. Cops entering and leaving the building. A man upset about an aggressive dog in his building. Another lawyer. Jerell Moore.

Josh had met Jerell ten years ago working on the case of a popular UW athlete found drowned after a night of drinking. Jerell had been leader of the Jet Brodies. Jerell had a litter of pups at his feet when

Josh met him. That's where he got Fig. Jerell found religion and now preached the gospel of Christ while instructing boys in martial arts.

Josh waited until Jerell turned toward him. He stood.

"Brother Josh. What are you doing here?"

"Have a seat."

They sat. Josh told him. "Lawyer friend trying to spring two veterans. Gang took over their building and busted into their apartment. They fought back. So the cops arrested them. Why are you here?"

"One of my boys tried to hijack a car."

"Oh man, I'm sorry. What are you going to do?"

"Imma going to talk to his public defender who's supposed to come in any time."

"You had any run-ins with this Venezuelan gang?"

"Not me, but some of my boys. They live in the projects up on Millard Avenue. Got into a spat with four of those motherfuckers looking to take over an apartment. I think my boys ran 'em off. Haven't heard about them in a while. Most of the gangs are fed up with those motherfuckers. There's talk of Murder Crows hooking up with West Side Bluds to run 'em out of town."

"They got ARs."

"So do my boys. I can't tell 'em what to do, but I warned them the police aren't going to cut them any slack just because they have a mutual enemy."

Fleiss came out with Garretson and Briggs. Josh stood.

"Here come my boys. Let's get together one of these days."

"Anytime, brother. You're always welcome."

Fleiss and the vets came over. Garretson and

Briggs were grinning. Garretson's teeth looked like an abandoned cemetery. Briggs's were perfect.

"Josh Pratt?" Briggs said.

Josh stuck out his hand. "Yes sir."

Briggs bypassed the hand and embraced Josh in a bear hug. Garretson did the same.

"We can't thank you enough," Garretson said.

"Happy to do it. Steve, how'd you do it?"

"I suggested that the *Milwaukee Post* was interested in the details of their incarceration, and news station WTMJ wanted to have them on to discuss their ordeal. Sergeant Ordway wasn't too happy. He agreed to drop the charges and said he will try to step up surveillance in that neighborhood."

"You boys hungry?" Fleiss said.

"Starving," Briggs said.

"Where are you going from here?" Josh said.

"We thought we'd go to a local VFW that has a couple rooms upstairs."

"You might be better off in Madison."

"Why would we be better off in Madison?" Briggs said.

"Reduces chance of retaliation. I'm thinking about your situation. What we can do about it."

Briggs's forehead wrinkled. "What do you mean?"

"People trapped in gang-controlled buildings. They're living on borrowed time. There's a VFW in Madison that offers accommodations. I'm having a barbecue tomorrow. You boys are invited. We're going to talk over the situation."

"You need anything?" Fleiss said.

Garretson nodded. "Yeah. My meds. Some clothes."

Fleiss held the front door open. "I don't think you

should go back there. That gang will have taken over your apartment by now. You can call your doctor from Madison. I know a decent restaurant in Wauwatosa. We'll stop on the way."

The Copper Kettle in Wauwatosa served traditional Wisconsin fare: fish boil, cheese curds, bratwurst. Everybody ordered cheeseburgers. Garretson and Briggs drank two beers each. They weren't driving. They were celebrating. They were alive. Garretson set his glass down.

"Guys, I hesitate to bring this up, but we have friends in a building up the block who are under siege. They've called the cops over and over, and the only time the cops showed up was this last time, when they arrested us."

"How many friends?" Josh said.

"The Welch family on the third floor. Both folks are in their forties, they have two girls. They're struggling. Johnny used to be a manager at some big box store, but it went under during the COVID. He and Helen are both taking on temp jobs. Their girls are fourteen and eighteen, and they're afraid to leave the apartment. Daryl, you got some friends on the seventh floor."

"Yeah. Esther Mills. She's widowed. Lives on a pension. I was doing her shopping. I should call her right now. Excuse me one minute."

"What building?"

"The Abbott."

Briggs pushed back and went outside.

"We need an accurate count of gang members living in that building," Josh said. "Is there video?"

Garretson folded his napkin. "There used to be.

There's a camera in the lobby, but the gang controls it."

"What about the footage? Does that exist?"

Josh wrote it down in his pad.

Fleiss put a hand on his arm. "What are you planning? Haven't you done enough? You're not a vigilante."

"What else I got to do?"

CHAPTER TWENTY-TWO
A QUIET EVENING
AT HOME

THEY GOT BACK TO MADISON AT ONE. FLEISS HAD contacted the local VFW, and Post 1318 in Fitchburg agreed to put the two veterans up if they could share a room. It was an apartment but there was only one bedroom. Garretson and Briggs were happy to have it. Fleiss took them to the VFW, stopping at a supermarket along the way so they could stock up. Mostly vitamins and over-the-counter meds. Garretson had phoned his physician on the drive home and filled him in on the situation, and he agreed to issue fresh prescriptions once Garretson found a pharmacy.

They pulled into the VFW parking lot. A man wearing civvies and a campaign cap came out of the two-story red brick building to greet them.

"Gentlemen, I'm Werner Grosz, chief cook and bottle washer. Welcome to VFW post 1318. I'm sorry you had to go through this. I applaud you on your resourcefulness, and you're welcome to stay here as long as you like."

Briggs put his arm around Fleiss. "We wouldn't be here if it weren't for this guy."

Grosz stuck out his paw, enclosing Fleiss's hand. "Thank you, counselor, for all that you've done."

"Happy to do it."

Josh invited the vets and the lawyer to his cookout the next day. "Take an Uber. I'll pay for it."

They agreed to come. Fleiss begged off. "I can't make it tomorrow. I have to be in court."

"Thanks, Steve. I really appreciate it."

"Happy to do it."

They drove to Fleiss's office. Josh got on his bike and was home by three. Ray's Prius was in the driveway. He went in through the kitchen where Fig sat begging at Ray's feet as she cut up asparagus. Fig paddled backward with her forepaws, an endearing habit designed to evoke sympathy. Josh kissed Ray and looked down.

"You're a beggar. You're not starving."

"Oh, give her something."

Josh opened the cupboard, pulled out a chunk of turkey jerky and tossed it to the dog. Snap. Gone. Paddle.

"What's cooking?"

"Chicken apple sausages from Whole Foods and asparagus marinated in olive oil, balsamic vinegar, and pesto. It's all going in this cast-iron pan."

"When do we eat?"

"Not for a couple hours. Why?"

"Good! Let's take advantage while we have the house to ourselves."

"He's seventeen, Josh. He may not be a virgin."

"Says he is."

"Where is he?"

"He's at that electronic repair store at West Towne. He'll be home around five thirty."

"Give me one minute."

She placed the cast-iron pan on top of the refrigerator and went into the bedroom. "You know where to find me."

Josh went onto Amazon and ordered a Pyle megaphone for thirty-six bucks. He went into the bedroom. They tore each other's clothes off. They lay in bed, Josh staring at the ceiling, Ray with her eyes closed, while the radio softly played Miles Davis, "On Green Dolphin Street." It was a dream state, a fugue state.

The sound of the garage door rumbling jarred them out of their stupor. Josh had given Dolan the code. Fig fired a fusillade of barks. The kitchen door opened and closed. Josh eased out from under Ray, swung his legs over the edge and pulled on his pants and shirt.

"I'm having some friends over for a barbecue tomorrow, if you want to come."

"Who?"

"Three vets we rescued and two bikers. Christ's Warriors."

"Ooooh, scary."

"You should see them."

"How did you rescue these vets?"

"Dolan told me about one, lived in his building. The building was taken over by a Venezuelan gang who is terrorizing everyone, demanding protection money, etc. So a friend of mine and I got him out, and he told us about two more vets in a building down the street, same sitch. So, we got them out, and they told us about two more people in another building and so on and so forth, and the fucking cops won't do jack shit."

"Well, what are you planning to do?"

"Get them out."

"And how to you plan to do that?"

"The power of persuasion. How to win friends and influence people."

She gave him the side eye. "Riiiiiiiight. I worry that you're going to get killed."

"I think we can do this without either side firing a shot."

"How do you figure?"

"They're terrified of biker gangs."

"How do you know?"

"I know from experience and getting Alfred out. He was the first. You coming or not?"

"I'd love to, but I have too much to do. Zoom meeting with an agent. Dinner with Idaho."

"Okay."

"Turn the oven on, please," Ray said.

Dolan was in the kitchen glugging down a glass of orange juice while Fig sat at his feet thumping and paddling. He put the glass down. "Should I feed Fig?"

"Yes please. There's an open can in the fridge."

Dolan pulled the can of Purina True Instinct, took off the plastic cap and scraped it into Fig's bowl. He set it on the floor. The food was gone in four seconds.

"Is that enough?"

"Vet says she could lose a few pounds. Dogs never get enough. You could put all the food in the world in front of her, and she'd eat until she got sick, throw up, and eat some more. It's just the way they are."

Josh turned the oven on. "Ray's cooking."

"You're cooking."

"Ray made it. Dinner in twenty."

"Okay." Dolan went downstairs.

Josh phoned Baker. "I'm having a barbecue here tomorrow at two. Bring Alfred."

"You want me to bring anything?"

"Bring a six-pack."

"Mind if I bring my camera?"

"What for?"

"I'm making a documentary."

"About what?"

"How to get gangs out of an apartment building without the police."

Josh thought about it. "Will you take my suggestions on the edit?"

"Well, yeah. You'll have to sign a waiver. Everybody will, or I can't use them."

Eight guests. Everybody loved ribs. He drove to Safeway and got five pounds of ribs and two pounds of potato salad. When he returned, Ray had pulled the pan. Six chicken sausages and asparagus.

She pointed to the pan. "It's hot."

Josh put three plates on the counter. He went downstairs where Dolan sat at the computer looking at the Christ's Warriors home page.

"These guys seem solid," he said.

"You a Christian?"

Dolan swiveled. "Not so you'd notice. I don't know what I am. Mom wasn't very religious. She swore a lot. So, if you hear me taking the Lord's name in vain, that's where I got it."

"After I found Christ, no more fights. I learned to turn the other cheek. Couple times, I even talked the other guy into doing the same. If Christ hadn't found me, I probably would have killed myself."

"But you still fight."

"When I have to. I'm not a pacifist."

"I wish I could fight."

"Nelson will teach you. I'll take you over Saturday after work. We're gonna get you a license too. Then we're gonna get you some cheap piece of shit that when you run it into an Armco barrier, it won't seem so bad."

Dolan laughed.

"Dinner is ready."

CHAPTER TWENTY-THREE
A GATHERING OF THE TRIBES

BAKER DROVE HIS TRUCK AND BROUGHT LONGCHAMPS. Garretson and Briggs took an Uber. Paul and Terry rode their bikes. They gathered in lawn chairs on the deck. Josh put Dolan to work grilling the ribs. Baker brought a quart of coleslaw and two bottles of bourbon. Paul and Terry brought a six-pack of Tyranena IPA. Garretson and Briggs brought a six-pack of We're a Rap Rock beer. Josh did the math. Twelve bottles of beer. Average alcohol by volume: 8.5%. Two bottles of bourbon. Seven drinkers.

"Gentlemen, if we drink all this, we'll be drunk."

Paul and Terry wore their colors. Paul took a Rap Rock and twisted the cap off. "I'm good for one. After that I can't ride."

Terry took a Tyranena. "Same here."

Josh handed beers to Garretson, Briggs, Baker, and Longchamps. He raised his beer in a toast. "To the ride."

"Hear, hear."

"Always and forever."

They drank.

"The reason I asked you here," Josh said, "is we need to know of other apartment buildings in the vicinity that this gang has taken over. Mainly for the vets. We're not the Milwaukee Police Department. It's not our job to clear these fucking gangs out. But we can't just stand by while they're terrorizing innocent people, particularly veterans. We're looking at the Wayzata on Wayne and Darryl's recommendation."

Briggs pulled a folded sheet of paper out of his jacket pocket. "Wayne and I figured you were gonna say that, so we made a list. We're mostly concerned about the Wayzata Arms. There are three veterans living there. I've met two. They're there for the same reason we were at the Abbott 'Cuz the Veterans Administration has a deal with the landlords to house veterans."

"Don't forget the widow and the Welch family," Daryl said.

Josh rubbed his temples. "Well we can get 'em out, but where will they go?"

"If your plan works, they can go hang for a couple hours and then come right back."

"Give me a list and room numbers. Is the VA unaware of the situation?" Josh said.

Garretson belched. "We musta told those dumb sons a bitches a half dozen times what was going on. It's always some flunky. Says they'll relay the message to the boss. Went down there once, and all I got was a runaround. Called Washington. Same thing. We're on our own."

"Tell me about the Wayzata."

Briggs set his bottle on the table. "Three guys. Hiles, Blankenship, and Johnson."

"You got phone numbers?"

"Just Hiles."

"Give him a call."

Briggs pulled out his phone. "Hey Harry, it's Briggs. You heard about me and Garretson?"

Beat.

"We're out of the apartment. We're in Madison. They tried to break down our door. Garretson and I subdued three of them and when the cops came they arrested us for kidnapping."

"What?!"

"Yeah. Crazy, huh? But this guy Pratt knew a lawyer. He got us out."

Beat.

"Yeah? Funny you should mention that. We were just talking about that. Got a guy here who wants to help."

Beat.

"I'll let him talk. His name's Josh."

Josh took the phone. "Hello, Harry?"

"This is Harry."

"Briggs tell you how we got him out of jail?"

"He mentioned it. What happened?"

Josh gave him the condensed version. "Like to help you and your buddies."

"Well yeah, we got to do something, but where will we go? The VA doesn't give a shit. I don't have any relatives who'll have me."

"We're thinking of a solution that would clear all the gangs out. Permanently."

"I'm listening."

"Can you do FaceTime?"

"Yeah. Gimme a minute."

Harry looked to be in his sixties with a shock of white hair and a red face. A drinker's face.

"I'm putting together a gang. Bikers, veterans, and maybe some local street gangs who aren't too happy about these foreigners."

"Are you serious?"

"Yeah. We already rescued these guys, but we don't want you living on the street corner. The goal is to clear these gangs out permanently. Make them go somewhere else."

"Then they'll be somebody else's problem."

"Maybe not. What we're planning, we get publicity. The kind of publicity the city doesn't want. Especially the police department 'cuz it'll make them look bad. Talk to your buddies. See if they're down. Can you get out of your apartment?"

"Yeah, during the day. Too risky at night."

"Okay. Let me see what I can put together. Let me give you my number."

Harry wrote it down. "I'll tell the others."

"Okay. I'll get back with you shortly."

Josh handed the phone back to Briggs. Fig went crazy, running back and forth at the fence facing the street. Josh excused himself, went through the house and opened the front door. His bullhorn had arrived. He took it inside and returned to the deck.

Baker stood with his camera. "Guys, I'm a film-maker. I've made a half dozen feature films. Grade Z horror. *The Hodag* is the most famous. I'm going to make a documentary about getting these assholes out of the building. I want you all to be in it. In order to do that, you have to sign a waiver giving me permission to use you. I'm not trying to sabotage anybody. I'm interested in the truth. If you don't like to be on camera, I won't use you. I'm going to pass these waivers out. Read 'em, consult a lawyer if you like, and get 'em back to me."

"Terry and I are in," Paul said.

"I'm bringing a drone. Does anybody here know how to operate a drone?"

"I do," Paul said. "I operated one in the sandbox."

"Great! It's a Ruko. Pretty simple."

"No prob. I've worked with Rukos."

Josh looked at Briggs. "How 'bout it?"

"I can do that."

"Okay," Baker said, "With your permission, I'm gonna do a little recording. I'll be discreet. Just act natural. I won't release anything you don't sign off."

He sat down. Josh stood.

"Anybody hear speak Spanish?"

Terry raised his hand. "I was stationed in San Diego. The Army taught me."

"When we get to the apartment building, I'm going to speak, then I'm going to hand you the bullhorn, and you repeat what I said in Spanish."

"I can do that."

"Tell me about the building."

"It was elegant in the thirties. Nine stories, hardwood floors, beautifully finished foyer which they ripped apart to install brass mailboxes. Not quite a slum but close. Mostly working-class families and a few veterans. Six apartments per floor. So thirty-six apartments total. The gang started moving in a year ago. One of the tenants died, and the landlord hung a unit For Rent sign out front. They went door to door making a lot of noise until they found the empty unit, broke down the door, and that's how they started.

They've driven out five other families and taken over their units. Drugs. Women. Kids."

"Kids?" Josh said.

"Yeah. Really young kids. Asian and Latino. I think they got a bunch of them up from the border before Trump took office, and the rest are coming in through Canada."

"How many gangbangers?"

Briggs looked at Garretson. "Figure they're crashing four and five to a unit, 'cept for the head honcho. He gets one by himself. So about twenty. Heavily armed. Our pals say they're carrying AKs. Not all of 'em. About half. The others got knives and hammers. They use sledgehammers to break into units. Now they're doing it to occupied apartments. They break in, tie up the tenants, soak them for everything they've got, then kick 'em out and warn 'em. One word to the authorities and they're dead. If a family has any girls, they stay."

"Who's the head honcho?"

"Dude named Luis. That's all I know."

Dolan waved his spatula. "These ribs are ready."

"Put 'em out, Dolan. We'll get 'em in a minute." He turned back. "Well, we gotta do something. Would any of your brothers be interested?"

Terry's forehead wrinkled. "Well, here's the problem. The club's on a run in Texas. We're all ex-Marines. Paul and I rode up here to visit family. The brothers might want to help, but most of us have day jobs, families, and who knows how long it would take for them to their shit together? Also, with the police being as they are, we might get a repeat of what happened to Wayne and Daryl."

"Our pals say they called the cops numerous times, and all they got was a drive-by," Daryl said.

"Would you boys be willing to go over there and give 'em a little push?"

"Fuck yeah," Briggs said. "Wayne here can hardly walk."

"What about you, Albert?"

Longchamps nodded. "Yeah. I'm fed up. I'll back ya."

Josh turned to Baker and the Warriors. Baker grinned. "I'm down. But I don't want to go in there guns blazing. I'd rather do it the old-fashioned way. Clubs. Knives."

"The problem is," Josh said, "they're heavily armed."

Briggs leaned forward. "Yeah. But they know if they have a firefight, that will bring the cops. They think they're tough. They think they can strong-arm any good Samaritans."

"That's why we ride up on bikes. You boys'll have to take the baffles out. The louder the better. I'm no psychologist, but I think we can get them out without violence just using a show of force. I'm trying to line up some allies."

"One of those guys is a Native American," Briggs said. "Ojibwe, I think. Name's George Nelson."

"Yeah? So?"

"So there are Native American motorcycle clubs."

"We don't want to get anyone shot," Josh said.

"Least of all ourselves," Briggs said. "I know where we can get ballistic vests."

"How many?" Josh said.

Briggs looked around. Did a count with his fingers.

142

"I know where to buy as many as we need. But who's gonna pay?"

Dolan waved his tongs. "Come on guys. The ribs are getting cold."

They heaved themselves to their feet, grabbed paper plates, and walked the buffet line loading up with ribs, potato salad, coleslaw, barbecue sauce, and paper towels. Josh waited until everyone had gone before filling his plate. He sat in a chair with a folding TV table and chowed down. Everybody but Dolan went back for seconds. Fig sat hopefully at his feet.

"Can we give Fig treats?" Dolan said.

"Nah. Barbecue ain't good for dogs. Go inside and get her some Pupperoni."

Josh wiped his mouth. "How much for the ballistic vests?"

Briggs poked his phone. "They're two bills, but then you gotta buy plates for the big stuff. Add the plates, were looking at five bills a set. So we're looking at around thirty-five hundred for everyone here who's up for it, but I may know a guy who can get them cheaper."

Josh waved his fork. "Hold off on that until we decide what we're gonna do. Daryl, why dontcha call your friend George and sound him out."

"George is a fighter. I'm surprised he hasn't killed somebody already."

"Ask him about any Native motorcycle clubs that might be interested."

"Yeah, I can do that."

"Ask him now. See how's he doing."

. . .

BRIGGS HELD UP A FINGER. "OKAY. GIVE ME A minute. I gotta get his contact info." He got up and walked into the yard. The boys talked bikes. Paul, Terry, and Arthur went through the house to look at their bikes. Josh helped himself to more ribs. The boys came back. Briggs came back and sat next to Josh.

"Says the situation is dire. He's packing, and he had to show it the other night to get through the lobby. He's worried about some of his neighbors. Hears pounding and screams at night, sees strange girls in the hallways, creeps coming and going. He would love to see a show of force."

"Know any Native bikers?"

"The Bisons. They got a chapter in Eau Claire. Got a name and phone number." Briggs handed Josh a folded-up piece of paper. Leonard Two Hawks.

CHAPTER TWENTY-FOUR
MAKING PLANS FOR DOLAN

SATURDAY MORNING JOSH AND DOLAN DROVE TO THE Zhong Yi Kung Fu Center on East Washington. They parked in the strip mall lot and entered the storefront. The school was between a consignment store and a liquor store. A dozen cars sat in front of the school, from a beat-up VW bug to a new Porsche. Inside students wearing loose-fitting sweats stretched, worked out on the kung fu wooden man, or practiced weapons.

Shifu Nelson Ferreira, a bear of a man wearing traditional Chinese kung fu dress came out to greet them. "Josh. Good to see you! Who's this?"

"This is my son Dolan."

Dolan bowed. "Pleased to meet you, sir."

Nelson bowed. "I didn't know you had a son."

"Neither did I until last week. He showed up on my doorstep. Long story. I'll tell you later. Dolan's interested in learning self-defense."

"We teach that along with traditional Chinese martial arts. Do you have any experience?"

"No, but I've watched a lot of kung fu movies," Dolan said with a straight face.

"He's kidding. He wrestled in high school."

Shifu smiled. "Okay. Wrestling is a combat sport. Why don't you hang around. You can watch the first class or participate if you like. Did you bring any workout clothes?"

Josh hefted a gym bag. "Old sweats."

"Very good. No street shoes on the mat but you can wear martial arts shoes. I think it's warm enough you won't need them."

"I gotta run some errands," Josh said. "Okay if I pick him up around one thirty?"

"Sure."

Josh stopped at Fleiss's office. Fleiss stayed out of court on weekends and spent his time going over depositions, examining evidence, or playing golf. The office was empty except for him, and the front door was unlocked. The door to his office was open.

"Hey, Steve," Josh said as he entered.

"What?"

Steve went in the office where Fleiss sat at his desk poring over papers with a pen.

"Need your advice."

"Shoot."

"These Venezuelan gangs taking over apartment buildings."

"What about 'em?"

"Some friends of mine and I are planning on getting more people out."

"Yeah?"

"Yeah. Here's the thing. This gang patrols the building. It's their turf. They terrorize the people who remain. They've driven several tenants out so they can take over their units for drugs and prostitution. They're heavily armed. The police pretend there's nothing going on. So a bunch of us are going in to kick ass and escort the gang out."

"How many in the gang?"

"At least a dozen."

"And you're going to do this without guns? What happens when they start shooting?"

"We're going to wear ballistic vests. We're taking bear repellent and shit, and we think that when faced with a group of determined bikers, they're gonna cave. I mean, even these scumbags have seen *Sons of Anarchy*."

Fleiss ran a hand across his head. "That's the stupidest thing I've heard all day."

"These people are in fear for their lives. They include a couple veterans."

"Call the police."

"They've called the police. The police won't do shit. They don't want to be involved. You know the drill."

Fleiss sighed. "Milwaukee's been Democrat for years. They've made it clear that in a dispute between the cops and Attila the Hun, they'll back the Hun. Don't do it."

Josh turned to go. "Yeah, thanks."

"Josh."

He stopped. "What?"

"Don't be a fool. I don't want you as a client. You're about to get married. What would Ray say?"

"I hear ya, I hear ya."

"Awrite. Keep your nose clean."

Josh drove home. He went into his office and phoned Jerell.

"Brother Josh. What can I do for you?"

"You can help me clean Tren de Aragua out of an apartment building."

"Say what?"

"When I saw you at the police department, we were springing two veterans who'd been arrested for kidnapping. The reason they were arrested for kidnapping is that two gangbangers forced their way into their apartment. With guns. My boys overpowered them and tied them up while they waited for the police. When the cops came, they took one look and arrested my boys for kidnapping. Both veterans."

"I wish I could say I'm surprised, but that sort of behavior has become the norm in recent years. I'm a guidance counselor these days. I might be willing to assist, but I don't see how that's going to help. These gangs are heavily armed and stoned to the gills."

"Right now, we got seven, including two Christ's Warriors. That's a motorcycle club."

"I'm familiar with Christ's Warriors. How many gang members in the building?"

"Maybe two dozen."

"Are you out of your mind?"

"We're hoping the bikers' reputation will give us some juice. We're recruiting."

"Up until they start shooting."

"Aren't you still in contact with some of the old gangs? Murder Crows? Westside Bluds?"

"Well yeah. Those are my boys. The boys I'm trying to reach."

"Aren't they just a little miffed about these newcomers, all of whom are in the country illegally, encroaching on their turf?"

"Yeah, I've heard that from boys I know."

"What if we were to form a temporary alliance with some of these gangs just to get these mother-fuckers out of the neighborhood? It would be good public relations. The cops might start looking at them in a new light."

"Let me think about it. I have to admit, it might work. But we're talking about kids."

"Violent kids."

"Let me think about it and get back to you."

"Thanks, Jerell."

"How's my dog?"

"She's fat and happy. Well, she's not fat. Vet says she could stand to lose a couple pounds."

Jerell laughed. "Stop feeding her five times a day."

He checked his email. Eugenia Hawkins wrote, "Confirming your appointment with Dolan for April 25."

Monday. He checked his watch. Dolan would still be working. He'd need to tell John. Josh didn't feel like cooking, so he drove to Trader Joe's on Monroe Street and bought two packages each of frozen Steak and Stout Pies, Chicken Pot Pies, Family-Style Meat Lasagna, and Chicken Burrito Bowls. They barely fit in his freezer.

Dolan phoned at one thirty. "I'm done."

"You ready to come home?"

"You bet."

"I'm on my way. How'd you like it?"

"Man, I had a blast! I can't wait to do it again! But I have to work on Monday."

"Nelson has evening classes. We'll figure some-thing out. Also, you see the guidance counselor on Monday."

"What about my job?"

"I'll explain to John about your job. I really respect your work ethic, but right now you have to go to school and learn."

"Learn what?"

"Readin', writin', and 'rithmetic."

"What about all the genders and how the white man is oppressing everyone?"

"Fuck that shit."

Dolan laughed. "Okay. See you soon."

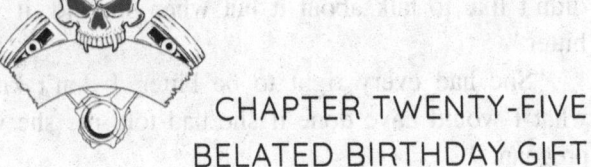

CHAPTER TWENTY-FIVE
BELATED BIRTHDAY GIFT

On Sunday, Josh took Dolan to West Towne to practice driving. At ten in the morning most cars were parked close to the mall leaving vast stretches empty. Dolan took the wheel. Hands at ten and two.

"Okay, drive up that light post, turn around and come back."

"How fast will this baby do? It's got a V8, right?"

"Faster than you want to go. Just take it easy, pal. You have to crawl before you can walk."

"Can I turn on the radio?"

"No. Just drive. Use your turn signals."

"We're in a parking lot!"

"Get used to it." They drove in silence.

"Did your mother know I was in Madison?"

"Yes."

"How did she know?"

"I told her."

Josh sighed. A harpoon of regret penetrated his heart. "She must have hated my guts."

"That's one way of putting it."

"I wish I could go back in time and right the many wrongs I committed. All I can do is try to be better."

"Honestly, you're not the man she described. She didn't like to talk about it but when she did, it was bitter."

"She had every right to be bitter. I don't know what I would have done if she had told me she was pregnant."

A man on an electric bike crossed in front of them. Dolan jammed on the brakes.

"Always brake slow. Never slam on the brakes unless you must. You'll be surprised at how much more effective it is."

"Okay."

"You go to school tomorrow. Memorial. I'll drop you off. Call me when it's over, and I'll send an Uber."

"Is it close enough to ride a bike?"

"Maybe. Let's drive first."

Twenty minutes later Josh pointed to an empty parking spot in front of Mooyah. "Let's eat."

They went in and sat at a table. A smiling waitress came up and handed them menus.

"Get you boys something to drink?"

"Just water."

"I'd like a chocolate shake."

"I'll be right back," she said, turning on her heel and heading to the counter.

"Wait persons wanted," Josh said quietly. "Must be fully inked."

Dolan laughed. "I want to get a tattoo."

Josh crossed his index fingers. "Ix-nay. You can think about it when you're eighteen. When's your birthday?"

"December twenty-third."

"That's rough. Did your mother pass off one gift as two?"

"She gave me clothes when I needed them. She never gave me a gift."

Josh's heart sank. He wanted to crawl into a hole and die. He offered a silent prayer. *Lord forgive me*. That night, Dolan retreated to the basement. Josh heard him watching a movie with a lot of shooting but didn't want to force himself on the boy. Better to let things happen gradually.

Josh decided to give Dolan a knife. The boy had demonstrated maturity. Josh wasn't worried that he'd gut someone on the bus. Josh always had knives. He had so many knives he kept them in a big plastic bin in the garage. He went out to the garage, dragged the bin out from under some boxes and opened it beneath the fluorescent lamp. He pulled over a plastic stool and sat. So many knives.

He had three balisongs, also known as butterfly knives. They were flashy blades with a split handle so you could flip them open, closed, twirl them around. No. Nothing but trouble for a teenager. He picked up the kukri. Massive. Full tang. Forged in Nepal. No. The temptation to wave it around and cut something was too great. Then there was the Puma, a hunting knife in a leather sheath. A handsome, faceted blade. Not exactly a pocketknife, but a beautiful tool. No. A boy needed a pocketknife, a tool at hand. Something practical that didn't cry out for blood. He had a half dozen flip lock blades he'd taken from hoodlums threatening him or someone else. He opened a weird sandwich blade from China. Its handle was split, but unlike the balisong, it was made of two halves like loaves of bread that folded up the side of the blade. It was a good knife, but it was weird. Finally, there was the Kershaw, a high-class thumb propelled switch blade. Yeah. He'd trust Dolan with the Kershaw. He'd give it to him after he picked him up from school.

He didn't want Dolan trying to impress his new classmates with a switchblade.

Maybe the sandwich blade.

No, the Kershaw. To demonstrate his trust.

He put the blades back in the box and the box back in the stack. He went inside. He went to his bedroom, turned on the light, and picked up a book he'd found at a Little Free Library in the neighborhood. They only popped up in upper middle-class neighborhoods. The book was *Flyboys*, about the war in the Pacific. It was about the development of naval airpower and how hundreds of kids, some Dolan's age, risked their lives to defeat the Japanese. It was mind blowing and made him think how worthless and indulgent most kids were these days, and he thanked God Dolan was not among them.

That made him think about what a wild, heedless punk he'd been and the awful things he'd done. To men. To women. Going to prison had been a blessing in disguise. Were it not for Chaplain Michael Dorgan, he'd be dead by now. Shanked in the yard. He'd first gone to one of Dorgan's Sunday prayer meetings out of curiosity and because a man named Dozer, one of the biggest, meanest sumbitches he'd ever known, invited him. Dozer was six-six and weighed two hundred and eighty pounds. He looked like the Incredible Hulk. He was Caucasian, but his body was so heavily inked he looked like a Native American at first glance. Black hair.

They sat on folding chairs in a circle in the chapel

while Dorgan explained passages in the Bible. Low key. Matter of fact.

"*Though I walk through the valley of the shadow of death*," Dorgan began. "It means, even during the darkest days of our lives, we experience God's protective care."

And, "*A friend loves at all times*. That one's easy. It means what it says."

And, "*Call to me and I will answer you*. It means, if you're wondering where your pizza is, the delivery driver has it."

The cons loved and respected Pastor Dorgan. Some of them still got shanked. Josh was one of the lucky ones. His lawyer at the time, Daniel Bloom, was good friends with the governor and got Josh pardoned. So Josh was out. And he believed in God. Life was good, for a while. Until he met Charlotte Newton. Everybody called her Fig. A maniac named Wayne Culligan killed her.

Josh was working himself into a bad place, but he caught it in time. Got out of bed and down on his knees. Thanked the Lord for his manifold blessings. Got back in bed and turned off the light. Tried to sleep. It was a long time coming.

JOSH DROPPED DOLAN OFF AT VEL PHILLIPS Memorial High School at seven thirty, as a yellow school bus pulled out of the drive. Formerly James Madison Memorial, the city council had renamed it Vel Phillips in honor of civil-rights activist Velvalea Hortense Rodgers "Vel" Phillips.

The renaming process was sparked by former Memorial student Myra Berry's proposal. James Madison's ownership of slaves prompted her suggestion. Committee member Shawn Matson thanked Berry for starting the process.

"If she didn't do that, we may not be sitting here today, and we may be just kind of pretending that there isn't a potential problem here that needs to be solved or a wrong that needs to be righted," Matson said.

Dolan was late. He wore clean khakis, a Green Bay Packer T-shirt, and carried a backpack in which Josh had packed a sandwich. Dolan entered the mostly empty main entrance. He could feel the place humming like a beehive. A floor to ceiling glass cabinet held hundreds of trophies earned by Memorial's Spartans and individual gymnasts. The place smelled of Pine-Sol and mac and cheese. A man in a beige suit, balding with glasses stood in the entry to a hallway.

"What can I do for you, young man?"

"Sir, my name is Dolan Pratt. I'm a transfer student from Milwaukee. Eugenia Hawkins said I should come today and experience class before starting my senior year."

"I see. Come with me. I'll take you to her."

Dolan followed the man down a side corridor opposite the classrooms to an office with an open door. He knocked on the door. "Eugenia, there's a young man here who says this is his first day."

"Come in, Dolan."

Dolan entered the room to find a prim, smiling older woman with short hair and glasses.

"Thank you, Roger. Dolan, have a seat. I'm Miss Hawkins."

"Please to meet you, ma'am."

Her smile broadened. "You're coming into the school year rather late. I'm going to give you some forms to fill out. You don't have to do it today but overnight would be good. Return them to me tomorrow." She handed him a clipboard with eight pages of questions.

"Should I take the clipboard?"

"No. Why don't you put them in your backpack. There's also a list of classes you'll be attending. That's on the blue card."

Dolan unclipped them and slid them into his backpack.

"You're too late for social studies, which would have been your first class, so we'll start you with your second class. You're a junior. We have your transcripts from your last school. There are a number of gaps in your scholastic record."

"Yes, ma'am."

"Your father told me that your mother recently died. I'm so sorry, Dolan. That must be hard."

"Thank you, ma'am."

"Well, you've got thirty minutes before the bell. You can wait in the cafeteria, or you can stay here."

"Thank you, ma'am. I brought a book." Dolan reached into his backpack and pulled out *Crime and Punishment*.

Hawkins pursed her lips. "Are you trying to impress me?"

"No, ma'am. I found this in my father's basement, and it looked interesting."

Hawkins turned to her work. Dolan read. The bell rang.

"You want room 214, okay? Ed Cummings."

"Yes, ma'am. Thank you, ma'am."

She pursed her lips again as he left. No one paid any attention as he went up the stairs to the second floor, swimming against the tide until he came to room 214. He was the first one there. The teacher, a middle-aged man with a slight paunch wearing a tweed jacket sat at his desk going through test results. He looked up.

"You must be the new kid."

"Yes, sir. Dolan Pratt."

"This is World History. I'm Mr. Cummings. Do you have this book?" He held up a softbound copy of

Manifest Destiny: Democracy as Cognitive Dissonance.

"No, sir."

"Well, it's rather late in the semester but you should read it to prepare you for your senior year. I'll loan you this copy. You can probably find a used copy online for about ten bucks."

Dolan took the book. "Thank you."

Students filtered in, giving Dolan the once-over.

"Take a seat."

Dolan took a seat in the back. The chairs were made of formed wood with an attached desktop that hinged upward. A big kid with short curly hair came up to him.

"That's my seat."

"Andrew, the seats are not reserved. Take another desk."

With a surly glance, the big kid moved two rows away and sat next to a weasel-like kid with acne and whispered something. The weasel looked over and snickered. The bell rang. Most of the seats were taken. Cummings stood.

"We have a new student joining us today, Dolan Pratt. Dolan, why don't you stand and say something about yourself."

Dolan stood. "I'm Dolan Pratt. I just moved here from Milwaukee. I'm grateful for the opportunity to learn in a school where I won't get shot. I look forward to meeting you all."

Some students laughed, including a stunning redhead at a desk near the front.

Cummings tapped his wood pointer on the desk. The class fell silent. "All right. Who can tell us how the United States acquired California, New Mexico, and Arizona?"

A boy in the front with curly black hair and glasses raised his hand.

"Cyrus?"

"The Treaty of Guadalupe Hidalgo, 1848."

"Very good. And how did that come about?"

Cyrus's hand shot up.

"Let's hear from someone else. Anybody know how that came about?"

A thin girl with short hair and a pierced nose raised her hand.

"Stella?"

And so it went until the bell rang. Dolan consulted his blue card. Next class was Business Management and Administration. Dolan picked up his backpack and headed out. Andrew was waiting in the hall. He got in Dolan's face. He was two inches taller.

"See you outside, faggot."

Dolan stared back. The staring contest lasted five seconds before one of Andrew's jock pals pulled him away.

"Come on. Don't do anything stupid."

Andrew backed away aiming a finger.

The red-headed girl came up to him. She wore denim coveralls over a pink T-shirt, and her face was unpierced. "Don't mind him. He's a jerk. Just a big dumb jock. He'll go to college and play football and try to join the NFL. I'm Mabel."

"I'm Dolan."

"Where'd you come from?"

"Milwaukee."

"Did your family move here?"

"No, my mom died, so I moved in with my dad."

"Oh, I'm so sorry to hear that."

"I gotta move. I don't want to be late for Business Management."

Mabel rolled her eyes. "My favorite. See you around."

"Hope so."

CHAPTER TWENTY-SEVEN
FINAL BELL

THE NEXT TO LAST CLASS OF THE DAY WAS PHYS ED, taught by Coach Moynihan. Coach Moynihan also coached the Spartans football team and had played one season for the Minnesota Vikings before an ankle injury derailed his career. Dolan read it in the awards case. Coach Moynihan was a stolid six feet, thick but not fat, wore cargo pants and a button-down shirt with a whistle around his neck on a lanyard.

Outside on the athletic field, the students lined up. Andrew was at the head. Dolan was at the foot. Everyone else was wearing sweats and tennis shoes. Dolan wore khakis and tennis shoes.

"Boys," Moynihan said, "it's April twenty-fifth, and you know what that means. For the benefit of any newcomers, it's time for the second six-hundred-yard walk/run of the season. We hold this event twice every year, the first in August, at the start of the school year, and the second today. Each time, we record your time to see if you have improved during the year. Sidney, come up here."

A slight youth wearing a vest and glasses took his place beside the coach. He had a slight limp.

"Sidney will wait at the finish line to record the numbers. I see we have a new student, Dolan Pratt from Milwaukee. Everyone give Dolan a warm Memorial welcome."

A few people clapped. Andrew lisped, "Oh, I'm tho exthited!"

"Dolan, if you want to sit this one out, you may."

"That's all right, sir. I'll run."

"You got anything in your pockets?"

"No sir. I left everything in my locker."

"Excellent. Six hundred yards is five times around the athletic field on the track. Don't worry about getting to the front of the line. This is not a race. This is simply an exercise to determine if you have improved during the school year. It's called the walk/run for a reason."

Dolan noticed a couple overweight boys shifting uncomfortably in their sweats.

"Okay, everybody on the track behind the black stripe."

Jocks jockeyed. Andrew was first in line due to his aggression and everyone else's deference. Coach Moynihan held his whistle. "Everybody ready? Okay?"

He blew the whistle, and the pack took off, separating instantly, jocks and jackrabbits to the front, brains and blobs to the rear. Dolan maintained a comfortable pace mid-pack. He'd run a lot in Milwaukee. Beggars and grifters were reluctant to approach a running man. He ran to the grocery store and the pharmacy. Most of the students weren't jocks, and with little effort, he found himself approaching the front of the pack. There were several students who could have easily outpaced Andrew but held back as a sort of praetorian guard.

Dolan didn't have that problem. He soon found himself at Andrew's heels. He could have passed him, but he needed time to think about it. The downside was it would cement the jock's antipathy, and that of his sycophants. On the other hand, the school year was almost over. He could gut out the six remaining weeks, and he would demonstrate contempt and fearlessness to someone who'd behaved badly for no reason.

What the hell. They were on the fifth lap, and Andrew was unaware of Dolan running ten feet behind him. As they rounded the final turn, they saw Sidney waiting with his stopwatch, table and clipboard at his side. But no Moynihan. Where was the coach? Dolan wasn't familiar enough with the school or the coach to know whether this was a frequent occurrence or some kind of emergency. He didn't care. Fifty feet from the finish line he turned on the gas, sweeping by Andrew ten feet from the finish.

He zoomed over the line with arms raised like an Olympic winner, slowed to a stop, breathing hard, but not hard enough to bend over and rest on his knees like so many others. He turned around grinning to see Andrew staring at him slack-jawed. Dolan wasn't even winded. He went up to Sidney.

"Where's the coach?"

"He got a phone call from his wife. Some kind of emergency. Said he'll be back in a minute."

Sidney opened his mouth, but nothing came out. A violent shove in the back threw Dolan to the ground. Rolling over, he saw a red-faced Andrew staring down.

"Think you're hot shit? Think you can make me look bad? I wasn't even trying. Get up. I'll show you what I can do."

Dolan scrabbled backward to give himself room before getting to his feet. Andrew was in his face throwing jabs. The first one whipped Dolan around, followed by intense pain in his jaw. Stopping, he felt his jaw. It wasn't broken. Before he could straighten up, Andrew grabbed him in a headlock holding Dolan's head by his hip. Dolan flashed back to his Zhong Yi and wrestling. Only one day and already useful.

Dolan stepped back with his left leg, reached down with his right arm and reached under Andrew's knee, jerking Andrew's foot up and twisting Andrew counterclockwise. Andrew fell heavily to the ground. Dolan was on top of him instantaneously, crouching, wrapping both arms around Andrew's right arm above the elbow, sitting back with his butt against the bigger boy's ribs. He held Andrew's hand in both of his, thumb up, and brought it down heavily against his thigh. He exerted pressure.

"Ow! Ow!" Andrew tapped frantically with his left hand on Dolan's calf.

The students formed a circle, all but Sidney and a couple loners who weren't interested. Andrew's pals looked shocked. Others barely concealed smirks. A shrill whistle split the air. The students turned. Moynihan strode toward the combatants with a red face.

"What's going on here! Dellinger! Pratt! Get up!"

Dolan sprang to his feet. Andrew was slower.

"You know the rules about fighting. I want both of you in the principal's office. Now."

"He started it," Dolan said.

"What's that?"

"Nothing."

Sidney stepped up and spoke softly in the coach's ear. Moynihan stared at both boys. "That's all. Phys ed is over. Go wait in study hall for the school day to end."

Moynihan marched them like a corrections officer through the halls to the principal's office. A sign on the door said PRINCIPAL DIANE SCHAEFFER. Inside was a waiting room with a middle-aged man at a desk wearing a white shirt and blue tie. He had a bad combover and was typing on his computer.

"John," Moynihan said, "would you tell Dianne that we've had our first fight of the school year?"

John looked up, nonplussed. "Oh dear. And we almost made it all the way to the end. Boys, what are your names?"

"Dolan Pratt, sir."

"Andrew Dellinger."

"Of course. Andrew, I'm disappointed to see you involved."

Dolan snorted. He couldn't help himself. John pushed on the intercom.

"Diane, Coach Moynihan has a disciplinary problem he'd like you to handle."

"Show them in."

John nodded to the door. Moynihan held the door open as Dolan and Andrew filed in. Principal Schaeffer was a handsome woman of about fifty, her brunette hair worn long and held in place by an elastic band.

"Sit," she said. "What happened, Coach?"

"I had to take a call from my wife during the six-hundred-yard walk/run. When I came out, these two were on the ground. The newcomer there was applying some kind of joint lock to Andrew."

Andrew grabbed his elbow and winced. "It still hurts."

"Andrew, why don't you tell me your version of events?"

"This gob shows up today and takes my seat in Mr. Cumming's history class. When I asked him to move, he gave me some lip. During phys ed we're running the six hundred yards, and he comes up behind me, and he shoves me. Then he knocks me to the ground and gets me in some kind of judo grip. I thought he was going to break my arm."

Dolan was silent.

"Dianne," Moynihan said, "I think I'd like to speak to you in private for a minute."

"Boys, go wait outside. Don't talk to one another."

Dolan and Andrew filed out and sat on chairs on opposite sides of the room. Dolan could hear Moynihan speaking but couldn't make out the words. A moment later he appeared.

"Come back in."

They sat with an empty chair between them. The principal looked at them sternly.

"Coach Moynihan says an eyewitness contradicts your testimony, Andrew. He said that Dolan there passed you in the home stretch, and when you caught up to him, you shoved him to the ground. When he got up, you hit him, and then you put him in a headlock. Is that true?"

Blood rushed to Andrew's face. For an instant Dolan thought he was going to get up and slug the coach or storm out of the office. He looked out the window.

"I may have exaggerated a little."

"Dolan, why don't you tell us your version."

"Ma'am, that's exactly what happened."

Beat.

"I see. Well, you leave me in a difficult position. Students caught fighting are automatically suspended for the semester. However, considering that you're new here, Dolan, and you did not instigate this incident, and that Andrew was essential to the Spartans' success as a football team and has good grades. He's been accepted at UW. I'm going to overlook this. Once. I expect both of you to behave with decorum for the rest of the school year, or you will be expelled. Do I make myself clear?"

"Yes, ma'am."

"Yeah."

"All right. You can sit in the outer office until the final bell rings."

The final bell rang as they stood.

CHAPTER TWENTY-EIGHT
EASY RIDER

I<small>T WAS THREE FORTY-FIVE BY THE TIME</small> J<small>OSH</small> <small>PULLED</small> up in front of the school, fifteen minutes after the final bell. Dolan stood alone, holding his backpack. He got in the car.

"How'd it go?"

"Did the school phone you?"

"No. Why?"

Dolan sighed. "Okay. I'll tell you what happened. I go to my first class. I sit down. This big jerk comes up to me and says that's his seat. Teacher told him to sit down. The last class was phys ed. We had to walk or run six hundred yards. Big jerk was in the lead. I passed him in the home stretch and crossed the finish line first. He didn't like that, so he shoved me down on my ass, and when I got up, he slugged me. Then he put me in a headlock. I just did what Nelson taught me to do on Saturday. I took him down and put him in an arm bar. He tapped out. Then the teacher comes out and sends us both to the principal's office. Another kid told the teacher what happened. I don't think I'm in any trouble, but I wish I hadn't started this way. My first day at a new school."

"Are you shitting me?"

"No, sir."

Josh drove in silence to the southwest side.

"You're not mad, are you?"

"No, of course not. I'm just sorry you had to put up with that shit."

"Well hopefully that dude won't bother me again."

"I can practically guarantee it."

Dolan went downstairs. Josh went into his office. His phone rang.

"Pratt."

"Mr. Pratt, this is Eugenia Hawkins. Do you have a minute?"

"Sure. Dolan already told me what happened. Of course that's his version, but I have no reason to doubt him."

"Yes, well I think we all agree that it was an unfortunate incident. The boy with whom he fought, Andrew Dellinger, has a reputation as a bully. Normally, we would suspend both students for fighting, but that really isn't fair to Dolan, and it's too close to the end of the school year."

"This isn't going to affect Dolan's curriculum, is it?"

"No. Not at all. If either he or Andrew request to be placed in a different class for second period, I would be happy to oblige."

"I think that might be best."

Ray sent a text. Her folks had chosen the Blackhawk Country Club for the reception. They were members. Ray wanted Josh to hire a band.

He phoned her. "What band?"

"I would like to hire the Poudre Valley Playboys, a rockabilly trio. Is that all right with you?

"Bobby Hines has offered to play. With bass and drums."

"Ohhhh."

Beat.

"Oh what?"

"You know, my folks are real jazz nuts, and Bobby's great. Let's go with Bobby."

"I'll let him know."

"What about the honeymoon?" she said.

"Our lives are a honeymoon. Where would you like to go?"

"Hawaii."

Josh did a quick mental calculation. There was no place he had to be. When Stoeckle put him on retainer as a National Security adviser, they'd paid him $185,000 a year. He'd socked it away with his financial planner who presciently bought Microsoft and other tech stocks that had ballooned. He never had to work again. He didn't work for money. He worked because a man couldn't just sit around.

"Why don't you make the arrangements and send me the bill. I gotta warn you, though, I can only stand a week in paradise before I start to go crazy."

"Baby, I feel exactly the same way."

"Okay. When do you want to go?"

"Some time in July. I'll check with you before I finalize arrangements."

"Groovy."

"How's it going with Dolan?"

"First day of school. He got in a fight."

"Oh no!"

"It wasn't his fault. He handled it like a gentleman." Josh left out the part about the arm bar. He heard Dolan come up the stairs. Dolan appeared in the office entry. "Can I call you back?"

"No need. We're good to go."

Josh ended the call and turned toward Dolan.

"Josh, I'd like to go through your computer and remove malware."

"What's malware?"

"Parasite programs that follow you home, gum things up, slow things down."

"Yeah sure. What do you want to do about dinner? We could go out."

"Sure. I don't care."

"There's a place in Mt. Horeb you'll like. Burgers and stuff."

"Sounds fine."

"Dolan, you behave with maturity and wisdom beyond your years. How'd you get that way? Was it your mother?"

"No, sir. It was a book."

"What book?"

"*Finding Fish* by Antwone Fisher."

"What about that book?"

"It's the story of this guy's life. His childhood was a lot more difficult than anything you or I experienced."

"That's hard to believe."

"Read it and judge for yourself."

"Maybe I will."

"He turned his life around. He didn't want to be like the other losers in Cleveland. That's where he grew up. He ended up homeless on the streets, so he enlisted in the Navy. They helped straighten him out. He's also a devout Christian."

"How'd you pick that book up?"

"Somebody left a box of books out on the sidewalk."

"Why that one? Why not a mystery or something?"

"I went through a bunch of books. That one seemed the most interesting. I also took a copy of *The Official John Wayne Handy Book for Men*."

Josh laughed. "Never heard of that one."

"You know who John Wayne is."

"I've heard the name."

Dolan put his hands on his hips and cocked his head. "Oh, come on."

"Yes, I know. He was a movie star. I've even seen some of his movies."

"Like?"

"*True Grit*."

"That's a great one."

"Mr. Rat, I have a writ here that says you are to stop eating Chen Lee's cornmeal forthwith. Now, it's a rat writ, writ for a rat, and this is lawful service of same!"

Dolan laughed. "What about *Red River*?"

"Nope."

"*The Man Who Shot Liberty Valance*?"

"Nope."

"Maybe we could watch those sometime."

"Sure. I don't know where to find them."

"I can probably get them out of the library. What streaming services do you have?"

"Fuck if I know."

"Gimme a minute."

Dolan went into the living room and grabbed the remote. He returned shortly. "Dude! You have Netflix, Tubi, Freevee, YouTube, and a bunch of others!"

"I don't remember signing up for all that."

"What do you watch?"

"Football and biker movies. If you want to talk biker movies, I'm your man."

"I don't think I've ever seen any biker movies."

"Well, that gives us something to do. First up, *Easy Rider*."

"Never heard of it."

"Well, it ain't gonna be tonight. We'll head out for dinner in about an hour, okay?"

"Sure."

Josh went to Amazon and ordered *Finding Fish* and *Easy Rider*. He had one credit card. He wondered why some people needed more. His phone rang. Jerell.

"Josh, I mentioned your idea to a couple of friends, and they're very eager to meet with you."

CHAPTER TWENTY-NINE
THE SUMMIT

Tuesday morning Josh headed east with Baker and Briggs. Paul and Terry would meet them at Grace Baptist on West Atkins, where Jerell ran his youth club. Grace Baptist was an old-fashioned gray stone church with oak pews, a nave, a bell tower, and a chancel. A half dozen young men were playing a pickup game on the half court at the far end of the parking lot. Josh parked next to the church. The players stopped the game to watch and resumed when Josh and his friends went inside.

They took the stairs to the basement. Jerell was waiting for them in the gymnasium with four gang-bangers. Years ago, Jerell had headed the Milwaukee chapter of Blackstone Nation. They dealt drugs. It was before the cartels had sunk in their hooks. Jerell found religion. His conversion was similar to Josh's, except he never went to prison. They'd stayed in touch over the years and helped each other out.

"Hey, Jerell. Thanks for seeing us. This is Baker and Briggs."

"Hey," Jerell said. "How you doin'?" They bumped fists. "Boys, introduce yourselves."

A tall, thin man with a throwback 'fro shook Josh's hand. "I'm Corey, and these sad ass motherfuckers are Javon, Edgerinn, and Benton. You the biker, huh?"

"Yes, sir. Baker's also a biker. More bikers on the way."

Paul and Terry entered the room. They wore their colors. "That's Paul and Terry."

"Well come on back," Jerell said. "Let's figure this out."

They followed Jerell into his office at the back of the basement, just big enough to hold them all. Jerell had set out folding chairs and brewed coffee in a big urn on a table. They lined up and got coffee. There were only eight chairs. Javon and Edgerinn stood. Jerell had prepared a PowerPoint presentation. He turned down the lights and brought up the first slide, a ten-story red brick building. The concrete arch over the entrance said Wayzata Arms in bas relief.

"This is the Wayzata Arms on Ridley," Jerell said. "This is one of the apartment buildings Tren de Aragua has taken over. They're driving out the legit tenants one by one so they can use the building to deal drugs and traffic boys and girls. Cops won't do shit. Josh here has successfully liberated several parties from another building, but the problem is, now his friends are homeless, and the gang has taken over their apartments. Josh, what's the goal here?"

Josh stood. "The goal here is to drive this gang out of the neighborhood so they don't come back. They're used to intimidating normal people. They weren't prepared for bikers. Even in Venezuela, they've seen *Sons of Anarchy*."

Jerell's pals laughed.

"I'm hoping they've also seen *Menace II Society* and *New Jack City*."

"Fucking A," Corey said.

"That's right," Javon said.

Jerell switched to the next slide, a still shot of four Venezuelans standing in the lobby. Two of them held baseball bats, the other two carried AKs. "These guys are carrying. We can't be carrying."

"Huh?" Corey said.

"Say what?" Javon said.

"In order for this to work, we can't use lethal force. That way we get public opinion on our side. The police will be forced to support us."

"That don't make no sense," Corey said. "We're not going on a suicide mission."

"We can do this without casualties. One, the gangs know the moment they start shooting, the cops will have to respond. Two, we're gonna have enough ballistic vests for everyone."

"What happens if they shoot us in the head?" Edgerinn said.

"We're gonna have to take that chance. However, bear in mind that we're planning a display of force that will intimidate them into leaving with no shots fired. Corey. How many men can you bring?"

"A dozen."

"Paul and Terry?"

"We got four brothers ready to ride when we give the word. We reached out to the Bisons and they say they're in. That's at least a half dozen more, some veterans."

"Who the Bisons?" Corey said.

"Native American gang out of Eau Claire."

"That's thirteen bikers," Josh said. "Add in a dozen homies, it will be intimidating as hell. Don't forget. They know you don't mess with biker gangs or inner-city gangs. Notice they haven't moved in on any apartment buildings in your neighborhoods. Plus, Art's gonna record what goes down and post it."

"I know a reporter who'd appreciate an invite," Jerell said.

"Who'd you have in mind?" Josh said.

"Sharon Simmons. She did a piece about me a couple years ago about my journey from thug to social worker for the Trib. She's Black and has a big following, so they're unlikely to bury the story."

"Why would they do that?"

"Because the Trib is a leftwing propaganda organ. They just print DNC talking points, but even they can't ignore the impact these gangs are having. There have been too many stories, especially on WMTJ, conservative talk radio. Sharon's a semi-regular on the evening news."

"She's warm for your form, Jerell!" Corey said. Edgerinn and Benton hooted and pumped their fists.

"Settle down, gentlemen."

Josh grinned. He had a similar situation with a reporter in Madison. "I don't think that's a good idea, Jerell. Once we're done, you offer her an exclusive. I guess the next step is to get everyone together and hammer out a plan. Can we use the church?"

Jerell grimaced. "The church tries to stay out of politics."

"This isn't politics. It's survival. These fucking gangs are taking over sections of the city, and nobody does anything about it."

"It might be better if we meet in Madison. That's kinda midway for the Bisons anyway."

Josh pointed a finger. "If Madison got wind of this, every lefty would march on the Square demanding that we respect the dreamers' rights to take over neighborhoods. I'll find us a place."

"Maybe the VFW," Briggs said.

"Maybe."

Josh pointed a finger at Baker. "Art, you're the writer. You want to put together a summary of what we agreed upon here today? Something we can show whoever's in?"

Baker looked up from his tablet. "I'm on it. You just gave me the idea for my next movie. I'd like you all to be in it."

"Let's not get ahead of ourselves. The main goal is to liberate this apartment building. We'll start there and see where it goes."

"I'll talk to Sharon, see if she's interested in a documentary."

"It would make a hell of a documentary," Baker agreed.

"Wait until it's over," Josh said.

Jerell clapped his hands. "Inna meantime, you keep this to yourselves, right?"

"What if some of the brothers want in?" Corey said.

"I'll want to meet 'em," Jerell said." We don't want any hotheads. We don't want any guns. We want to accomplish this with no violence. Think of it as a psyops. The goal is to freak 'em out so they leave willingly."

"Once we liberate this apartment block," Josh said,

"we might want to think about doing it again. That'll be hard to ignore."

Jerell flashed perfect teeth. "I like it! Grass roots kind of thing."

Edgerinn pumped his fist. "Fucking A, bubba!"

Jerell looked around. "Is that it?"

Josh stood. "That's it. Paul, Terry, any good barbecue around here?"

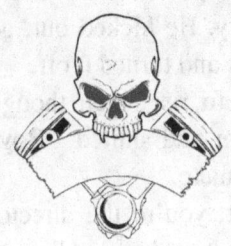

CHAPTER THIRTY
SOFTBALL

THE MEETING WAS SET FOR WEDNESDAY, MAY 10, AT Stewart Lake County Park outside Mt. Horeb. Parking lots on the west and east side gave access to the lake, a clear water swimming hole. Josh had often stopped at the park while roaming around southwestern Wisconsin. The park had a beach at one end and a pier at the other. By eleven, the west side parking lot was jammed with chops, low-riders, and a van Jerell had driven with charcoal and food. Baker, Briggs, and Garretson rode with Josh. The presence of biker gangs usually attracted police, but the fact that some of them were veterans would mitigate the circumstances.

The West Side Bluds and Murder Crows had brought the low riders and hot hatches. Christ's Warriors had ridden up on their bikes. The Bisons arrived. A boom box spewed Snoop Dogg.

A faint rumble grew like an oncoming locomotive. The Christ's Warriors roared up. Three Harleys, two Indians. They wore their colors. To the uninitiated, they were big scary bikers. But to those who bothered to read the colors, they were disciples. Terry was six-four and weighed about two-fifty. He kicked out, got off, walked over to the boom box and turned it off.

Two of the bangers started to rise, then thought better of it. Terry turned to them and smiled. "Boys, we got a few announcements to make."

Josh sat next to Baker. "Art, you're the director. Why don't you tell them what we have in mind."

"I can do that. In fact, imma record this event for posterity."

"You're going to film?"

"Sure. I brought my Sony F3. Why not?"

"Well do me a favor. Keep me out of it."

"This is your idea."

"You can say it's your idea. You put me in touch with Alfred."

"Actually, it was Dolan's idea. He put me in touch with Alfred. Alfred got the ball rolling."

"Where's Alfred? I'll interview him."

"He's at the VFW in Fitchburg. I'll text you his phone number."

A state police car pulled into the lot. Two uniformed cops. Josh headed their way. The driver lowered his window. "What's going on?"

"Sir, we're having a prayer meeting. Those are Christ's Warriors. They look bad, but they're all veterans devoted to the teachings of Jesus."

"May I see an ID?"

Josh forked over his driver's license.

Jerell joined him. "Officer, I'm Jerell Moore, a counselor at Grace Baptist in Milwaukee."

The other cop was Black. "I know you. I've seen you on Sharon Simmons's show."

"Sister Sharon has been kind enough to have me on. My goal is bringing people together. The brothers whom you see are interested in what the Christ's Warriors have to say. Then we're going to play softball."

"Yeah, okay," said the driver. "Just checkin'."

"'Preciate it. You brothers want some coffee?"

The driver raised a cardboard cup from Dazbog. "We're good."

They drove out of the lot and headed east.

Four motorcyclists passed them heading for the park. The cop car stopped, sat there for a minute, then moved on. The Bisons pulled into the lot and kicked out. Three of them were big, like their namesake. The fourth was a skinny little guy. They wore goggles. No helmets. The skinny little guy strode toward the awning. He wore a denim vest with their colors, a buffalo wearing a headdress. On the front, it said, "TWO HAWKS. PRESIDENT." He walked up to Paul.

"You in charge?"

Paul pointed to Josh. "He is."

Two Hawks faced Josh. "Two Hawks. Bisons."

They shook hands.

"Thanks for coming."

Two Hawks smiled, dazzling white teeth against his café au lait skin. "We are happy to oblige. I'm a veteran. Big Bob's a veteran. Got a minute? I have something to show you."

"Sure."

Two Hawks returned to his chop, dug through the black leather saddlebag and took out a Mason jar. He walked down toward the beach. Josh followed. They were far enough from the crowd so that no one could hear them. No one was interested. The rest jabbered up a storm. Two Hawks handed Josh the jar.

"Open up and take a whiff."

Josh unscrewed the cap. Stench rose from the jar that would gag a dog off a gut wagon. Josh held the jar away, turned, and sneezed.

"Jesus! What the fuck is that?"

"It's durian. A fruit native to Southeast Asia. Thailand mostly. Some people love it."

"It stinks!"

"I know it stinks. I can get my hands on ten pounds of durian. We let it ferment for a week. We take it to the building. We uncork it in the foyer. We spread it wherever this gang is. I got tubes that can shoot the juice."

"That's a brilliant idea, but if we're successful, nobody will be able to live in the building. Better leave it at home."

"You sure? We can transport it in our saddlebags. A little durian goes a long way."

"Two Hawks, I love the idea. You mind if I hang onto this?"

"Take it. I can always get more."

"Imma file it away for something more appropriate. Let's stick to visuals. Let's get this meeting underway." They walked uphill to one of the shelters jammed with veterans, bikers, and gangbangers.

"Gentlemen, gather round," Josh said loud enough for all to hear. The gangs gathered. Some sat, most stood. There weren't enough seats. Baker slowly rotated his Sony.

"We're here to liberate an apartment block from a foreign gang. Tren de Aragua has taken over several buildings on Milwaukee's northwest side. We got some veterans out, and some of them are with us. Boys, identify yourselves."

Garretson and Briggs raised their hands. Everyone looked around.

"Some of us are local boys who don't appreciate a bunch of foreigners taking over their turf."

Edgerinn stood. "Wait a minute. Don't assume that we're involved in illegal activity. Some of us have put that behind us, and we're here because Jerell asked."

"Fair enough. Thank you, Edgerinn."

Another lanky banger stood. "Demarius Tucker. Orchard Avenue Killers. OAK."

A young man rose and thrust a fist in the air. "Strong as oak!"

"That's right!" others echoed.

"Okay, good enough. We're here to get to know each other too. So, here's what's happening. The address of the building is the Wayzata Arms at 1225 Ridley Boulevard. Put that in your phones. Put it in the map app and take a look at it right now. Write it down if you want.

"There may be as many as two dozen foreign criminals living in that building. We know of at least six units they've taken over. They took them with threats of violence. The people they drove out can't afford to move anywhere else. Some of them are in shelters. Some of them are on the street."

"When we gonna do this?" Jerell said.

"Sunday, May 14. Now that you've looked at the address on a map, see that strip mall on Cramer? It's been boarded up for a quarter century. Bikers will meet there. Street gangs will meet at Menominee Park. Both places are a few blocks from the Wayzata, opposite one another. We'll meet at nine a.m. The front door is open. First thing these gangs do is disable the locks. Not all of us will go into the building. Most of you will gather in front of the building. Some will gather in the parking lot. At nine-fifteen, we're gonna make a hella noise. We're going to chant 'Hey ho! Hey ho! Tren de Aragua has to go!' We brought thirty ballistic vests. They're in Jerell's van. Thank you, Christ's Warriors! If you don't have a ballistic vest, ask the Warriors. There will be no firearms. You all know that Tren is likely to be armed. It's our hope that a show of force from groups not known for their pacifism, will convince them to leave."

"Yeah, but what if they start shooting?" a banger said.

"Arthur will be recording. He'll zero in on faces. I've also asked the veterans who live in the building to come out and use their phones. Even the dumbest thug doesn't want his face on the evening news. Which reminds me. Art's going to pass out forms. You have to agree to have your likeness used, or it will not be included in the final cut. Those of you who are in the documentary will have bragging rights. It will redound positively on your organization."

"What's redound mean?" a banger said.

"Contribute greatly to a person's credit or honor."

"Speak 'Murican, damn ye!" Paul said.

Josh laughed. "That's the spirit! Bisons Prez Two Hawks brought a jar of magic ointment. This is sacred to the Indians, and those who inhale its heavenly scent are blessed by the Great Spirit. I'm going to pass it around. Unscrew the lid and take a whiff. Pass it on." Josh handed the jar to Art Baker. Art unscrewed it, turned away, and sneezed.

"Holy fuck!"

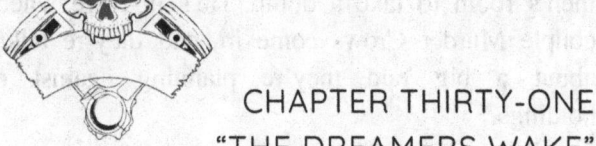

CHAPTER THIRTY-ONE
"THE DREAMERS WAKE"

LUIS SPRAWLED ON THE SOFA IN HIS STOLEN apartment getting a blow job from a nineteen-year-old from Honduras. She was a little old for him, but he wasn't really looking at her. Someone knocked on the door. Two slow. Three fast.

"Momento!" he cried, putting his hand on the girl's head. "Faster, chiquita! I got things to do!"

Again, the knocking.

Grunting, Luis came. Gasping, he handed the girl a towel. "Help yourself to a gram, baby doll. Now you got to excuse me. I got business."

The girl grabbed a tiny Ziploc off the table and went into the bathroom. Luis wiped himself off, pulled up his pants, and opened the door. Delcey looked like an idiot with his pants hanging halfway to his knees. He wore a Kansas City Chiefs' hoodie. He swooped in and went straight to the table. He sat on the sofa, shook a line out on the mirror, wrangled it with a credit card, and hoovered it up.

"What?"

"We got to get out of here."

"What are you talking about?"

"Jesus was in Lock's last night. He goes to the men's room to take a dump. He's in there when a couple Murder Crows come in, and they're talking about a big raid they're planning against our holdings."

"What holdings?"

"Like this one right here."

"What are you talking about?"

Delcey looked up. "This apartment building, chamo! They're getting a gang together to kick us out of this apartment building!"

"The Wayzata? They said that?"

"Yes."

"They say when?"

"No. Soon. They're waiting to get the word."

"What are they going to do? Come in blazing like some fucking commando movie? We got the guns. They try anything, bang, bang."

"Luis, think for a minute. How often the cops come by? Just that one time, and it was because those *mamarrachos* started shooting. We start shooting, they'll come for us."

"I think it's because the policia are on our side."

"They're not on anybody's side. They're on the side of whoever gives them *plata*." He rubbed his fingers together.

Delcey was bringing down Luis's high. Luis frowned. "You got any ideas?"

"Yeah. That guy? The biker? I found out who he is."

"No shit. Who is he?"

"Josh Pratt. Private investigator. Lives in Madison. And get this. He's fixing to get married."

"How the fuck do you know that?"

"Niefred, hombre. He's an expert at internet security. He found the guy with facial recognition. We put La Raza on him. They followed him. They drove to Madison. He's seeing this bitch got a dance studio."

"How you know they're getting married?"

"They went into the dance studio. They want to be dancers, y'know?"

Delcey held up his arms and spun flamenco style clicking his fingers. "Dreamers, y'know? Young. Sexy. All tatted up. They look like theater people. They hear the bitch talking to the dancers. Making plans."

"Do you know where she lives?"

Delcey smiled. "She bring this copy of *Dance* magazine to her theater. Got her address right here." He pulled out his phone.

"What about the boyfriend? Where does he live?"

"I'll get that for you."

CHAPTER THIRTY-TWO
CONFAB

THURSDAY MORNING JOSH DROPPED DOLAN OFF AT school. "Stay out of trouble."

"I will."

"I'll pick you up at three forty-five."

"Okay. Thanks, Dad." Dolan got out of the car and headed toward the entrance with dozens of other students. Josh sat there a minute. Dad. It was so unexpected. He'd have to get used to it. He could tell Dolan to call him Josh. It felt more natural. But who was he to deny his own child?

Dear Lord, please don't let there be any more surprises like Dolan.

Shame.

Dear Lord, please disregard that last prayer. Whatever happens, it's Your will.

Ray called on his way home. He pulled to the side of Ptarmigan, the trees in the first blush of spring. "What's up, babe?"

"I just talked to Melvin Hyman! He's sending me a

contract! Five thou with an option to renew at ten thou!"

"That's great! Is he in LA?"

"No, he's in New York. But he's got a place in LA."

"And it will star Idaho Mongoose?"

Ray laughed. "No. She doesn't even know about it. He likes the songs! Says he's working with an arranger to flesh it out."

"Whassat mean?"

"He watched the live performance several times on my website and thinks it's too short. It's only ninety minutes. He wants more songs."

"Who wrote the music?"

"I did. Mostly on piano. Now I have to come up with four more songs."

"Is that a problem?"

"Well yeah. Music writing doesn't come easy to me. I can write plays. I can direct, but coming up with new songs is a bitch. I wish I had a collaborator. Someone who's a real musician."

"Bobby Hines."

"Bobby the pianist?

"That's the guy."

"Has he written songs before?"

"He released a CD last year. *In the Tradition*. I'll get you a copy."

"Thanks, babe. It's worth a shot. How can I get in touch with him?"

"I'll email you his contact info."

"Mom and Dad want us over for dinner Sunday night."

Sunday was D-Day. They were going to meet in

Wauwatosa at nine and drive to the Abbot. It was a cinch, since the Venezuelans slept late. They needed to do it in broad daylight.

"Yeah, I should be back."

"Back from where?"

"Oh, I'm visiting some friends in Milwaukee on Sunday. But I should be back. What time?"

"Seven."

Josh drove home, changed into sweats, and took Fig for a jog. They ran northeast along Ptarmigan to the convenience store, turned around and ran back. Six miles. Josh showered and checked his email.

"Pump Up Your Erection Muscle by 67% Using This Simple Trick."

"Join 1,000,000+ People Building Credit with SELF. The Card for Credit Builders. Managing finances shouldn't be difficult. Get the card that helps you build credit responsibility while preparing for your future. YOUR CARD IS WAITING!"

"BACK IN STOCK! These lids won't stay on the shelf for long! Alpine Stars Supertech R10 Carbon Helmet. 999.95 to 1399.95."

"Dear Sir: I am Gwendolina Ammerstrach, the wife of the late Soviet Oligarch Overseer of Uzbekistan, Frankophile Ammerstrach.. My beloved husband transferred thirty-three million dollars to the Bank of America before his death, but unfortunately, I cannot access it, stuck as I am in Uzbekistan. I have it on good authority…"

"Dear Mr. Pratt: I got your email from Wayne Garretson. My name is Bill Hiles. I am a veteran living in the Wayzata, at 1225 Ridley Ave. I am sixty-seven years old and served in Operation Desert Storm. There are three veterans living here, including my friends Tom Blankenship and Darren Johnson. There are thirty-six units in the nine-story building This gang has taken over six of them, and they are making life very miserable for the rest of us. Sometimes they offer to buy us out, but their offers are laughable. Sometimes they pound on the door and threaten to kill us. I still have my Army issue Colt .45, and I had to show it to them to get them to back off. Now I'm concerned that they intend to kill me.

"Wayne told me about your plan to liberate us. For this I am extremely grateful. I have spread the word to as many of my neighbors as I can, but some don't speak English, and I don't speak Spanish. I want to tell you about the laundry room in the basement. It has a separate entrance in the alley that runs behind the building, between Harvard and Beck Streets. The lock has been inoperable for years.

"The fire escape in the rear alley leads to the roof. One of those gangbangers fell off the roof a couple weeks ago and killed himself. I saw the body from the fire escape. No police. Don't know what they did with the body. They get high a lot. Now they're staying off the roof. I don't know if this information is helpful. Please feel free to call me at (414) 223-1959. Yours, Bill Hiles."

"Dear Mr. Hiles: Thank you for writing me. We plan to liberate the building this Sunday at nine o'clock in the morning. We are a coalition of veterans, bikers, and local street gangs. We will not have guns. We hope to scare the Venezuelans off with a show of force. Please remain in your apartment and tell the others to do the same until we give you the all-clear sign. We will go door to door if we are successful. If you hear gunshots, they won't be coming from us. If your friends are armed, ask them not to come out of their apartments until we give the all-clear. Of course, if the gang tries to break in, that's a different story. Best, Josh."

Josh picked up the phone and called Hiles. "Sir, it's Josh Pratt. It might be better if we talk. I'll give you a heads up when we're ready to move, and you can alert the others."

"Well, most of these people who are still here, I don't have their phone numbers."

"I understand. If you get an opportunity, tell them to just sit tight until we give the all-clear."

"How will we know when that is?"

"I have a bullhorn."

"I'll do that as soon as I get off the phone. Why are you doing this? Are you a veteran?"

"No, sir. I'm an ex-con. I got out nine years ago. I'm not the man I used to be. I'm a soldier of Christ."

"That's great!"

"Some of the bikers are veterans and Christians. They're wearing their colors. Christ's Warriors. They're based in Texas, or there'd be more of them."

"How many people are you bringing?"

"At least two dozen. How many bangers are in the building?"

"I would say no more than a dozen, but I heard some shouting last night, and I looked outside, and some bangers I've never seen pulled up and came inside. Do they have any idea what you're doing?"

"I doubt it. But it's not like they're gonna flee in a panic. They're arrogant and defiant. The cops won't touch them. I think they're unprepared for what's coming. As I said, we're not planning on hurting anyone unless we must. And that depends on whether they'll go peacefully. If they won't go peacefully, we'll have to persuade them the biker way."

"Well good luck. I'll pray for you."

"Thank you, sir. If you have any more questions don't hesitate to call."

CHAPTER THIRTY-THREE
MABEL

DOLAN SAT IN CIVICS CLASS STARING AT A BLANK sheet of paper. It was the last class of the day. Ms. Considine required hand-written statements because she didn't want students accessing the internet to plagiarize. Ms. Considine arranged the desks in pairs. Dolan's desk butted up against Mitchell Harkins's. Mitchell wore Coke-bottle glasses and guarded his paper like a hungry dog. Dolan's paper was fair game. As soon as Dolan began to write, Mitchell looked over. He tried not to be obvious which only made him more obvious.

The subject was, how did the US Constitution upend the divine right of kings. It was a peculiar question coming from the blue-haired Ms. Considine, an attractive woman in her early thirties. At least she hadn't pierced her nose. If she had tattoos, they were well hidden. The usual subjects fidgeted. Some surreptitiously peered at their phones. The rule was no phones in class. There were always scofflaws. Dolan had seen teachers confiscate phones, then those same students looking at phones in classes later that day.

The US Constitution, Dolan wrote, *upended the divine right of kings by putting the individual first. No longer was the government the most important body. The Constitution says that our rights, the right to free speech and self-defense, do not come from government but from God. Therefore, the government can't take them away. These rights are outlined in the Bill of Rights. The First Amendment guarantees our right to free speech. This is the most important right. If we can't speak freely for fear of being arrested, or worse, we don't have a free country..."*

Mitchell stopped pretending he wasn't looking at Dolan's paper. Dolan drew the paper in and hid it with his arm. Ms. Considine walked down the aisle toward them. Mitchell's attention fixated on his own desk. Ms. Considine inspired lust among the boys. Dolan included. He limited himself to masturbation once a day. He wasn't worried about going blind. He was worried about his humanity. It probably would have been a lot more if he hadn't read that book. If Antwone could control himself, so could Dolan.

Ms. Considine stopped next to Mitchell and crossed her arms. Mitchell bent way over his essay. He looked like The Hunchback of Notre Dame.

"Mitchell, go sit in that desk in the corner."

Without a word, Mitchell gathered his stuff and slunk off. Classmates tittered.

"Plagiarism will not be tolerated," Ms. Considine said. She returned to the front of the room.

Ten minutes passed.

"Class, stop writing. Georgia, will you gather the essays please?"

Georgia, a tall girl who played center for the Spartan Girl's Basketball Team, went up and down the aisles gathering all the essays. All were written on yellow legal pad pages, which Ms. Considine had supplied. As Georgia laid the stack in front of Ms. Considine, the bell rang.

Dolan unlocked his locker, took out his backpack, and headed for the front. He always left his phone in his backpack to avoid interruptions. Mabel walked beside him.

"Hey."

"Hey, Mabel."

"How's it going?"

"It's going."

"Is that clown giving you any more trouble?"

"No. Oddly enough, he doesn't even look at me when we pass."

"Well, that's good. He's picked on a bunch of kids. Maybe what you did to him will teach him a lesson."

"It is devoutly to be hoped."

Mabel grinned at him. "You talk funny."

"I just read a lot."

"I was wondering."

"What?"

"Would you go see a movie with me?"

"Depends on the movie."

"*La La Land* at Point Cinema."

"What's it about?"

"It's a musical about a jazz pianist and a struggling actress who fall in love. It's a matinee. They're only charging five bucks."

"When?"

"Saturday at one?"

"Sure. You want to meet me there?"

She took his hand and quickly let go. "It's a date."

Dolan's phone buzzed. He took it out.

"I'm out front."

"My dad's out front. You need a ride?"

"Well sure. I'd like to meet your dad."

Josh's silver Chrysler was in line behind a couple other helicopter parents. Dolan and Mabel walked up.

"Dad, this is Mabel. Can we give her a ride home?"

"Sure."

Dolan held the front door open. "You sit up here. I'll sit in back."

He got in the back seat. Mabel hesitated. "You don't have to do that. I can walk."

"Where do you live, Mabel?" Josh said.

She pointed across the street. "Right over there on Honey Locust Trail."

"Get in."

"Turn right and take the first street on the left."

They exited the school lot and turned right. Josh then turned left as instructed.

"How was school?"

"Okay. I wrote an essay about the Constitution in Civics."

Josh caught Dolan's eye in the rearview. "Have you read the Constitution?"

Mabel leaned forward and pointed. "That's it. First driveway on the left."

Josh pulled into a cul-de-sac with three duplex condos. It was directly across the street from the school, pushed back by a broad green park.

"That's it with the juniper."

Josh stopped. Mabel got out.

"See you Saturday. Thanks for the ride."

Dolan got in the front seat. Josh waited while Mabel unlocked the door and went in. Josh turned around and went back to Gammon and turned right.

"What's Saturday?"

"We're going to a movie at Point."

"Don't you have to work?"

"I'll get in at eight and work until noon. John won't mind."

Josh turned right on Mineral Point. "She's cute."

"Yeah."

"You got any rubbers?"

"Daaad…"

"What? You think I don't know what goes on? You been laid yet?"

"No."

"You just want to go and get it over with? I can make that happen."

"I think I'll wait."

Josh grinned. "Well, that's different. You mind telling me why?"

"I almost got laid in Milwaukee, but she was Black, and her big brother scared the crap out of me."

"What's wrong with Mabel?"

"Then I read that book."

"What book?"

"The Antwone Fisher one."

"You still have it?"

"I'll get you a copy."

They passed the Circle K and turned south on Ptarmigan.

"So have you read the Constitution?"

"I read it last week. I got it at Westfield Comics."

"Got what?"

"The comic book." Josh reached into his backpack

and pulled out a square, bound graphic novel in a plastic sleeve. Josh pulled over to the shoulder and stopped.

"Can you take it out of the plastic?"

Dolan slipped it out and handed it to Josh. The cover showed the Founding Fathers looking down like Mt. Rushmore on a bespectacled Black man holding the original document above the capitol building. Two howling mobs faced off below. Josh opened it. The dreadlocked citizen gave a brief history lesson. The Founding Fathers hammered it out. Article One appeared on page six. The First Amendment appeared on page twenty-seven. Josh handed it back.

"You know, if they gave these out to our duly elected representatives, maybe some of them would actually read it."

"I wouldn't know. I never watch the news."

"Smart kid."

"I want to come with you on the raid."

"Forget it, pal. Why the hell would you want to do that?"

"So I can tell my children about it."

"No way. You can watch the documentary."

"What documentary?"

Josh pulled into his driveway and opened the garage. "Baker. He makes cheap horror movies. He's gonna shoot the whole thing."

They entered through the kitchen. Fig barked and grinned. She sat and paddled backward with her front paws.

"All right. All right." Josh opened a cupboard and gave her a piece of beef jerky.

"Why's he shooting a documentary?"

"Because it's interesting. We're gonna show how to get rid of maggots without violence."

"Dad, those guys have guns!"

"Okay, without guns."

"What if you get shot?"

"We're all wearing bulletproof vests."

"You guys are crazy."

"Maybe. Me and Fig are gonna go for a run. Want to come?"

"Sure."

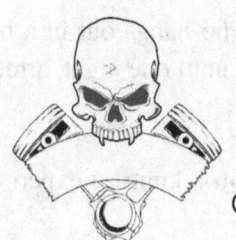

CHAPTER THIRTY-FOUR
THE SNATCH

MELVIN HYMAN SAT BEHIND A DESK THAT LOOKED like an aircraft carrier. Behind him, a window showed the studio. A patio for the restaurant, a swoopy administration building, and, peeking out between two office buildings, a Western set. Golf carts carried visitors up and down the immaculate streets. Hyman was a stolid middle-aged man with graying hair and square horn-rimmed glasses. He smiled benevolently at Ray.

"Phil Marcuso brought this to my attention. He thinks this is the perfect vehicle for Tom Highland."

"I don't know either of those people," Ray said from the office in her condo.

"Well, they know you. They love the score. You have a flair for the hook."

"Thank you. Idaho helped me."

"Is she a composer?"

"Yes. She's also an actress. We've been working together for five years now. She starred in my production of *Drunk Octopus Wants to Fight*."

"What's that about?"

"It's about a bitter ex-cop who hangs out in a bar every night. Filled with self-pity until one night, armed robbers invade the bar."

"Does he get into the act?"

"Boy, does he! We brought in a kung fu expert to choreograph the fight scenes"

"Why would an old drunk cop study kung fu?"

"He was a tournament fighter before he joined the police. One of those guys who's living on borrowed glory. Rueful. I have all my productions on video, if you'd like to see it."

"You know, that sound like something we might be interested in. Please send me the script."

"Part of the appeal is seeing this drunk old fat man throwing people around."

"How old and how large is Ms. Mongoose?"

"She's a hundred and twenty-five pounds. Forty."

"I'll withhold judgment until I see the video. It does sound interesting."

"Will do."

"Phil Marcuso represents Jason Statham. He'd be perfect for that."

Ray laughed. "I love Jason Statham, but he's not a very good actor. He talks like a Cockney. He made a movie, *Homefront*, based on Chuck Logan's novel. Logan's protagonist is a Vietnam veteran and a native Minnesotan. Backwoods. Sly Stallone bought the rights and moved the setting to Louisiana. Okay, he came from somewhere else. Every time he opens his mouth it's, 'Oi! Let's get you up those apples and pears! Don't forget your 'at!' Then he makes *A Working Man*, based on Chuck Dixon's Levon Cade novel. Levon Cade's supposed to be this good ol' boy from Georgia. And it's all, 'Oi! Let's take the Mickey!' Sylvester always options novels by writers named Chuck and always casts Jason Statham."

Hyman laughed. "I know. But people love him."

"You've got English actors you'd swear were American. Charlie Hunnam. Kelly Reilly. Tom Hardy."

"The people love Jason. They can't get enough of him."

"In *Homefront,* he was supposed to be a good ol' boy. 'Ol roight, just think for a minute what you're doing.'"

"He's a star. Like John Wayne. He only plays himself."

"And then *Working Man,* where he's supposed to be a good ol' boy from Alabama. 'Ere's your 'at. Put it on your 'ead.'"

Now Melvin was laughing. "All right, all right. Where'd you get the kung fu instructor?"

"My fiancé."

"Is your fiancé a martial artist?"

"He was in a motorcycle gang. He went to prison."

"Why was he in prison?"

"Atrocious assault."

"What did he do?"

"I'll tell you that when I sign a contract."

"We'd like to fly you out here for a story conference."

"When were you thinking?"

"First week in June."

"I'm getting married June fourteenth, and then we're going on a honeymoon."

"Hmmm. Well, we can't do it any earlier. Let me check with my colleagues and see what we can find."

"We could just do a Zoom meeting like we're doing now."

Hyman laughed. "Oh no! They'll want to meet you in person! Who turns down an all expenses paid trip to Hollywood?"

"But the fires…"

"We'll be nowhere near the fires. The fires are over. We'll put you up at a five-star hotel. You'll love it."

"Well thank you, Mr. Hyman. I should be free by June 20th. I have a production in the works, but I can get away for a couple days."

"Excellent. Would you be so kind as to send me an invitation? I'd like to send you a gift."

"That's not necessary."

"I'll email you my address."

"Well thank you!"

Ray was walking on air. She never dreamed that her little neighborhood theater would launch her into the stratosphere. Sure, she dreamed of making it big. She considered herself lucky to make a living doing what she loved. Teaching dance. The theater was an afterthought, after watching *Kiss Me Kate* on Tubi. Ann Miller's opening number blew her mind. She ordered the DVD and planned to watch it with Josh the first chance she got. Even a hardened ex-con would melt at that movie.

She called him.

"What up, girl?"

"You busy tonight?"

"Never too busy for you."

"How about I come over around five and make dinner for you and the boy."

"Or we could go out."

"I feel like cooking."

"No Chinese."

Ray laughed. "I don't like it either. Don't tell anyone. We'll become outcasts. What's the boy like?"

"Meat and potatoes. Me too."

"So be it."

"Anything you need me to get?"

"No. You have beer?"

"Got beer."

"Okay. See you at five!"

Sid Vicious twined between her feet howling for food.

"All right. All right."

Sid followed her into the kitchen. Ray grabbed a can of Friskies out of the cupboard. Someone knocked at the door. She looked at Sid.

"That better not be Joan." She went to the front door and looked through the peep. A young man in a UPS uniform holding a package. She wondered what in hell she'd ordered. She opened the door. The young man dropped the box, scooped her up around the waist, pinning her arms as she kicked and flailed. Another slapped Gorilla Tape over her mouth. They forced a black cloth bag over her head and pinned her wrists behind her back with zip ties. Then her ankles. They picked her up and carried her out.

"Coge su bolso!" someone said.

Ray had studied Spanish in high school. *Grab her phone.*

It was three in the afternoon. No one else was around. She heard the door to the stairs open. They carried her down four flights of stairs. Their footsteps reverberated. Outer door. She could tell by the scent.

Through a tiny gap at the bottom of the bag she glimpsed sunlight on asphalt. Springs on a car. They threw her into a dark empty space and slammed the lid. The car started up and drove away.

CHAPTER THIRTY-FIVE
THE CRIMINAL EMPIRE STRIKES BACK

JOSH, DOLAN, AND FIG RAN TO THE CONVENIENCE store where they splurged on mineral water, pouring some into a dog bowl the owner left outside. They ran back. It was six miles round trip. They ran on the wrong side of the road facing traffic, on the shoulder. They got back around five. Josh showered. Dolan showered in the other bathroom. Fig licked herself.

Josh put on clean clothes. He was hungry. He hoped Ray would arrive soon. He'd left his phone on his dresser. He picked it up. There were two calls. The first was from Ray's neighbor, Hayley.

"Josh, call me back."

He called Hayley. "What's up?"

"Josh, I don't want to alarm you, but I found Sid Vicious roaming the halls meowing. And when I took him back to Ray's, the door to her apartment was open. She wasn't there. It's not like Ray to take off and leave her apartment door open."

A chill ran down Josh's spine. "Thanks for telling me, Hayley."

The second call was from an unknown number. "Hey, motherfucker. We got your bitch. You ever want to see her again, you do what we say."

A vast gulf opened beneath his feet. Not again. He couldn't do this again. He'd lost too many. The man spoke with a South American accent. Josh didn't have to see him to know he was Venezuelan. His first instinct was to call back and find out what he had to do. His second was to contact one of his tech guys and see if they could trace the phone's location. His third was to call his friend, retired police detective Heinz Calloway, whose daughter they'd saved from a doomsday cult.

He called Heinz.

"Josh. What's up?"

"Heinz, I need your help."

"Anything you need."

"Ray's been kidnapped."

"What?!"

"Yeah. Her neighbor told me she was missing, and her condo door was wide open. Then I got a phone call from Tren de Aragua telling me they had her."

"Have you told the police?"

"I'm telling you."

"I'm retired."

"I don't know how they got on to me. Some friends of mine and I escorted sp,e veterans out of gang-controlled buildings in Milwaukee. We did it as peacefully as we can. We're doing it because the Milwaukee police won't. I don't think they know about it yet, although they arrested two veterans for kidnapping. It was a bullshit charge. They detained two gangbangers who broke into their unit."

"Well, what do you want me to do?"

"I don't know. Can I come over?"

"Yeah. Come on over. I want to hear these phone calls. Then we can talk about what we're going to do about it."

Josh hung up. He wondered if calling Heinz had been a smart move. He had the resources if only he knew how to use them. Finding where they were holding her was everything. He went to the head of the basement stairs.

"Dolan, I gotta run out for a while. I may be late. Don't wait up."

Dolan came to the bottom of the steps. "Where you going? Can I help?"

"No. Don't worry about it."

"I heard you talking on the phone. What's going on?"

Josh paused. "Can you trace a phone? Tell me where it is?"

"Maybe."

Josh was torn. He didn't want to drag Dolan into this. But they were just going to talk.

"All right. Grab what you need and let's go."

Heinz lived on the west side near Owen Park. It was a neat two-story white brick colonial with Heinz's Tahoe parked in the driveway. Josh parked on the street. Heinz opened the front door as they approached. He was the color of café au lait, gray hair cut short, still slim and athletic at age sixty.

Josh and Heinz shook hands.

"Who's this?"

"This is my son Dolan."

Heinz's eyebrows raised. "I didn't know you had a son."

"Neither did I until about ten days ago."

"Let's go out on the deck. You want something to drink? Dolan?"

"I'd take a soda, sir, if you have any."

They went through the kitchen. Heinz handed out ginger ales. The deck looked out on trees.

"Doreen's at work," Heinz said. "I did a little research. Milwaukee's not a sanctuary city, but the mayor's made a big deal that he won't prosecute dreamers. Or illegal aliens, as we used to call them. However, things are reaching a boiling point. You'd never know it reading the Journal or watching the television shows, but the gangs have moved into neighborhoods, particularly on the upper west side, and the natives aren't happy. The police have been understaffed since the pandemic, and since the jackasses in the legislature voted for the George Floyd Justice in Policing Act, twenty-five percent of the department resigned. Fifteen more took early retirement. The cops have been operating at sixty percent ever since."

Dolan hunched over his laptop.

"Play it."

Josh pulled out his phone. "Hey motherfucker. We got your bitch. You ever want to see her again, you do what we say."

"What did he sound like?"

"South American accent. I'm no expert, but it was probably Venezuelan."

"I told those fools not to ignore this. What happens if you find the location?"

"I don't know. I don't think the cops can handle this."

"So why'd you call me?"

"I don't know. Moral support. I have a few guys...

we pulled some veterans out last week . Even these fucking gangbangers have heard about bikers. They've all seen *Sons of Anarchy*."

"You're going after them with a bunch of bikers?"

"Heinz, I'm making this up on the fly. You ever hear of the Christ's Warriors?"

"I have. There one of the clubs that is most definitely not on the watch list."

"Well, I got a couple warriors, and some West Side Bluds and some Murder Crows."

"That sounds like quite a coalition."

"The enemy of my enemy is my friend."

"You show up with a mob, what's to stop them from chopping off fingers and throwing them out the window?"

"I don't know. I don't know."

Dolan held up a finger.

"You got something?"

"Yeah. I'm using a GPS location tracker. I have it narrowed down to a three-block area in Milwaukee."

"You're shitting me."

"No. These guys aren't that sophisticated. They may not even be aware you can track a phone by its number. On the other hand, maybe they do know, and it's a red herring. What about Ray? Would she have her phone with her?"

Josh smacked himself in the head. "Six oh eight, two four nine, eight seven eight seven."

Dolan focused on the laptop. Birds chirped in the trees. Sounds of a lawnmower up the block.

Dear Lord, please look over and guard Ray. Please return her to me unharmed. I won't insult you by offering any services. I'm doing all I can.

His stomach churned.

After what seemed like an eternity, Dolan looked up. "The reading I'm getting is the same reading as the other phone."

CHAPTER THIRTY-SIX
MY PAL LUCIFER

RAY WOKE IN A DARK ROOM. SHE FELT AND SMELLED the building's age. The window to her left looked out on an old red brick apartment building separated by an empty lot. A concrete wall rose from the parking lot to the second floor. Two bangers swinging rattle cans, covering Murder Crows. Replacing it with Tren de Aragua. They let Shred Hustl stand.

The lights went on. Ray blinked, putting a hand to her eyes. A lizard entered. He was five-nine with a shaved skull covered with tats. He wore a wife beater. Anybody that inked up had given up on society. It's what lifers did in prison. Even young women covered everything but their faces. Ray had four tats. The lizard grinned, showing a gold tooth. A skull watched from above his eyes.

"My name is Luis."

"What are you doing?"

"Hey, maybe you don't know this, but your old man has been making our lives shit! I want you to call him and tell him what's going to happen to you if he doesn't leave us alone."

Ray's smile was dazzling. "No, thank you."

"Excuse me?"

"I don't need a phone call."

"Lady, are you out of your mind? One word from me, and my boys will eat you alive. I might take a bite myself. You're a little older than I like, but you're looking good."

"Do you know who my old man is?"

"Yeah. Some biker muthafucka. Thinks he's tough."

"Do you know how many men he's killed?"

"How many?"

"I have no idea. Do you know what they called him in prison?"

"He went to prison?"

"That's right."

"What did they call him?"

"Chainsaw."

That smile.

"Would you like to know why they call him Chainsaw?"

"You tell me, lady."

"Because he cut a man's arm off with a chainsaw."

Luis grinned. "Is that all?"

"Josh served five years. How long were you in prison?"

"What makes you think I was in prison?"

"Your face."

A gorilla with crossed pistols. An upside-down cross. Scroll work. The skull. His eyes were inked so his face resembled a skull. The ink went down his body, disappearing into his shirt.

Luis laughed. "You are brave. American women are not brave."

"What do you think of American women?"

"They are weak and scared. They do what we say."

"Those aren't women. They're girls. Most of them have led terrible lives. By the time you get your hands on them, they're ruined. They're probably not American either. You prey on those who are in the country illegally. Like you are. You know they can't go to the authorities. So, you take young girls and force them into prostitution. You turn them into drug addicts. Tell me something, Luis. Are you Catholic?"

Luis's face froze. "My parents were Catholic."

"Are they still alive?"

"I don't know."

"Do you go to church? Do you take confession?"

"When I was a child, my parents made me and my sister Alejandra go. She prayed, but I didn't. They stopped taking us. My father struggled to feed us. I left when I was thirteen. I found a gang. The gang is strong. I am strong."

"Do you believe in the goddess Hecate?"

Luis's mouth opened. "How do you know about Hecate?"

"I know she is the goddess of witchcraft, the night, moon, ghosts, and necromancy. Many Venezuelans worship here. They worship her in Louisiana. If anything happens to me, you pray to Hecate and see how that works out. Josh is a proud Christian. He once told me he'd killed twenty-two people," she lied, "that he could remember. Are your parents still alive? You don't know, do you? Alejandra? If anything happens to me, Josh and his friends will track you to the ends of the earth. They will wipe out your family. They will kill your parents and your sister and any bastards you may have accidentally brought into this world."

Luis swallowed. He hadn't expected this. He was starting to sweat.

"All you have to do is let me walk out of here. You don't even have to take me back to Madison. In fact, I would prefer making my own way. You will give me three hundred dollars for food and transportation."

"Oh, lady. What's your name?"

"Ray."

"If we do that, will your man call off his raid?"

"I'll ask."

Luis fished around in his pockets and pulled out Ray's phone. "Call him now. Tell him we are turning you loose."

"No. Give me the phone and the money, and I'll call him when I am convinced you have really let me go."

Luis froze. Ray stared at him without blinking. She put her palms together in front of her interlocking the fingers the way her yoga teacher taught. It was meant to promote tranquility.

"Stop. What are you doing?"

"Josh is Christian, but I am not. I'm a Luciferian. I am Shiva, the Destroyer, death, the shatterer of worlds. I have been Shiva since I was eighteen. I am consecrated in the rituals. I caused a woman whom I didn't like to drive into a bridge abutment at ninety miles an hour. There wasn't enough left for an open casket. When I was twenty-five one of my teachers tried to rape me. I took his balls. I still have them in a jar of formaldehyde in my closet. I have never mentioned this to my fiancé for fear he would reject me. Now watch."

She separated her fingers and rotated her palms so one middle finger pointed up, one down. She moved them like a teeter-totter. Luis went white.

"Stop."

"I am in touch with Shiva now. Shiva comes to me when I'm in danger. She asks me what I want. I asked her to clasp onto your groin. It won't happen today. Nor tomorrow. But soon. Maybe next week. Maybe next month. You'll feel a pain in your testicles, but you'll be afraid to visit a doctor. Maybe you'll visit an herbalist. Or a witch doctor. They won't be able to help. The cancer will spread swiftly. Your friends will abandon you. You will reek of death. They will smell their own deaths in you, and they will abandon you. Now watch."

She put a finger beneath her right eye and drew it down exposing the red. She didn't blink.

"Please stop."

"Give me my phone and five hundred dollars and let me go."

"You said three hundred."

"The longer you delay, the greater the amount. Now watch."

She steepled her hands, in, out. In, out. What her brother used to call a spider doing push-ups on a mirror. Luis went white.

"Please stop."

"Give me my phone. Give me five hundred dollars. I won't call Josh right away. I will wait one hour. You will give me a ride to the bus station downtown. Do you know where it is?"

"No!"

"I will find it for you. I will not phone Josh until I'm on the bus."

"Will you tell him not to come?"

"For one thousand dollars, I will tell him not to come. I will tell him that you and your gang are too dangerous. You know, he only has a handful of men coming. Maybe five. I will convince him not to come."

"How do I know you'll keep your word?"

She clasped her hands and bowed her head. "My lord and savior, Lucifer. If I fail to convince my novio not to come, you may have my soul."

Luis gaped like a guppy. Ray stood and pointed to the door.

"Give me my phone. Get me my money. Take me to the bus station. Go."

Luis was frozen like a carved monkey.

"Go!"

He leaped out of the chair and left the room.

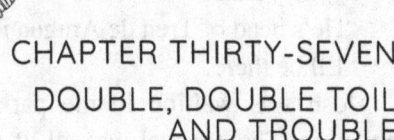

CHAPTER THIRTY-SEVEN
DOUBLE, DOUBLE TOIL
AND TROUBLE

RAY PHONED JOSH AS SOON AS LUIS DROPPED HER OFF.

"Where are you?" he said, trying to control his fear.

"I'm fine, baby. I'm on the bus back to Madison. You can pick me up at the bus station at eleven thirty. Six hundred Highland Ave. In the hospital parking lot."

"What happened?"

"Those thugs you confronted. I never should have opened the door. I was so stupid. They grabbed me, drugged me, and took me to Milwaukee. They wanted me to phone you and tell you not to come or they were going to kill me."

"Jesus Christ! How did you get away?"

Ray laughed. "You wouldn't believe it! The greatest acting of my career. I'll tell you when I get there."

"Why did you take the bus? I could have been there by now."

"I didn't want you in Milwaukee when I tell you

what happened. At ease, big guy. I'm fine. And I have a thousand dollars in my pocket."

"Where'd you get that?"

"Luis gave it to me."

"Who's Luis?"

"He's head of Tren de Aragua in Milwaukee."

"I'll be there."

Josh was waiting in the parking lot as the bus pulled in. The hospital was all lit up. He'd been there twenty minutes and seen two ambulances pull up to the ER entrance as medics rushed in and out with gurneys. The Greyhound chuffed to a stop and opened its doors. Out came a student with hair like Trotsky, followed by a grandmother type, two Asians clutching backpacks, and finally Ray, still wearing the capris she'd had on the previous night and clutching her phone. She rushed into his arms.

They squeezed the air out of each other and kissed. She pulled back.

"Let's get out of here."

"My place?"

"Yes. Grace is taking care of Sid Vicious."

They drove west on University Avenue. "What happened?"

"They stole a UPS uniform. I stupidly opened the door, and they jumped me. They used chloroform, I think. I didn't wake up until I was in this shitty, dark apartment in Milwaukee. They took my phone. Luis comes in. Looks like a vandalized statue. I mean, he had more ink on him than *The New York Times*. Tells me I have to call you and tell you not to come or they're going to kill me."

"I don't understand. How did he know we were planning to come?"

"I don't know. Maybe off the internet? If you're not tech wise these days, you may as well live in a log cabin in the mountains. Maybe he deduced it from your previous actions."

"What did you do?"

"I told him I was a witch, and he'd better cut me loose, or Hecate would strike him deaf and dumb and rip off his balls."

"No really."

"That's what happened. One look at him and I knew he was superstitious. They all are. They're a traditional people from a developing country. Half his tats were demonic. It was the greatest acting job of my life! I wish I'd recorded it, but he didn't give me my phone back until he set me free. And he paid me a thousand dollars."

"Huh?"

"I told him to throw in a thou, or I'd cause a stroke. He'd be alive, but unable to move. I have to remember this shit. I'm going to write it down. It would make a terrific play! Witch! Sorceress! Conjurer!"

"Baby, you're a fuckin' genius."

Josh turned into his driveway. The lights were on in the living room. He rolled into the garage. As he was about to get out, she put a hand on his arm. She held out a pair of soiled white briefs.

"I brought you his underpants."

"Huh?"

"They belong to Luis. I found them on the floor. They might come in handy."

"How will it come in handy?"

"I'll explain."

Fig barked as they entered through the kitchen.

"You want something to drink?"

"Scotch on the rocks."

Josh grabbed the bottle and two glasses. Ray went into the living room where Dolan sat on the sofa watching ultimate fighting. He stood.

"Hey! I'm so glad you're all right!"

"You should see the other guy."

Josh handed Ray a glass. "Thank God you're safe."

"Hey, are you still gonna take a gang and force those bangers out?"

"That's the plan. Ray can stay here 'til we get it settled."

"Oh, they're not coming back for me. They may even clear out before you get there."

"Why would they do that?" Dolan said.

"They think I'm a voodoo priestess. They think I can make their cocks shrivel up and fall off."

Dolan sorta half-smiled. "Huh?"

Josh pointed at Ray. "She's good. Show him how good you are."

"Double, double toil and trouble," Ray said in an old woman's voice. "Fire burn and cauldron bubble!"

"Ha!" Dolan said. "Is that what you said?"

"No, that's Shakespeare. Shakespeare has all the best lines." She switched voices. "Hail to thee, Thane of Glamis!"

Josh sipped his scotch. "Show off."

"You know Shakespeare?" Ray looked at Dolan.

"I saw *Romeo Must Die*," Dolan said. "Does that count?"

"I'll loan you my DVDs. *Hamlet*. *Richard III*. *Hamlet*. *Romeo and Juliet*. *Hamlet*."

"*Hamlet*, *Hamlet*, and *Hamlet*?" Dolan said.

Ray counted on her fingers. "There are over fifty film versions. I have Mel Gibson, Nicol Williamson, and Laurence Olivier."

"I've heard of Mel Gibson. I saw *The Road Warrior*."

"Dolan's only seen six movies."

"Is that true?"

Dolan grinned. "I've seen more than that."

"Did Luis indicate he knows what's coming?"

"No, not specifically. But he knows you're coming."

"How does he know that?"

"I don't know."

"I mean the longer we wait, the more they may do something stupid. They knew where you lived. They may know where I live."

"Trust me, darling, some Venezuelan gang isn't going to drive to Madison to attack you in a ritzy neighborhood."

"It's happened before."

"That was before all these millionaires moved in."

"Maybe. I would just as soon get it over with. The longer we delay, the more danger those tenants are in."

"I want to come," Dolan said.

"I told you, you can't come. You have to stay here and take care of Fig."

Dolan stretched. "G'night. I'm glad you're okay."

Ray pulled him in. "Gimme a hug."

She hugged him. Dolan colored. He went downstairs. Josh and Ray went into his room.

"How soon are you planning your raid?"

"Tomorrow."

"Tomorrow?"

"Yeah. We can't wait. The longer we wait, the crazier they get."

"Don't you want to wait and see if I scared them off?"

"I love you, babe, and you put the fear of God into that creep. But they have a reputation to uphold. They're not going anywhere. At least not until tomorrow."

"What time are you going?"

"We're meeting a block away at nine. As soon as we're all there, we march."

"Oh god. I'm going to be a wreck until I hear you're okay."

"We're gonna be fine. They have to know the tide is turning. The cops came for them in Colorado. The cops came for them in New York. We're just further down the list. Prob'ly be safer. None of us are carrying guns."

"But they are."

"That's why we have ballistic vests."

"So, you're not riding your bikes."

"No, but the Warriors and the Bison are. They're gonna make a noise. That's the point."

"Then we'd better make this a night to remember."

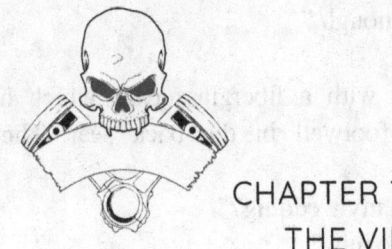

CHAPTER THIRTY-EIGHT
THE VIDEOGRAPHER

JOSH WAS ON THE ROAD BY SEVEN. HE CARRIED SIX ballistic vests in the trunk and twelve more in the back seat along with the bullhorn. He wore a denim vest with a dozen patches, including the names of lost friends and what used to be his tag. Enforcer. The back showed his colors, "Bedouins" over a bearded rider wearing flowing white cape like Lawrence of Arabia. He hadn't put it on in years.

Baker was waiting when he pulled into his driveway. Baker wore his Devil Dog colors and aviator shades and carried a Canon FX100.

"Pop the trunk."

"What you got?"

"My drone."

"Might not be room. Can you fit it in the back seat?"

Baker looked in the back seat. "Can I move those vests around?"

"Sure."

Baker went back to the garage. Alfred came over.

"Wish I could come."

"You've done enough."

"Stay safe."

Baker returned with a fiberglass case which he jammed into the footwell in the back seat. They headed east on 90.

"You coming to my wedding?"

"Can I come like this?"

"No."

"Kidding. Of course I'll come. I'll even shave."

"Let's not go hog wild."

"I have a sports coat and some decent pants. I'd love to come. I'll take pictures."

"Great! I'll send you an invite soon as I get back."

As they headed east on the interstate, Josh pointed to the glove compartment. "Would you open that and take out the tags?"

Baker opened the hatch and brought out three Apple AirTags. "What do you want me to do with them?"

"I'll take them." He tucked them in his vest.

An hour later they drove down Cramer to the strip mall. One-story, plywood sheets covered with graffiti covered with more graffiti. The graffiti artists covered up the day's work every night. They probably took turns. Shred Hustl was always part of the design.

"Who's Shred Hustl?" Baker said.

"Shred Hustl is the fictional hero of a series of hard-boiled crime novels written under the pseudonym 'Curtis Mack' from 1971-1973. All are set in the world of Black pimps, players, and private eyes and were published by the Onyx Press. Titles include *Tear the Roof Off the Sucker*, *Take It to the Max*, and *Stop*

Killing Me. Modern scholars compare Mack to Donald Goines, Icepick Slim, and Malcolm X."

"How do you know that?"

"Believe it or not, it was part of a case I worked on soon after I became a PI. Turns out Curtis Mack was a pseudonym for a white guy. But Donald Goines is the real deal. I've read several of his novels. Whoever keeps painting Shred Hustl is a reader."

"Man, I love those old blaxploitation movies. *Hell Up in Harlem*, *Black Caesar*, *Superfly*. Me and my buddies used to go see them in Milwaukee at the old Roxie. No longer there."

"The brothers always wanted to watch those in prison. Wouldn't do it. The closest we got was *In the Heat of the Night*."

"Well, I dig Sid, but that's not exactly blax-ploitation."

"They screened *The Sound of Music*."

"What? No!"

"I know." Josh parked in front of a store that had been stripped of its identity. They were early. Baker talked movies. Josh had not seen most of them. Baker described them.

"I'll loan you my copies. You have to see Sorceror!"

The roar of unmuffled Harleys droned and grew. Five Christ's Warriors pulled into the lot and backed their bikes to the curb. Paul, Terry, and three other guys. They had that military bearing. You could tell. The Jugan had it. Non-military bikers swaggered. Five Bisons pulled in. They all wore war paint. Two Hawks pulled a compound bow and a quiver of arrows from his saddlebags. Josh frowned. Two Hawks shrugged. "It's just for show."

Baker unpacked his drone. Paul came over.

"Can you do a slow fly-by, from fifty feet?"

"Yeah, I can do that. But don't you need me on the line?"

"Bring the drone with, get her up there before Josh starts talking. When he starts talking, that's when you fly the line. It doesn't matter if they see you. In fact, it's good if they see you."

"Gotcha."

"Guys," Josh said. "Thank you for coming. I have twelve bulletproof vests in the car. Who wants one?"

Everybody raised their hand. Josh opened the trunk and handed them out. Everybody took off their colors, put on the vests, and then back to the colors. Josh's phone rang. Jerell.

"Brother Josh. I have twelve brothers with me, waiting on your signal."

"Do you have bulletproof vests?"

"Some of us do. Other are convinced these gang-bangers can't shoot straight."

"No guns."

"No guns."

Josh looked at his phone. "It's nine twenty. Let's meet at nine thirty. We'll take the front. You take the back."

"What if the back door's locked?"

"It's not. Trust me. But don't barge in. Stay at least thirty feet away. Give them room to leave. All you got to do is stand there and look menacing. You start shooting, that's on you."

"Brother Josh, I have impressed upon the brethren the necessity of leaving their firearms at home."

"I sure hope so."

"How's my dog doin'?"

"She's doin' great for a senior citizen."

"How long has it been now?"

"Ten years."

"Awright. See you in a bit."

Josh circled his arm. "Let's go."

Clutching the bullhorn in his right hand, he walked across the street and turned left toward the Wayzata, followed by Baker, the Warriors and the Bisons. Traffic either slowed down or speeded up. They passed a hot Civic hunkered inches above the pavement. Josh held his hand up. He got down on his knees and slapped the tag beneath the rear bumper. He pulled out his pen and pad and wrote down "018 blue Civic" and the license plate number. He tagged two more cars before they got to the Wayzata.

As they neared the building, a banger sitting on the front stoop did a double take, coughed a cloud of dense gray smoke, tossed the vape to the street, and went inside.

Except for Baker, Josh and his companions formed a semi-circle facing the building. Josh turned on the bullhorn.

"ATTENTION. ATTENCIO. YO YO YO! WILL ALL GANG MEMBERS WHO ARE IN THE COUNTRY ILLEGALLY PLEASE VACATE THE BUILDING. IF YOU ARE IN THE COUNTRY ILLEGALLY, PLEASE VACATE THE BUILDING. THANK YOU."

Baker faced them from two steps up filming. He came down to street level and walked the line, training the Canon on faces. He took up position at the end midway between the line and the building. The sound of windows screeching open pierced the air. They looked up. A man whose head looked like a well-used eraser trained an AK on them.

"GET THE FUCK OUT OR I START SHOOTING."

Two Hawks stepped between two cars into the street and unfolded his bow. He plucked an arrow from the quiver across his back. Josh didn't notice. He focused on the building as four armed bangers came out on the front porch. Two held automatics. The others AKs.

Josh handed the bullhorn to Terry. Terry lifted the bullhorn.

"¡ATENCIÓN! ¡ATENCIÓN! ¡YO YO YO! ¡TODOS LOS PANDILLEROS QUE SE ENCUENTRAN EN EL PAÍS ILEGALMENTE, POR FAVOR, DESALOJEN EL EDIFICIO! SI SE ENCUENTRAN EN EL PAÍS ILEGALMENTE, POR FAVOR, DESALOJEN EL EDIFICIO. GRACIAS."

The banger on the third floor adjusted his rifle. Two Hawks crouched between two cars unnoticed. A slight man covered in ink wearing a Braves hoodie came out. Josh knew who it was the second he appeared, since Ray had described his ink.

"Which one of you cabrones is Josh?" he said.

Josh raised his hand.

"You think you're some kind of bad motherfucker, don't you? You think you can just run us out of town."

"Well, you are in the country illegally. We'll provide free transportation to El Salvador."

Luis laughed. "We ain't from El Salvador, pendejo. You know, I thought about what that bitch said. And I gotta say, she was a fine bitch. Now I'm sorry I didn't take a piece of her when I had a chance. Now how's this. You got five minutes to clear the fuck out, or we'll mow you down like sugarcane."

"We're not armed. Cops left you alone so far. You open up, and they'll be forced to respond. And who do you think they're going to arrest? A bunch of Native Americans and veterans? Or a bunch of tattooed cretins in the country illegally?"

Luis wrinkled his nose. Josh pulled the underpants from his pocket and held it up.

"Are these yours?"

Luis did a double take. "Where you get that?"

"My woman brought them home. She gathered some of your pubic hairs. How do you have pubic hairs? You don't have enough hair to cover your balls."

Josh tucked the bullhorn under his arm and displayed the underpants, turning them around and inside out. "You ever do laundry?"

Some of Luis's gang snickered. Luis tensed.

Bang. The bullet whistled past Josh's ear. He didn't hear the bow twang. He sensed the arrow. The AK fell out of the window and hit the concrete. There was an instant of silence. Josh walked up the stoop. He towered over Luis. "Get out now," he said softly.

Luis stared back. They held each other's gaze. Luis blinked. He turned white, looked around, gestured down the street. "Let's go."

He spoke into his phone. They began to file out. Some wore backpacks. Some carried duffel bags. A handful. Then several more. Josh counted. Nineteen males, all inked. Twelve females. They all looked underaged.

Baker filmed the whole thing.

Delcey fell into step beside Luis. "Where will we go?"

"My cousin Alejandro has a place in Chicago."

"But our cars."

"We'll take the cars. They won't stop us."

They walked in silence and shame.

"There is one more thing you must do for me," Luis said.

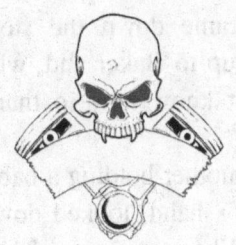

CHAPTER THIRTY-NINE
THE WALK OFF

JOSH PHONED JERELL. "WHAT'S GOING ON BACK there?"

"They came out, took a look, and went back inside. What's going on out front?"

"They're clearing out. They're taking their shit. They're taking a bunch of girls."

"You gonna let them do that?"

Josh thought about it. He didn't want it to explode just when they were leaving, but he didn't want them to take their sex slaves with them. On the other hand, most of those girls were addicts. They were just following the dope. He didn't have the facilities to straighten them out. He'd leave that fight for another day. It killed him, but it wasn't his fight. He'd share his tagging information with the police. If they were interested.

The bikers stood like a praetorian guard as the gang loaded their low riders and hot hatches and took off, spinning their tires, gassing their mills, and slithering down the road. No one spoke until the sound of glass packs died away. The apartment's legit renters filtered out. An old woman came down the steps hanging on to the rail, walked up to Baker and, with tears in her eyes said, "I don't know how to thank you."

A young Latino family, the mother holding a baby, the father holding a young boy's hand, looked down from the stoop. "Who did this? Whose idea was it?"

Josh swept his arm. "Everybody. Christ's Warriors. The Bisons. Show 'em your colors, boys." The bikers turned around, arms crossed and faced the street. Residents continued to trickle out until there was no room on the street, and they spread up and down the sidewalk. Some brought folding chairs. Some brought coolers. They passed out beers. Someone set a boombox on the riser. "Disco Inferno" filled the street. It was ten fifteen. Two Hawks started dancing like John Travolta in *Saturday Night Fever*. Paul and Terry joined in. Couples from inside the building joined them. Baker stood on the riser to film. Windows opened across the street, and throughout the building, residents leaned out, waving.

A gray-haired Latina in a blue dress swayed on the stoop singing, "Burn, baby, burn! Burn that mother down, y'all! Burn, baby, burn! Disco inferno, yeah!"

Josh noted the window from where the AK fell. He went inside, up two flights of stairs and found the apartment door open. There was blood on the floor next to the window, a trail of blood to the door. Whoever dropped the rifle was gone. Two Hawks hit his target. Josh was glad the shooter had removed himself. It saved him a lot of trouble when the police showed up, if they did show up.

Paul took the bullhorn. "Any veterans here? Please come forward."

An old man with white hair and a cane came carefully down the stairs, aided by a middle-aged man wearing carpenter pants. Paul went to them.

"I'm Paul Wyrich, Christ's Warriors. We're all ex-military. We're here to help in any way we can."

The man in carpenter pants kept his hand on the older man's arm. "I'm Barry Sandoval, Army. Desert Storm. This is Tim McNab. Tim's a Korean War vet. Navy."

Paul shook their hands. "Great to meet you. We don't know what's going to happen, but we're pretty sure that gang is never coming back. We're going to share what happened with the media. Don't worry. Your names and faces won't appear. Are you both doing all right? Do you have funds for food and lodging? Do you have funds for medical?"

"I've been trying to get scheduled for shoulder surgery for six months," McNab said. "The fuckin' Veterans Administration doesn't know its ass from its elbow."

"I've heard that before. We'll work with you to try and make that happen. Are you comfortable here? Now that the gang is gone, assuming they don't come back, do you want to stay?"

Sandoval shrugged. "My friends are here. I like the local VFW. My daughter lives in Wauwatosa. I see her once a week. She wants me to move in with her, but I don't want to give up my independence. I used to walk every morning, but I stopped when those scumbags took over the building. Maybe now I can start again."

Baker approached, camera at his side. "Hi, guys. I'm Arthur Baker. I'm making a documentary about today's events. Would either of you gentlemen be interested in participating?"

McNab shook his head. "No thanks."

Baker turned to Sandoval.

"Well yeah. I got a few things to say. Not just about what happened, although I gotta tell ya, that was unexpected. And welcome. We heard how you guys got a couple other guys we know out of a similar situation, but clearing out that whole hornet's nest…wow."

"Let me get your contact information, sir, and I'll get you a waiver. Of course I'll only include you with your permission. If you fuck up and start cussin' and stuff, we'll cut that out. Unless you want it in."

"Fuck that," Sandoval said.

"Well now," McNab said in a phlegmy voice. "Maybe I will participate."

"We're gonna take off," Josh said. "Maybe the police will come, maybe they won't. The plan is for Art to get this edited and release it to the media within twenty-four hours. Once that happens, they'll come around. They can't afford to look flat-footed."

"This will attract national attention," Baker said. "It's just too good not to show. So be on your toes." He made quote marks with his fingers. "Media personalities will want to talk to you. You must stress that we had no firearms, and the gang had plenty."

Nobody mentioned the arrow. Maybe they didn't see it. The injured party left and took the arrow with him. There would be no blowback. Josh caught up with Two Hawks as he got on his bike.

"I went to the shooter's room. A little blood, but he's gone. And he took your arrow."

"That's good. I didn't want to kill the guy."

"You did good. We never touched that AK he

dropped. It's gone. One of the tenants grabbed it. It's their problem now. Say, man, I owe you one. What's your contact info?"

Josh wrote it down in the little notepad he kept in his jacket. He handed Two Hawks his card. "You need anything, don't hesitate to call."

"You going to Sturgis?"

Josh looked up. Looked down. "Haven't in a long time. Last time I was there was kind of rough. But I do ride, and we should get together. I'll be in touch."

Two Hawks slipped out of his vest. "Here."

"You keep it. Everybody hangs on to their vests in case we have to do this again."

"I'll bet you we won't."

"I'm not gonna take that bet. I think you're right."

Josh and Baker returned to the mall and booked. Once they left the city, Baker picked up his camera and turned it on Josh.

"What are you doing?"

"I'm making a documentary. This was your idea, wasn't it?"

"Yes, but you were there from the beginning. This is your documentary. I think you should narrate it, and you can describe how it came about."

Baker held the camera silently. He turned it off and placed it in the back seat. Josh dropped Baker off just past noon and drove home. Dolan and Fig were gone. There was a note on the kitchen table. "Went running. Back soon."

Josh phoned Ray.

"How'd it go?"

"We did it. The whole gang left, and Baker taped the whole thing. He's cutting it right now into something he can send to the media."

"Will he send it to your admirer, Katy?"

She said it with a smile, but there was a hint of jealousy. Katy Varner of WMAD had been an admirer of Josh for years. More than an admirer. "Probably."

"Oh goodie. Expect a phone call."

Josh laughed. "Don't worry about Katy. She's dating a millionaire."

"Do tell."

"Brian Bascomb. Vice President of something or other at Epic Systems."

"Well that's exciting."

Epic Systems was a massive health insurance data factory that had built a campus in Verona.

"So what are you doing tonight?"

"Why don't you and I go to the Old Fashioned and then go back to my place?"

"What time should I pick you up?"

"Pick me up at the studio at six."

"It's a date, babe."

The front door opened. Fig sat at Josh's feet wagging her tail and back pedaling. Her forelegs lifted and retreated, a quarter inch at a time. It was her feed me dance. Josh found it endearing. Dolan came in the room, flushed and sweating.

"What happened?"

"Complete success. The whole gang walked away like a group of tourists heading for the bus. Wait 'til you see the video."

"That's great, Pop!" Dolan threw his arms around his father who felt a flash of embarrassment before returning the embrace.

"What have you been up to?"

"Practicing my martial arts." Dolan made some Elvis-like moves. "I looked at your computer and removed a shitload of malware. Should be a lot faster now."

"Great! Hey, I'm going to have dinner with Ray tonight. You good on your own?"

"Fig and I will manage."

"Awright. I gotta take a shower."

"Yeah, man. I can smell you from here."

CHAPTER FORTY
THE HODAG

RAY CAME OUT OF THE STUDIO AS JOSH PULLED TO THE curb. She wore dance clothes and a short leather jacket with a fur collar, her long auburn hair falling down her back. She slid in.

"Mmm," she said, leaning over and kissing him. "You smell good."

"You should have smelled me before! You hungry?"

"You bet."

They drove to the capitol square and parked two blocks down on Butler Street, in view of the Frank Lloyd Wright-designed Lamp House, which occupied an odd spot in the center of the block. Hand in hand, they walked up East Washington to the Capitol Square. The Old Fashioned on North Pinckney was a la-de-da version of a Wisconsin tavern serving brats, fish fries, twenty-seven local brews, and cheese sticks. The hostess was a willowy young woman with a nose ring and inked sleeves.

"Hello! Do you have a reservation?"

"McRaney," Ray said.

"Right this way." The hostess led them to a booth in the back. The decor was aged wood, wood floor, walls covered with framed photographs. Vince Lombardi. The Steve Miller Band. Robert LaFollette. Jessica Lange. Their waitress was a slim person of indeterminate sex with a nose ring. Josh thought it was a guy. Then he saw the tag reading she/her.

"What can I get you folks?"

"I'll have a Giant Jones IPA," Josh said.

"I'd like a nice glass of Chardonnay."

"Perfect. I'll be right back."

"I'm so excited!" Ray said. "The wedding's in two weeks!"

"Yeah. Bobby Hines is gonna play at the party."

"Wonderful. Mongoose has written a song."

"Oh no."

"She's got a great voice!"

"What's the song about? The patriarchy?"

"No! It's a love song."

"Transgenders in love?"

"It's not specific."

"I'll believe it when I hear it."

"Great! Because she uploaded it to YouTube. I'll play it for you when we get back to my place."

Josh spread his hands. "I look forward to it with the keenest alacrity."

Ray laughed. "Oh Josh! Those words don't belong in your mouth!"

The waitress returned with their drinks. Josh ordered the pork schnitzel. Ray ordered the chicken-fried steak. They were halfway through their meal when Ray looked up, eyes wide and stopped chewing. Josh twisted in his seat to look at the big flat-screen behind the bar. Someone had recorded the Tren de Aragua walk from that morning and sent it to a local station.

The sound was off, but a scroll bar ran along the bottom. "This scene unfolded this morning in front of the Wayzata Arms, an apartment building in Northwest Milwaukee. What you see are members of the notorious Tren de Aragua gang voluntarily leaving this building, which they had taken over, due to a show of force by Indigenous peoples, local Milwaukee gangs, and a group of Christian bikers."

Josh turned back in disbelief. "Voluntarily?!"

"They're idiots. When does your friend's video come out?"

"Knowing Art, he's editing as fast as he can. He'll upload it as soon as he's done, and then we'll see. He has a YouTube channel with thirty thousand followers. You mind if I call him?"

"Knock yourself out."

Baker answered on the first ring. "I see it. Nothing to worry about. I saw several residents recording this morning. Didn't say anything. They can do what they like. What I present will be a thirty-minute documentary providing context and interviews."

"What interviews?"

"I'm going back tomorrow. Wanna come?"

"Can't do it, pal. Got too much going on. Good luck."

"How's the wedding coming?"

"It's coming. You gonna wear a tie?"

"Of course I'll wear a tie. I'm not a complete idiot! Who's your best man?"

"Dolan."

"Later."

They returned to Ray's apartment. Sid Vicious twined between their legs, purring. They made mad love and turned on the late-night news. Katy Varner at the desk.

"Startling news out of Milwaukee where a group of bikers and local street gangs convinced a Venezuelan street gang to abandon the apartment they had taken over. Residents of the Wayzata Arms claimed that they had been living in fear for over a year, ever since Tren de Aragua had moved in, chasing out several tenants, and using their units for drugs and human trafficking.

"Mayor Peterson has long denied that Milwaukee has a gang problem, even as homicides and convictions for drug trafficking have steadily grown. We reached out to the mayor for a response but have not yet heard from his office."

"I'm surprised she hasn't called you."

Josh's phone rang. He picked it up. He pressed a button.

"Guess who that was?"

"What are you going to tell her?"

"I'm going to stall as long as I can. Art says he'll have an edited version to release by Friday. If we can just keep the lid on until then, everything will be fine."

"How long will it be?"

"He said around thirty minutes. That's the short version. He's turning it into a feature-length documentary."

"What do you want to do now?"

"Let's watch one of Arthur's movies."

"All right. Where can I find it?"

"Speak into the remote."

Ray grabbed her remote, switched to apps and

clicked on her streaming services. "What am I looking for?"

"*The Hodag*."

"It's on my list."

"In American folklore, the hodag is a terrifying beast resembling a large, bull-horned carnivore, with a row of thick curved spines down its back. The hodag was said to be born from the ashes of cremated oxen, as the incarnation of animals which had suffered abuse at the hands of their masters."

"It's an animal rights thing!"

"Bingo."

Ray thumbed the voice command. "*The Hodag*."

An image appeared on screen. An outlandish creature with enormous fangs and claws.

"It's on Tubi."

Ray hit the button. They went to Tubi. A clearing in the forest. A wedding party. The guests were dressed as German immigrants with Tyrolean hats and white shirts as a band played polka music. The band consisted of a tuba, an accordion, a drummer, and a bass player. Close in on the married couple, a plump, rose-cheeked girl and her mustached groom, wearing shorts held up with suspenders.

The music fades as a crone invades the scene. Baba Yaga. A long-haired witch in a black robe, her hand raised like the hodag's claw.

"Do you not know whose land this is?"

The astonished groom confronts her. "Why, this is our land. We just bought it!"

"This land belongs to the hodag," the witch responds in a sinister tone. The polka music faded into something ominous. Minor chords foretelling evil.

"You dance on the graves of the slaughtered. Not

just the animals, but the Ojibwa as well. And now you
must pay the price!"

Ferocious snuffling, screams, the camera veers to
show a guest tossed high in the air, blood arcing from
her wounds. The main title begins.

THE HODAG
A FILM BY ARTHUR BAKER

"OH MY GOD!" JOSH WAILED, LAUGHING.

"You ain't seen nothin' yet."

CHAPTER FORTY-ONE
SMOOTH

JOSH WOKE TO SID VICIOUS PURRING LOUDLY IN HIS ear. Sid had come a long way since the days when he pissed on Josh's clothes. Ray was still out. Josh rose, took a shower, went into the kitchen and made coffee. He grabbed his phone and went out on the deck overlooking Lake Monona to the west, the capitol dome visible on the horizon. Katy Varner had called.

"Josh, I'd like to interview you for the station about your triumph in Milwaukee. Call me."

Triumph.

Baker called. "Hey, bro. You're not off the hook yet. I still want to interview you. You know you can trust me. It's not just because it's your idea, but because you're a fascinating character. At your discretion, of course."

Josh grimaced. "Art, I love you like a brother. I do not wish to become a public figure. Interview Jerell instead."

"I've already set that up. I'm talking to him tomorrow."

"You should talk to Ray. Some producer wants to option her Kung Fu Musical."

"Kung Fu Musical?! When am I going to meet this legendary creature?"

"Wedding rehearsal dinner. It's at the Hoity Toity in Middleton. We'll get the invites out this week."

"Who's throwing the dinner?"

"Normally, the groom's family. So I guess I am."

"You got any folks?"

"Never knew my mother. My father's in prison for murder."

"Jesus, I'm sorry, bro. I had no idea."

"It's no big deal. I've moved on. Let me know how it goes with Jerell."

"I'm also interviewing Two Hawks, Paul, and Terry."

"I have a feeling this doc's got legs."

"Me too."

Ray came out of the shower wearing a jumbo towel, her hair in a towel turban. "What are you doing today?"

"Mowing the lawn."

"Why don't you have Dolan do that?"

Josh snapped his fingers. "Good idea!" He checked the clock. It was nine a.m. He phoned Dolan.

"What's up, Pop?"

The word gave him a little burst. "Not much. You see the news last night?"

"I sure did. Proud of you, Pop."

Another burst. "When's your birthday?"

"July first. I told you."

"What about Mabel?"

"I haven't told her about my birthday."

"Maybe you should. You want to invite her to the wedding?"

"That would be great!"

"What do you want for your birthday?"

"A car."

"Okay. First things first. You have to take the test and get your license. You ready to do that?"

"You bet. I've been using AI to learn all about the driver's test. I know what to do. I may want to practice a little."

"Okay, we can work on that. I'll come with you. Don't want you driving around by yourself without a license. You home?"

"Yeah. I'm not going anywhere until noon."

"Would you mow the lawn?"

"Sure."

"Should start on the first pull."

"No worries."

"See you in a bit."

"Bye, Pop."

Pop.

Ray entered the living room wearing sweatpants and a UW hoodie with Bucky Badger on the front. "You want breakfast?"

"You don't have to cook."

"Microwave biscuit."

"Sure."

While the microwave hummed, Josh checked his messages.

PAYMENT AND TRANSFERS
10017WIRE TRANSFER/AUDIT UNIT

Our Ref: WB/NF/UN/XX02x79
ATTN: BENEFICIARY,
IRREVOCABLE RELEASE OF YOUR
PAYMENT

we have actually been authorized by the World Bank and international monetary fund (IMF), to investigate the unnecessary delay of your payment, Recommendation and approval of your claims for payment is certified as genuine.

During the course of our investigation, we discovered with dismay that your payment has been unnecessarily Delayed by corrupt officials of the Bank, who are Trying to divert your Fund into their private accounts, to forestall this, security for your funds Was organized in the form of your personal Identification number (PIN) and your transfer access code (T.A.C.), this will enable only you have direct Control over this fund.

We have also agreed with the World Bank and international monetary fund (IMF) that, we will handle this payment in ourselves to avoid the hopeless situation created by these corrupt Officials.

We have obtained an irrevocable payment guarantee on your Payment, from the World Bank and international monetary Funds (IMF).We are happy to inform you that based on our recommendation/instructions, your Entire contract fund/inheritance claim has been credited in your favour through our paying bank You are therefore advice to contact: MR.DOUGLAS BENSON, of African

*Development Bank Group the (un)paying bank
Liaison Office in Nigeria Lagos with the
contact informations stated below: PAYING
BANK: AFRICAN DEVELOPMENT BANK
GROUP EMAIL: adbg_bankplc@vipmail.hu
CONTACT   PERSON: MR.DOUGLAS
BENSON.   Phone   Number: +234-9047
7356 69*

*Make sure that you contact the above-
mentioned person to collect your original
payment slip with your pin and transfer access
code. As soon as you submit these codes and
your payment slip to your bank, they will credit
your account without any delay.*

*YOU ARE ADVISED TO RE-COMFIRM
YOUR INFORMATION TO AVOID TRANSFER
OF THIS FUND INTO A WRONG ACCOUNT.*

Your Bank Name:
Your Bank Address:
Your Bank Account No:
Routing No:
Swift Code No:
Account Name:
Age & Occupation
Your Driving license:
Full Name:
Home Address:
Your Direct Tel, Mobile & Fax No:
*NOTE:YOU ARE ADVISED TO CALL MR.
DOUGLAS BENSON ON HIS DIRECT TELE-
PHONE NUMBER +234-9047 7356 69 AS
SOON AS YOU RECEIVE THIS MAIL TO
CONFIRM THE*

MAIL TO HIM AND FORWARD YOUR

*DETAILS FOR THE PAYMENT TO HIM
IMMEDIATELY THIS IS DONE.
CONGRATULATIONS.*

HE DELETED IT.

"Breakfast!" Ray sang from the kitchen. Josh went in.

"The World Bank apologizes for the unnecessary delay of my payment. They only need my bank name, bank address, account number, Social Security number, age and occupation, driver's license, and home address."

Ray set a microwaved biscuit in front of him on a small dish. "How much?"

"Thirty million dollars. I had to turn them down."

"That's too bad. I had to turn down twelve million a week ago from the widow of Generalissimo Gerhard Fugazi of Uganda, who had chosen me as a worthy recipient. They wanted my Social Security number and bank routing information."

Josh wolfed down the tasteless biscuit. "Okay, babe, gotta run. I'm setting up the rehearsal dinner at the Hoity Toity in Middleton. Need a list of who you want to invite. Let's keep it to twenty people max. I'm inviting Dolan, Bobby Hines, Heinz and Doreen Calloway, Art Baker, and Steve Fleiss. Bobby may want to bring someone."

"What about Fleiss?"

"If Fleiss has a girlfriend, she's well hidden."

"Okay, that's seven. Does that mean I get to invite thirteen?"

"Yes. Not counting your folks."

"Okay. I'll put a list together and tell the folks. Love you!"

They kissed. Josh left.

He pulled into his driveway. Dolan was on the last square in the middle of the front yard, pushing the old gas-powered lawn mower. He finished, put the lawn mower back in the garage and came into the house.

"You want to practice driving?"

"Sure!"

"Let's go."

Josh let Dolan take the wheel as they headed west to the university golf course.

"Smoothness is the key to good driving. Be alert, eyes on the road, and make no sudden moves. That's why you have to be alert. You don't want to be surprised by someone lurching into your lane or a sudden red light. A light touch on the gas and the brake."

They approached a stop sign. Dolan gently feathered the brake to bring them to a joltless stop.

"Excellent. I hardly ever achieve a joltless stop."

"What about on a bike?"

"Same thing, only moreso. You ever see a good rider, a grand prix rider, lay it down so he's scraping a peg leaning into a curve?"

"Yeah?"

"He can do it because he feels the track, feels the bike, and is smooth."

"Can I ride that Hawk?"

"One. Get a driver's license. Two. Take a motorcycle safety class. Three. Ride the Hawk."

"Okay."

CHAPTER FORTY-TWO
THE TUX

ON MONDAY, MAY 22, JOSH RODE HIS BIKE downtown and parked on the Lake Street ramp. Wearing blue jeans and a white cotton pullover, he marched up Bascom Hill toward Bascom Hall. The statue of Abe Lincoln still sat at the top looking down State Street toward the capitol. Behind the statue was a curved concrete bench. If two people sat on opposite ends of the bench, they could lean into the back and whisper and hear each other perfectly.

Four previous student bodies had unsuccessfully petitioned to have the statue removed because of racism or something. The statue remained. Abe endured. The university had not been as successful with the racist rock, which had been put in storage, or the racist Civil War Memorial from Camp Randall, listing the names of Wisconsin volunteers who had fought for the Confederacy.

Josh entered the building holding a legal envelope. A clerk looked up from her desk.

"How can I help you?"

"Where can I find the chancellor, ma'am?"

"She's on the second floor. Is there something I can do for you?"

"I'm a process server. I have to deliver this personally."

"Well good luck with that. She's pretty busy."

"Thank you, ma'am."

Josh climbed the elegant sweeping stairs to the second floor. A free-standing sign pointed to the chancellor's office. The large oak door was open. A plaque on the desk said Chancellor Miriam Hotchkiss-Plowright. The chancellor, a prim woman in her fifties with tight gray hair, sat at her desk wearing glasses reading a document beneath a framed painting of Fighting Bob LaFollette. Josh knocked on the doorframe. She looked up.

"Yes?"

"Ma'am, I'm here to deliver a summons."

"What?"

He handed her the envelope and turned to go.

"Just one minute."

Josh paused. The chancellor removed a stiletto from her desk drawer and slit the envelope open. She pulled out the summons. "False pretenses?"

"Yes, ma'am. The professor claimed on her application that she was of at least twenty percent pure Lakota blood and therefore deserving of special consideration. As you can see, the Sioux Nation refutes that claim. They keep a registry of every Lakota in the United States. Not only is Professor Aushenker not listed, neither is any relative going back five generations. Whenever someone claims to be Lakota, the Sioux Nation looks into it. Professor Aushenker is teaching Native American history. The

Sioux Nation doesn't require such professors to be Native, but they won't tolerate someone claiming to be Lakota if they're not. Especially to gain special privileges."

"What special privileges? She's a full professor like most of the faculty."

"Her salary is $620,000 a year. They may be referring to that."

"How is it that I'm the subject of this summons?"

"You hired her."

Her phone rang. Old-fashioned desk phone. She picked it up. "Yes?" She listened intently. "All right. Give me a minute. I'm dealing with a ridiculous situation." She hung up, folded her hands and looked at Josh.

"All right. Sorry to go off on you. You're just the messenger. What should I do?"

"My advice would be to contact an attorney. I'm sure the university has one."

"All right. Thank you." She picked the phone up. Josh left. He rode to Lucca's Men's Clothing on East Main Street and backed up to the curb. It was in the Tenney Building. He went inside. A man sat behind the counter reading. He put his book down, smiled, stood, and stepped around the counter. He was in his mid-forties with white sidewalls framing dense brown hair and wore a blue sportscoat over matching trousers and a white shirt.

"Good morning, sir. How can I be of assistance?"

"I'm getting married. I need a tux."

"Well, you've come to the right place. Congratulations. How much are you looking to spend?"

"I don't know. I'm kind of new at this. I only expect to wear it once."

"I understand. Well, we have some very nice tuxedos in the four-to-five hundred-dollar range. Let me show you what they look like, and if you're interested, we can move on to measurements."

"Sure."

The man placed a loose-leaf binder on the glass countertop. Under the glass were bow ties, cummerbunds, and cufflinks. "Flip through here. See if anything catches your eye."

Josh opened the book to the first page. A nice black tuxedo worn over a smooth white shirt with tiny buttons. "This looks fine."

The clerk laughed. "You're easy to please. This is a Pronto Uomo Platinum on sale right now for two-fifty."

"That'll do it. You got one I can try on?"

"No sir. We tailor each tux to the man. Let me get my tape measure."

Josh stood still while the clerk pulled out a stool. As he measured Josh's inseam his cuff rode up his arm revealing a USMC tattoo.

"Thank you for your service."

The clerk looked up, surprised. He stood and stuck out his hand. "Robin Ryan."

"Josh Pratt."

"You serve?"

"No, sir. While you were fighting, I was in prison."

"Nice bike."

"Thank you. You ride?"

"Used to. Then I got broadsided by a little old lady in a Buick. Broke my leg. Gave it up. My wife insisted."

"I suppose if you're gonna sell tuxes, you should be married."

"When's the date?"

"June fourteenth."

"Well, we'd better put this on the fast track. You can pick it up Friday."

"Great."

"What do you do for a living?"

"I'm a process server."

"I can see why. Got a card?"

Josh pulled a card from his wallet. Ryan stared at it. "Says here you're a private investigator."

"I am, but process server sounds better."

Ryan laughed. "Good to know. Like Sam Spade, huh?"

"Not exactly. It's mostly pretty boring. Mostly people who don't pay their bills or going through a divorce."

"Did you see where a bunch of bikers drove one of those Venezuelan gangs out of an apartment complex in Milwaukee?"

"I heard about it."

"About time somebody did something. I wonder where they went."

"Let's just hope they don't come here."

"Amen, brother. Got a ring?"

Josh slapped his forehead. "D'OHHH!"

"Well, there's still plenty of time. I recommend Sutter's just off the Square on West Mifflin."

"Next stop."

Josh used his credit card, got on his bike, and headed west. A driver pulled out just as he was pulling up. He backed the bike to the curb and got off. The door jingled as he entered. A woman in a tight skirt, hands on hips, back to the door, green hair, looked at a selection of necklaces on a black velvet board. Behind the counter stood an old man with white hair wearing a gray suit, white shirt, and pink tie.

"Good morning, sir," he said. "I'll be with you in a minute."

The woman cupped her chin. "You know what? I'm just going to take a picture of these necklaces and show them to my friends." She pulled out her phone and took the picture. She brushed by Josh.

"Sir, how may I help you?"

"I need a wedding ring."

"Congratulations. Do you have an idea for the price range?"

"Well, I don't know. Something with a diamond, I guess. But not the Star of India."

The old man smiled. "Sold that last week. All right. Let me show you what I have."

He unlocked the sliding glass cabinet and pulled out a black velvet slab with sixteen velvet cones, each bearing a diamond ring. They started with a tiny diamond in the upper left corner and grew larger to a monster diamond in the bottom right. Josh knew that Ray's love for him did not depend on the size of the diamond. On the other hand, she'd be disappointed with a chip. He pointed to the middle ring on the bottom row. "Tell me about that one."

The jeweler removed the ring and handed it to Josh. The price tag became visible. Eleven thousand dollars. "Price is determined by the four Cs: carat, cut, color, and clarity, along with other factors like shape, fluorescence, and market conditions. That is high quality. Two point seven five karats."

"I'll take it."

"Do you know the bride's finger size?"

Josh was able to force the ring down on his left pinkie. "Yeah. This'll fit."

"Would you like to make a deposit?"

"Nah. I'll pay for the whole thing now." He reached for his wallet.

"I wish all my customers were like you."

Josh handed the jeweler his credit card. He tried to remove the ring. Stuck. The jeweler reached beneath the display case and handed him a squeeze bottle of liquid soap and a white cotton towel. Josh squeezed the soap on his finger, worked it back and forth, and pulled it off.

CHAPTER FORTY-THREE
FAME

THE REHEARSAL DINNER WAS SET FOR THE HOITY Toity. A week prior, Josh and Ray consulted with the chef, Rivera Ordóñez, who had studied at the Cordon Bleu in Paris. The Hoity served classic American fare with a Spanish touch. They sat in the spacious bar looking out on University Ridge. Golfers teed up or cruised by in golf carts, some wearing red ball caps with the UW logo. Chef, bride, and groom zeroed in on focaccia and carpaccio di scampi as appetizers, with duck breast, ribeye, or salmon for the main course.

"What about wine?" Josh said.

"You must ask our sommelier, Winston."

Ray put her hand around Josh's arm. "I'll take care of it."

"Tell me something, Rivera," Josh said, looking around.

Rivera leaned in, all ears. Josh lowered his voice.

"Is it true that you've served steaks from mastodons found frozen in Siberia?"

"I can neither confirm nor deny such rumors."

"If you were to come into some of these mastodon steaks, how would a potential diner know?"

"Would you like me to put you on the list?"

Josh handed the chef his card. "If you would."

Rivera looked at the card. "Ah. A shamus," he said in a Brooklyn accent. "You got a gat?"

"No gats."

"Well then, I'll see you Thursday."

When Josh and Ray returned to his house, Dolan was practicing kung fu in the backyard. Fig watched, tongue lolling. Fig erupted when Josh and Ray came out on the back deck. Dolan was working over an elm tree. Kicks. Hands.

"Hi!" He went back to the tree.

Josh got a bottle of bourbon and two red Solo cups, then poured some for Ray. They sat on the deck watching Dolan.

"You know, Dolan," Ray said, "you look pretty sharp."

"I just started."

"You could do a walk-on in Kung Fu Musical."

He stopped. "What's Kung Fu Musical?"

"It's a production I put on. Some big shot producer wants to turn it into a movie."

"Really?"

"For reals."

"And they want Jason Statham to play your father."

"Oh, come on."

Josh circled his temple with a finger.

Dolan came up on the deck and snagged a dish towel to wipe his face and neck. "Pop, can I order a kung fu wooden man?"

"Sure. I'll give you my credit card." He dug for his wallet and handed over the card. "Do it now and bring back the card."

"Yes sir."

Dolan went into the house.

"What's happening with the musical?"

"We have another Zoom meeting July fourteenth. Melvin wants me to meet his production partners. He said there might be a surprise guest, but he wouldn't tell me who."

"What about our honeymoon?"

"Honey, I'm so sorry. I'll make it up to you. Wait a minute. They want to fly us out. Give us the full first class treatment. Maybe that can be our honeymoon! We can go to Disneyworld, take in some shows."

"It that's what you want to do. So who do you think their surprise guest is?"

"Ryan Gosling."

"No."

"Jackie Chan."

"What part would he play?"

"The old guy."

"I doubt it."

"Will they use your script and libretto?"

Ray rolled her eyes. "I doubt it. They always want to put their stamp on it. He also wants to fly us out for a face-to-face meeting."

"Us?"

"Yes. I told him a little about you. He's dying to meet you."

"I don't know."

"Oh, come on. It'll be fun. Have you ever been to Hollywood?"

"Once. It was not a pleasant trip."

Dolan came out clutching the card. "Pop, it's four hundred and thirty bucks."

"Do it."

"Great! Thanks!"

He went inside. Ray regarded Josh with amusement.

"Pop?"

Josh shrugged. His phone rang. It was Baker.

"'Sup, Art?"

"The short version is up. It's fifteen minutes. I put it up at noon, and so far, it's had one million views."

"Oh, come on."

"I'm not kidding, man! I've scheduled interviews with Jerell, Two Hawks, Karenga, and Paul Price from Christ's Warriors."

"Who's Karenga?"

"Leader of the West Side Bluds. You're next."

"Oh no."

"Come on, man! This was your idea."

"Work around me. Where can I see it?"

"I'll text you the link."

Josh told Ray what Baker had said.

"Are you serious?"

"Let's find out."

Dolan came out with the credit card. Josh showed him the text. "Can you bring this up on your laptop?"

"Sure. I gotta go get it."

Dolan returned, put the laptop on the round metal table, opened it up, and entered the URL.

"Turn up the sound."

The theme to the Peter Gunn show hit them. An overview of the Wayzata Arms taken by a drone, lazily flying down the line. Red words appeared on the screen.

• • •

DEPARTURE DAY
A FILM BY ARTHUR BAKER

"For months, Milwaukee police have turned a blind eye to the presence of Venezuelan gangs in their city. Partly due to the defund the police movement, which found advocates within the Milwaukee City Counsel. Partly due to a reduction in force. Members of the notorious Tren de Aragua descended on the north side and began to take over apartment buildings via intimidation.

"This was the scene in Aurora, Colorado, two years ago as the gang went door to door to take over an apartment complex which they turned into a center for drug distribution and human trafficking."

The screen showed the famous footage from Aurora, Colorado, as Tren de Aragua went door to door clutching machetes and AKs. The view shifted.

"This is footage from the Wayzata Apartments in Milwaukee, Wisconsin as they did the same thing."

The video was shaky, shot by a resident. A gang leader, tats covering his face whirled to face the camera and point his machete. The resident fled inside his apartment and slammed the door.

"A group of veterans and bikers decided to do something about it. Christ's Warriors are a religious motorcycle club made up former Marines. They look menacing but abide by a code of honor. They were joined in this enterprise by the Bisons, a Native American motorcycle club, some of whom are also veterans.

Several Milwaukee street gangs, including the West Side Bluds and Murder Crows, agreed to participate.

"Their strategy was simple. A show of force demanding that the illegal-alien criminals leave the building. Although Tren de Aragua was heavily armed, those who confronted them were not. They believed they could accomplish this seemingly impossible feat, which has eluded the Milwaukee Police Department for years, through a simple show of unity. They counted on the popular image of motorcyclists as violence-prone hoodlums."

The camera cut to Jerell.

"Jerell Moore used to be a member of BPSN, Black P. Stone Nation. Nine years ago, he had a come-to-Jesus moment. Jerell, how did that come about?"

"I was fighting a rival gang member when this big dude comes along, beard like an Old Testament preacher, and pulls us apart by our collars. There was like ten brothers watching. He says, 'Youngbloods! What the fuck you fighting for? You think the Black man don't have enough on his plate just trying to make a living, take care of his family, get through the day? You think your minor tiff is more important than making peace with your neighbors and getting right with the Lord?'

"That was the Reverend Billy Spooner. We were so ashamed. About a week later I saw him preaching on a street corner. The Reverend Billy Spooner turned my life around the way Pastor Michael Dorgan turned Josh Pratt's around."

"And who is Josh Pratt?"

"Josh Pratt is the reformed motorcycle hoodlum who put this operation in play."

"Shit!" Josh exclaimed.

Ray put her hand on his arm. "What's the matter, baby?"

"I'm trying to keep a low profile. It's all right. I'll talk to Arthur, and he'll fix it."

"Do you want to? Think about it. Do you want more business?"

"No."

"You can leverage this fame. You could write a book."

"Ha!"

Dolan had paused the video. He turned it back on.

"And that's how I came to Jesus."

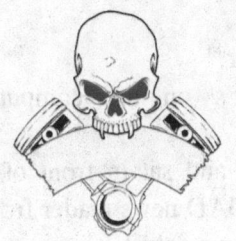

CHAPTER FORTY-FOUR
DEPARTURE DAY

BY THURSDAY MORNING, THE NETWORKS HAD glommed onto Departure Day. Baker's video had been viewed over five million times. News readers jammed Josh's phone with hundreds of requests. Josh didn't know what to do. He hated publicity. He thought about asking Baker to take it down, but this was Baker's biggest hit ever, and the full-length documentary would make him a millionaire. At nine a.m., someone rang the doorbell. Josh walked through the living room and saw the WMAD news van. He went to the basement stairs.

"Dolan, would you do me a favor?"

Doland appeared instantly. "Yes, sir?"

"Would you go outside and explain to Miss Varner that I'll give her an interview next week with my lawyer present."

Dolan bounded up the stairs. "Is Katy Varner the good-looking brunette standing at the front door?"

"How do you know that?"

"I rigged up a surveillance camera under the eave. It's tiny. You won't notice it."

"Grrrrrrreat. Yeah. That's her."

"You want to watch? It's on the computer downstairs."

Josh went to the basement and sat in front of a curving screen showing the WMAD news reader from an downward angle, svelte in a gray skirt, cameraman in tow. The door opened. The sound was crystal clear.

Dolan stepped out. "Good morning! What can I do for you?"

"I'm Katy Varner with WMAD. I'd like to speak to Mr. Pratt, if he's in."

"Mr. Pratt says he'll be happy to talk to you next week with his lawyer present."

Katy flashed dazzling teeth. "Who are you, young man?"

"Dolan Pratt. Josh is my father."

Her face froze for an instant. Hard to compute. "Really! I didn't know he had any children."

"Neither did he until a month ago."

"The interview will be nothing but positive. Your father's a hero."

"Well, if you know my dad, you know he hates publicity. All the credit goes to Jerell Moore, Christ's Warriors, the Bisons, the West Side Bluds, and the Murder Crows."

"I would be interested in speaking with them as well."

"Have you tried Arthur Baker? He's the filmmaker."

"We will be interviewing Mr. Baker this afternoon." She handed Dolan her card. "Please tell Mr. Pratt he's welcome to join us at that time. This will be at the WMAD studios on the Beltline at four p.m."

Katy turned, spun her finger in the air and returned to the van. The cameraman got behind the wheel, and they left. Josh came up the stairs.

"Thanks, pal."

"She's hot."

"She's too old for you. You seen Mabel recently?"

"We have a date this weekend to see the new Jason Statham movie."

"What's it called?"

"A Working Man."

"Is that the one about Levon Cade?"

"Yeah."

"I know that guy."

"What guy?"

"Levon Cade."

"I thought he was a fictional character."

"He's real all right. I'll tell you about him sometime."

Josh went out on the deck and phoned Baker. His line was busy. Josh left a message.

Ray phoned. "You're blowing up."

"I wish I wasn't."

"Listen, I just talked to my producer friend, and he brought it up! When I told him we were going to get married, he almost had a stroke. He's dying to meet you! I told him a little bit about you, and he thinks he might want to put you in a movie."

"Oh my god."

"Seriously. Think about it. You don't have to risk your life to make a living."

"I don't need to make a living. I like to help people."

"He says Frank Grillo might be interested."

"Who's Frank Grillo? Interested in what?"

"In playing you in the movie!"

"Oh please. What's this producer's name?"

"Melvin Hyman. I told you. Can I give him your phone number?"

Josh laughed. "If it will help you in Hollywood, you may."

"Thanks, baby! I'm going to be writing all day, but we should get together tonight. You're going to be on all the news."

"My dream come true. All right. I'll give you a call."

"Come over to my place. Let Dolan have some time to himself."

"What time?"

"Around six. I'll cook."

Josh felt antsy. He looked at Fig. "You want to go for a run?"

Fig barked. Josh changed into sweats and sneakers and told Dolan he was going for a run.

"Can I come?"

"Sure. Why not?"

The three ran on the broad left shoulder of Ptarmigan Road, Fig on a leash, tongue lolling, enjoying life. Louise Lowry passed them heading home and waved out the window of her Mercedes. Josh waved back. He'd met Ray at one of the Lowrys' parties. They were his across the street neighbors. Dave had been his first case when a dog fighting gang stole his two schnauzers, George and Gracie. He found the dogs. He found a girlfriend. The girlfriend had a friend whose child had been abducted by her boyfriend seventeen years ago. The boyfriend turned out to be a demon from hell.

Josh shook his head and picked up the pace. It had all happened so long ago. They reached the service plaza. It had been the lone outpost of civilization when Josh first moved into his modest suburban one-story brick ranch-style house. Now he was surrounded by multimillion-dollar mansions, each with at least three garage bays. Fountains. Swimming pools. Gates. At first the neighbors tried to buy him out. His house was out of place. He was a ruffian. Bit by bit his neighbors came to accept him, most notably Phil Bass, who'd built White Oaks.

They reached the 7-Eleven. "You want anything to drink?" Josh said.

"Yeah. I'll take a Coke."

The owner had placed a water bowl outside. Fig slurped. Josh went inside, bought a Coke for Dolan and a sport drink, then joined them on the bench. They drank, watching the steady flow of traffic. To the north lay Madison's west side, fancy neighborhoods, and Elver Park. Gangs used to hang out at Elver until the police woke up and showed up. They cruised the park regularly and had arrested dozens of gangbangers, including several from Venezuela. The Venezuelan gangs were like an invasive species.

A smartly dressed woman in a blue dress pulled up in a BMW and gassed up. Realtor, Josh guessed. Two guys on Harleys pulled in. No colors. Ordinary motorcyclists out on a beautiful day. Made him want to ride. He'd invite Dolan along except he didn't want to embarrass his son. The boy was too old to ride behind his old man. He needed his own bike.

All in good time.

Josh stood, stretched. "You guys ready?"

Dolan stood. Fig barked and wagged her tail. "Yes, sir!"

"Let's hit it."

They waited for the green light before running across Raymond Road. Back the way they'd come. Neither paid attention to the lowered Honda Civic S that passed them heading east.

CHAPTER FORTY-FIVE
AN IDYLLIC CHILDHOOD

DELCEY GUERRERO THOUGHT NOTHING OF THE TWO men and the dog he passed on his way from the house. You saw them all the time in America. Maybe not so much in the neighborhoods the gang frequented, where people were afraid to leave their homes. But out here in the white suburbs the well-fed, spoiled Americanus Caucasian took his liberty and safety for granted. They didn't know what it was like to live under a dictator, to have to fight every day for a place to sleep, a bite to eat.

Delcey's father Hector had been in Tocorón when he was born. His mother was a whore hired by Nino Guerrero himself. He grew up in a walled encampment in Tocorón, home to several women whose men were in prison. The number varied from time to time. Sometimes five, sometimes as many as nine. Some had always been there. Others disappeared in the night never to be heard from again.

His father ruled the prison. He used tribute sent to him from outside to build a zoo. A swimming pool. A playground, restaurant, and nightclub. Sometimes his mother Adriana would visit, and Delcey would wander through the zoo or swim in the pool with the gang, their women, and their children, under the watchful eye of the guards. A rival gang member killed his father when he was eight. One of his father's friends gutted the killer like a fish. One of the killer's friends hammered a rebar down the murderer's throat. And so it went.

Delcey killed his first man when he was fifteen. The puto fucked his mother and wouldn't pay. When she objected, he slugged her. Delcey beat him to death with a brick. Rio Herrera was now the man in charge of Tocorón. When Rio heard, he summoned Delcey and gave him a knife. Delcey turned the ten-inch blade over and over in his hands to catch the light.

"This is Damascus steel," Rio said. "See how each whorl is hammered out by hand? You have guts, boy. Soon you will have guts on this knife. When you kill a man, you tell him he should consider it an honor to be killed with this knife. This knife is worth more than most men make in a year."

Rio followed El Tiburon who'd been poisoned by the Black Thorn. A witch. There were few witches in Venezuela, but they were much feared. Why she poisoned El Tiburon no one knew. Some say he had disrespected her in some way. Refused a summons. Failed to tithe. It didn't matter. Being head of Aragua's largest criminal gang was always temporary.

Rio had ascended six months ago. In gang terms, an eternity.

When Delcey crossed the border, he brought the knife. No one challenged him. No one asked to see what he had in his backpack. Helpful Americans told him how to apply for Medicaid. Food stamps. Free housing. Social Security.

Delcey learned about cameras and facial recognition in Aragua. The prison had hundreds of cameras. The guards were corrupt, eager to teach a rising gang member how they worked. Tiburon and Rio used them to blackmail prison officials and rivals.

Delcey took a bus to El Paso. Rio told him to look up Luis, a young lieutenant on the rise. El Paso was hot and dry. Tren ruled a neighborhood of rambling shacks by the freeway. They set up a fentanyl factory and distribution center. Brothels, mostly filled with naïve girls who'd come north in search of a better life.

Luis had taken over a stucco two-story by the tracks. One night, one of his boys mooned the chief of police. They had to get out of town. Luis had heard Milwaukee was wide open. He took his pack, including Delcey. They caravaned north in stolen cars. That was sixteen months ago. The winters were hard, but the city was ripe for plucking. They took over four buildings before those fucking bikers showed up. The first time it happened, Luis went nuts.

"Find out why they came! Find out who invited them!"

Delcey and the others went door to door. They knocked and pounded. The tenants were afraid to answer. They promised free drugs. They promised free sex. Very few bothered to respond. Those who did claimed they were ex-military men, and if the gang persisted, there would be repercussions. Delcey had no idea what they were talking about. He told Luis.

"They're veterans, you mentecato! Look it up!"

Delcey looked it up. Men who had served in the armed forces. Venezuela had an army. The Bolivarians. They mostly fought the Columbian Army. They were arrogant and brutal. They sold weapons to the gangs. Their pension was one hundred percent of the minimum wage. Fabuloso. Delcey tried to get listings of every tenant so he could find out who were veterans.

The landlords didn't respond. One landlord told the policia that gangs had infiltrated his properties. The policia didn't respond.

When Luis left the gringa witch, he looked like he'd seen a ghost. Delcey asked him what happened. Luis made the sign of the cross and said three Hail Marys.

"What the fuck, Luis? Is she a witch?"

Luis nodded. Delcey laughed. He had no religion. A lot of ignorant atheists feared religion. They didn't understand it. They didn't take it into their hearts and souls, but they recognized a mysterious power, greater than themselves. Delcey never went to church. Who would take him?

They were making progress in Milwaukee. Living the American dream when those fucking bikers showed up. Now they had no home. They had to start over. The tide was against them. The mayor was talking about cleaning up the streets. That's when Luis told him, "You find that cabron who did this. Use your special knife. I give you five thousand now and five thousand when you bring me his head."

Delcey knew how to use the internet to run scams. OnlyFans accounts with AI-generated girls. He knew how to use facial recognition software. So he used facial recognition to find her lover.

And now he knew where he lived.

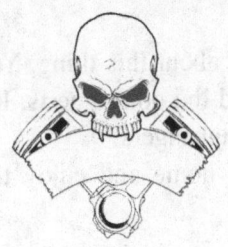

CHAPTER FORTY-SIX
THE TERRACE

DEPARTURE DAY WAS EVERYWHERE. IT LED THE evening news. Josh was unavailable, but Arthur Baker was exploding. CNN. Fox. ABC. Sixty Minutes. Joe Rogan phoned. Timcast. Baker was in a frenzy. He called Josh face-to-face on Facebook.

"Man, you gotta help me out here! They're chewing my leg off! They keep asking me about you! You're practically retired, why not cash in?"

"Art, I value my privacy. I have no intention of retiring. My job is helping people, and I'll never run out of people to help."

"But think! Think how much wider your reach would be!"

"Then I'll be swamped with thousands of people. How do I choose? I'll go into catatonic shock. I'll have to move to Bratislava and change my name."

"At least give me an interview. We can blur out your face like one of those witness protection guys."

"Let me think about it. Did you get the invite to the rehearsal dinner?"

"Yeah, yeah, I'll be there. You want me to bring my camera?"

"Not if you're going to talk about this thing. You can film as a memory for us and the other guests. It's about the wedding, not about gangbangers."

"Maybe I'll just leave it at home and enjoy the dinner."

"What a novel idea."

"Can I bring a date?"

"By all means. Bring a date."

Heinz Calloway wanted to meet for coffee at the Union Terrace, overlooking Lake Mendota.

They'd been meeting there for years. Heinz had retired two years ago, just before his daughter Ashley ran off with the cult leader Scipio. Josh and Heinz got her back. Not without a struggle. Heinz had called before The Departure, but now everybody knew about it. Josh was glad he was unknown. He rode downtown and backed into a slot on Langdon. He wore a Jellyfish T-shirt. He walked around the Union counterclockwise to the terrace, scanning the tables. Heinz stood at a round table near the giant oak and waved him over. Heinz wore amber aviator shades, a blue sports coat over a black tee, and jeans. They embraced.

"The man of the hour," Heinz said, sitting.

"Aw Jesus, I never thought it would blow up like that."

"It wouldn't 'cept for your friend's video."

"He's expanding it into a feature-length film."

"Well damn. You better get yourself an agent."

"I just want to be left alone."

Heinz laughed. "That's why you keep a low profile."

"Well, I was, up until this."

"I gotta hand it to you. Getting rid of those fucking scorpions like that was genius. No one else could have done it. You just scared them into leaving!"

"It all started with Dolan. He told me about Alfred who told me about a couple of other vets stuck in one of those apartment buildings. Sorta ballooned from there."

"Too bad the cops didn't do it."

"The cops can't do it. Those hoods are trained from birth to meet all police with defiance. How often have you seen a police officer with a gun telling a guy with a gun to just set it down. Just set it down. They seldom do. They aim the gun, and the cop shoots them. They all must have a death wish."

"Or they're too stupid to know what's going to happen. A lotta those guys, they're programmed to resist no matter what. Can't look weak to the homies. They don't think past their act of defiance. See how dangerous! How defiant!"

"You ever put someone down like that?"

"Yeah. Long time ago. When I was just a patrol cop. Ironically, it was in Milwaukee, before I moved here. Blackstone P. Nation. Just happened to be driving by when I saw them beating the shit out of someone on the sidewalk. South side. Pulled over. My partner and I got out, advancing separately. There were three of them. And this one loudmouth pulls out his pistol and starts yelling at us. 'Pigs! Get the fuck outta here, pigs! This is Blackstone territory!'"

"You kill him?"

"No. I shot him in the thigh. Nearly bled to death, but after a long convalescence he returned to the street where he resumed his career and was shot to death by a rival gang."

"You coming to my wedding?"

"Of course I am. Sent you an RSVP."

"Oh, you probably sent it to my future in-laws. The McRaneys."

"Looking forward to it."

"How's Ashley doing?"

"She's studying pre-law at Michigan State."

"Not here?"

"She wanted to get away from her old man."

Josh laughed. "I get it."

Heinz stood. "You want a brat?"

Josh stood. "Sure."

Heinz held his hand out. "It's my turn."

"You got it last time."

"Your money's no good here."

Josh watched him walk to the cart. He looked at the lake, where a series of white triangles played in the light breeze. Students in bathing suits threw themselves off the Union pier. To the left, Hoofer's Club members launched boats and brought them in. The giant chair beneath the oak was unoccupied. It was designed for Paul Bunyan. Students laughed and talked. Solitary students stared at their phones. One man was writing longhand in a legal pad.

Heinz returned with a cardboard box holding two brats and two beers in red Solo cups. He put them on the table along with a wad of napkins and some ketchup packets. He opened a packet and squeezed the ketchup on his brat. He paused, mouth open.

"You don't want ketchup?"

"Let's not get into that debate."

Josh ate without condiments.

"You oughtta write a book."

"About what?"

"Your life."

"Yeah no. I can't write."

"You could if you were forced to."

"What's that mean?"

"I call it Writer's Camp. You live in a dorm. Reveille wakes you at six. You run five miles. You sit at a desk under the eye of a watchful tutor. He corrects your spelling, grammar, syntax, and rationale."

"How does he do that?"

"He hits you with a stick to get your attention then patiently explains. I've got it all figured out. I'm writing a book."

"What about?"

"My life as a cop. There's a huge market. Mostly other cops."

"I'll buy one."

"You're in it."

"Oh no. Leave me the hell out."

"The rescue of my daughter is the centerpiece of the story. I already have a publisher."

Josh pinched his nose. "You're giving me a headache."

Heinz finished a beer. "You want another beer?"

"No, man. I'm on a bike. What's the alcohol content anyway?"

"Hazy IPA. Six point three."

"Oh hell no. How are you going to get home?"

"Uber. Uber down, Uber back."

"Where's Doreen?"

Heinz shrugged. "I think she's crafting with some pals."

"Crafting?"

"They get together, drink wine, and make cards. Need any cards?"

"Well yeah. I know Ray would appreciate a couple dozen to thank people for the wedding gifts."

"What should I get the happy couple?"

Josh shrugged. "Ray would love a bonsai tree."

"I'll tell Doreen."

Josh's phone rang. Ray. "What's up, babe?"

"Do you have time to come over here and read some lines?"

"What's it for?"

"*Release the Aardvark*."

"Who wrote it?"

"Idaho and me."

"I'll be right over."

Josh stood. "Thanks for the brew, Heinz. See you at the rehearsal dinner."

Heinz gave him the thumbs-up.

Josh straddled his bike across the street from the Union and phoned Dolan.

"I'm heading over to Ray's. Probably spend the night."

"Okay. Thanks, Pop."

"Have one of those chicken burrito bowls from Trader Joe's."

CHAPTER FORTY-SEVEN
RELEASE THE AARDVARK

IDAHO AND RAY WERE ONSTAGE WHEN JOSH GOT there. The theater was empty except for a couple technicians playing with microphone placement. It was bright outside, but the theater was dark, save for a couple spots shining from the projection booth in back. Josh sat in the front row. Idaho and Ray were in the middle of a scene. Idaho sat on a stool wearing baggy carpenter's pants and a Queen muscle shirt over her small breasts, leaning forward, one arm on her knee, the other pointing.

"Release the aardvark, or I call the cops."

"Call 'em. They'll tell you the same thing. The aardvark belongs to me."

"Bullshit. It's an exotic animal. You need a license."

"The hell I do. I need a license for apes, baboons, bears, cheetahs, crocodiles, constrictor snakes over three feet, coyotes, elephants, game cocks, hippos, hyenas, jaguars, leopards, lions, lynxes, monkey, piranha if they're over six inches, but not one word about aardvarks."

"What kind of woman are you? Why would you keep such an exotic creature? What kind of life do you think it will have in your cage? What do you feed it? Kibble?"

"It's none of your business what I feed it. The aardvark is happy."

"Show me."

Ray stiffened and pointed at the exit. "Get the hell out."

Idaho stood. "I'm leaving. When I return, it will be with a writ of habeas corpus." Idaho stomped off the stage. She returned and looked at Josh.

"Come on, Josh. We need you."

Josh smiled. "What's this play about?"

"It's about the absurdity of life."

Josh heaved himself out of the front row. "That's what I thought. What I gotta do?"

"Just come up here and read the lines. Your lines are all underlined in red." Ray plucked a script off a nearby desk. Josh stepped up on the stage and took the script.

Ray pointed to an X made with black tape toward the back of the stage. "Stand there."

"Don't you want me to come in with Idaho or something?"

"No, we just need you to read the lines. Idaho will feed you your line. 'This is Stanley Durkin, an officer of the court.' Then you read your line."

"This is Stanley Durkin, an officer of the court," Idaho said.

Josh looked at the script. "I'm serving you a writ of habeas corpus. Produce the aardvark at Dane

County Clerk of Courts at ten a.m. tomorrow, or Judge Foster will find you in contempt."

He looked up. "Uh, I work for a lawyer, and that's not how this works."

"Why not?" Idaho said.

"Because it's an aardvark. Not a person."

"Not a problem. The play's not to be taken literally. It combines elements of dada, Kafka, and absurdism to shine a light on universal truths."

"Okay."

"Just read the lines."

"You got it."

"Then you hand me some papers."

Josh handed her his script.

"Just fake it."

Josh forked over imaginary papers. Ray pretended to read them.

"This writ is invalid. You got my name wrong."

"How did I get your name wrong?" Josh read.

"It's Hawkens with an e, not an i."

"That doesn't invalidate this writ."

Idaho held her hand out. "Give me the writ."

Ray handed over imaginary papers. Idaho took out an imaginary pen and made a correction on the stool. She handed it back. "There."

Josh stuck the script in a back pocket and pulled out his phone.

"What are you doing?"

"I'm taking a picture. We're supposed to take a picture when we deliver a summons."

Idaho stood, put her arm around Ray's shoulder and posed smiling. Josh snapped a picture. He pulled out his script.

"I don't have any more lines."

"Not now, but we may write some later."

"You asked me to come over to read two lines?"

Ray put her arms around his neck. "Maybe I just wanted to see you, baby."

"Me too!" Idaho said.

"And now we want you to take us out to dinner."

"I just had lunch."

"Well, you have to eat eventually, and some of us have to eat now."

Josh threw his hands up. "Okay. Okay. Let's go."

"Not so fast, big boy. Idaho and I need to take showers and change our clothes."

Ray had installed a bathroom near the dressing rooms the previous year, flush from *Drunk Octopus* money and a grant from the Wisconsin Arts Board. Josh sat in the lobby on an old student moving day sofa. Threadbare. He thrust his hand between the cushions and retrieved seventy-six cents in change. There was a little library in an alcove. He plucked out *Driving Lessons* by Ed McBain, a slim volume. He was almost finished when Ray and Idaho emerged fresh and smelling great. Idaho had changed into baggy jeans and a French-striped long-sleeved T-shirt. No makeup. Ray looked like a million bucks in ladies Carhartt pants that cupped her ass and a loose white cotton sweater.

"I'll meet you there," Idaho said.

They went to Monty's Blue Plate Diner on Atwood and sat in a booth. Their waitperson was a slim, six-foot man with a long black ponytail, a nose ring, tribal tats covering his arms. He wore a nameplate. Cynthia. Idaho ordered the vegan Caesar Salad.

"Perfect."

Ray ordered the chicken, bacon, and goat cheese sandwich.

"Excellent."

Josh ordered a hamburger.

"Super."

"Josh," Idaho said, "I saw that clip of a bunch of bikers convincing all those gangbangers to leave that building. That was awesome. Was that your idea?"

"Well, I had a lot of help."

"Josh's friend Art, who made that film, is expanding it into a feature-length documentary," Ray said. "You're a star, baby!"

"I hope not."

"Why'd you do it?" Idaho said.

"Somebody had to do it. The cops weren't doing shit."

"Well they're all over it now."

Cynthia brought out their food. Ray insisted on paying. Josh and Ray went to her condo on the lake and sat outside watching the sun set smoking a joint. Josh didn't get stoned much now, unlike his life before prison, when he'd wake up and have a joint with his coffee. They went inside and tore each other's clothes off. As they lay in bed afterward staring at the luminescent stars Ray had pasted to the ceiling, she said, "You gonna let Art interview you about 'Departure Day?'"

"Nah."

"Why not?"

"Because, love of my life, I don't want publicity. I just want to help people. I don't need the money. I don't want fame. I just want to be left alone. I think most people just want to be left alone."

She snuggled in. "That's why I love you."

She turned out the light. She was asleep within
fifteen minutes. Josh lay on his back staring at the ceiling, a vague sense of unease churning in his gut. His
phone chimed. Ray turned over. Josh picked up his
phone. It was Dolan.

"What?"

"Dad," he said. His voice was dead. "Someone
broke into the house."

CHAPTER FORTY-EIGHT
THE ANTLER

DELCEY STOLE AN ELECTRIC HYUNDAI FROM POINT Cinema. He'd watched it arrive for an 11:30 showing. Hyundais were so easy. All it took was a flathead screwdriver and a USB-A cable. He used a flat plastic plank to spring the lock, slid into the driver's chair, yanked the bottom of the plastic steering wheel column housing off, ripped out the ignition cylinder, and used the USB cable to turn on the ignition.

He found a phone in the center console. He picked it up and held the button to trigger the automated assistant. "How do I get to 418 Ptarmigan Road?"

"To get to Ptarmigan Avenue, exit the lot and turn left. Proceed to Mineral Point."

He cruised Ptarmigan with his lights off. A faint glow emanated from the front window of Pratt's surprisingly plebian home. In Venezuela, it would be a mansion. It would also be concealed from the street by a nine-foot stucco wall. Here, in American, the fat, rich, lazy Americans took their security for granted. No longer. Delcey had met so many violent hoodlums on his long march to America it was hard to keep them all straight. Venezuela, of course. Columbia. El Salvador. Guyana. Honduras. Nicaragua. Guatemala. Dominican Republic. Belarus. Croatia. Bulgaria. Macedonia. Ukraine. Russia. Algeria. Tunisia. Morocco. Somalia. Lots of Somalians. Syria. Kurdistan. Pakistan. China. The whole world was invited to the feast. The big, gorgeous buffet that was America for the taking. Delcey would never forget the kindness of the volunteers he'd met upon crossing the southern border. How'd they given him a phone, paid for by the government. A gift card worth two hundred dollars at Walmart. Instructions in Spanish for how to apply for Social Security and small business loans.

The instructions came in dozens of languages. Portuguese. Arabic. Mandarin. Cantonese. Somali.

Delcey had walked from South America. The column grew the farther north he got. Many governments had laid out camps for the travelers under the condition that they stay the night and move on in the morning. Murderers, rapists, drug dealers, Chinese military, terrorists. Of course there were ordinary families. Mothers, fathers, children, who were invariably separated from their parents by the cartels and promised to be reunited with them on the other side. Just carry this package. Present it to our agents at the border. Your children will be returned to you.

Delcey had availed himself of the soft sweet flesh of underage girls offered to him by fellow gang members. They knew by his markings that he was high in the organization. They did it to curry favor.

Delcey wondered how Americans could be so stupid. How could the United States, the greatest nation on Earth, be so stupid? Did they not understand that their wealth, their success, inspired only envy and malice? Once over the border he headed for El Paso to hook up with Luis. Luis had a sweet deal going for a while. Drugs. Prostitution. But El Paso was a military town. A law enforcement town. And soon they had to move on.

He parked his car on a stretch of darkened road overhung with trees and crept a hundred meters back toward the house. He crouched in the bushes watching. It would be best to approach from behind, where they would be most vulnerable. With his precious Damascus in a leather sheath at his belt, he floated through the night like mist, circling the house clockwise until he came to the fenced-in yard. It was only six feet. He could leap it.

He ran at the fence, boosting himself on a decorative boulder, one hand on top and landed on both feet in the backyard. A barking dog shattered the night. The creature ran at him, fangs bared. Delcey drew his knife and kicked the dog savagely beneath the chin. It yelped and stumbled. Delcey was on it in an instant, circling his arm around his neck, using his full weight to pin it to the ground. He drew the blade heavily across its neck, cutting deep to the spine. The dog whimpered once and collapsed.

Delcey ran for the back door, leaping up the two steps. The door was open. He entered a dimly lit kitchen. Only the hood lights on over the stove. He paused. He listened. His heart beat loudly. He waited and listened. At first there was silence. He heard the creak of feet on the stairs. He stood to the side of top of the basement stairs. The door was open, dim light issuing from below. He watched the floor and when the faint shadow of a man appeared, he pivoted to the head of the stairs and kicked the figure solidly in the gut. A man. He tumbled down the stairs like a load of rocks. Delcey had played soccer his whole life and knew how to kick.

He flew down the steps two at a time as the figure lay groaning. At the bottom, he raised his knife, aiming at the man's chest. It took a fraction of a second to register. It was a boy. A young man. Maybe Delcey's age. Before he could act, the man hooked Delcey's left ankle with his right instep and yanked, sending Delcey in a pile on the ground. The man rose and ran toward the back of what looked like an office with two computer terminals facing a chair. The only other light came from a desk lamp with a green glass shade.

Cursing himself for his carelessness, Delcey ran after him. The kid grabbed something off the wall and faced him in a fighter's stance, right foot forward, holding something in his right hand. Holding it low, point up. Some kind of spike. Delcey grinned.

"You Pratt's kid?"

"Who are you?"

"I came here to give him a message. You will be the message."

Delcey lunged. The kid expertly side-stepped, going low and kicking Delcey in the knee. Delcey was surprised. Most Americans he'd fought were clumsy and stupid. The kid backed up, scraping his feet on the tile floor. He stopped next to a five-foot gun safe. Stupid. He'd backed himself into a corner. He reached behind the safe with his left hand and brought out a baseball bat. He jammed whatever he was holding in his belt and came forward swinging. Delcey brought his foot to chest height to block the swing. The kid reversed direction, did a three-sixty, and whacked Delcey in the side of the head. It was the end of the bat. Speed but not heft. It hurt. Delcey recovered instantly. He'd been hit harder in the streets of Caracas.

Okay. If the kid wanted to play games, Delcey would play too. He backed up to the table with the computers. There was a rock on the desk holding down papers. Delcey seized it and without pausing, hurled it fastball style at the kid's head. The kid got the bat up and bunted the rock to the floor.

"You got cojones," Delcey said. "You could hang with us."

"You can just hang," the kid said.

Delcey charged, whipping the knife in a figure eight, inside the bat's reach. He slashed the kid on both arms drawing blood. He went low, aiming up at the gut. The kid kicked his knife hand. Delcey hung on and pressed forward. He outweighed the kid by thirty pounds. The kid jerked the thing from his belt and thrust forward like a musketeer. Delcey felt something sharp penetrate his chest. He looked down in surprise. A sawed-off deer antler stuck out four inches.

"What the fuck is this?" he said, bewildered as his strength fled.

"A deer antler."

Delcey fell to the ground.

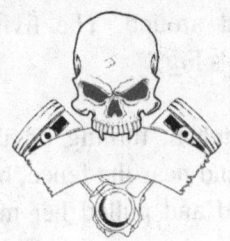

CHAPTER FORTY-NINE
CRIME SCENE

JOSH LEAPED OUT OF BED AND THREW ON HIS CLOTHES.

"Where are you going?"

"I have to get home. Someone broke into my house."

"What?! Wait! I'll come with you!"

"No way."

"Are you going to phone the cops?"

"Not until I see what happened."

"Phone the police, Josh!"

"No! I have to know what happened first!"

It was past midnight when he pulled into his driveway. The living room lights were on. There was no bark of greeting. Dolan opened the front door. He looked like a condemned man. Blood dripped from both arms. Josh saw gashes on his left forearm. He rushed to Josh and threw his arms around him, weeping. Josh held him tight.

"He killed Fig."

Josh went cold.

"Who killed Fig?"

"I don't know who he is. He's in the basement."

Josh ran inside and looked around. The living room looked untouched. "Where's Fig?"

"In the backyard."

Josh stormed out of the kitchen, turning on the porch lights. Fig lay on the ground near the fence, her neck slashed open. Josh kneeled and pulled her into his arms.

"No, no, no."

Dolan sat with him, arm around his shoulders for a long time.

"Breathe deeply," Dolan said. "That's what you always tell me."

Josh forced himself to draw a deep breath and let it out slow. He felt his heart abate. He cried. Dolan cried with him. After a while, he gently set Fig back on the grass and stood, lifting Dolan. His pants were stained with his dog's blood. He looked at Dolan.

"Oh my god. He I am weeping over a dog, and you're bleeding all over. I'll call an ambulance."

"I don't think you have to do that, Pop. He didn't cut very deep."

"Is he alive?"

"No. I killed him."

"How did you kill him?"

"You know that deer antler you had hanging on the wall?"

"Let's go into the bathroom and patch you up."

In the bathroom, Josh poured hydrogen peroxide on a clean washcloth and dabbed Dolan's wounds. Dolan grimaced. One of the slashes was deep. Maybe a quarter inch. "We have to go to the ER."

"They'll call the cops."

"I have to call them first." He pulled out his phone and dialed nine-one-one.

"What is your emergency?"

"We had a break-in. A man attacked my son with a knife. My son had to defend himself. The intruder is dead. We'll need an ambulance. My boy's pretty cut up."

"Who is this?"

"Josh Pratt. I live at 418 Ptarmigan Road."

"Stay on the line with me, Mr. Pratt."

"I can't. My son is bleeding." He set the phone down, pulled out a roll of bandage and wrapped it around Dolan's wounds. "What happened?"

Dolan recounted the fight.

"This is my fault. I should have known. I should have known that if they could find Ray, they could find my place."

"It's not your fault, Dad. He was a criminal. It's not your fault when some scumbag enters into the country and starts killing people."

"If I hadn't pulled that stunt with the bikers and the gangs..."

"That wasn't a stunt, Dad. You saved people's lives. The cops wouldn't do anything. I'm proud of you. You'd do it again."

"Maybe. Maybe not. Maybe I'll sell this place and buy a cabin up north. Would you come with me?"

"I'd visit."

"What do you mean you'd visit?"

"I know what I want to do. I'm going to enlist."

"Enlist in what?"

"The Marines, I think."

"What? Where is this coming from?"

"I've been giving it a lot of thought. I want to

make something of myself. I've been lucky so far but…"

"Lucky?!"

"I'm lucky I found you. I'm lucky you're not the man you used to be."

Tears ran down Josh's cheeks. The phone rang. It was Ray.

"Are you all right?"

"Yes. Dolan's all right too."

"What happened?"

Sirens. Louder and louder until they stopped in front of the house. Car doors slamming.

"We had a break-in. Listen. I gotta go. The cops are here."

They didn't bother to knock. Josh met them in the living room, hands open at his side. Three uniformed officers. Josh recognized one of them.

"Officer Natividad. Thank you for coming."

Natividad had a black brush mustache. "What happened, Mr. Pratt?"

"Gangbanger broke into the house. Killed my dog. Tried to kill my son."

"Where's your son?"

Dolan came out of the bathroom, arms bandaged. "Here I am."

"Get those paramedics in here," Natividad said.

One of the cops went out the door. Seconds later, two paramedics entered, one carrying a first-aid kit.

"Does this have anything to do with that stunt you pulled in Milwaukee the other day?"

"Probably."

"That was no stunt," Dolan said. "My dad saved those people from a living hell. Some of them are veterans. That's how this all started."

Two cops drew their flashlights and went through the kitchen into the basement.

"Sorry about your dog," Natividad said. "Sit down. Tell me what happened."

Josh and Natividad sat in the living room. The cop pulled out a notepad. Josh told him everything that had happened since Dolan had phoned him. Another cop interviewed Dolan in the kitchen. They strung yellow crime tape across the head of the stairs.

They heard shouting through the open front door. Ray was raising hell. Josh went outside where a female officer was trying to restrain her.

"Officer, that's my fiancée. She can come in."

"I'm sorry, sir. It's still an active crime scene."

"What about my son and me? Are we being forced to spend the night somewhere else?"

"Depends on how quickly we process the scene. A photographer has to take pictures. Detectives have to gather evidence."

"What evidence? We told you what happened."

"I understand, sir. But there are protocols. Where did all that blood come from?"

"The intruder murdered my dog. She's in the backyard."

"I'm sorry."

Natividad held up his hand. "Sarah, may I speak to you outside?"

They went outside. The paramedics wanted to take Dolan to the hospital.

"I don't need to go to the hospital. I probably just need to get stitched up. Can't you do that here?"

"Sorry, son. Rules say we got to take you to the hospital."

"Go on," Josh said. "Phone me when you get there."

Dolan went with the paramedics. Josh saw him get in the back of the ambulance through the open door.

A middle-aged man with a hairline mustache wearing a cheap suit approached. "Mr. Pratt, I'm Detective Oscar. Do you know the attacker?"

"I haven't even been downstairs yet!"

"Does this have anything to do with that video showing you and a group of bikers confronting a gang in Milwaukee?"

"Probably. You should ask Ray outside. My fiancée. They kidnapped her."

"Did she report it?"

"She talked her way out of it."

The detective regarded him dubiously. "How's that?"

"There she is. Ask her."

Oscar held up a finger. "I'll be right back."

Josh turned toward the basement. Natividad intercepted.

"You don't want to go down there right now."

"Can you identify him? Does he have ID?"

"We're looking into that right now. I can tell you that he's inked up the wazoo. That's not necessarily evidence of gang involvement, but it leans that way. We'll show you a picture."

Another detective came up the stairs. He wore nitrile gloves and carried an alligator wallet. He held the wallet open displaying a driver's license for to Delcey Guerrero, listing an address in El Paso. His birth date was 2004. His picture looked like a mug shot.

"We're checking to see if he's in the database."

"Do you recognize him?"

"No. Can I get a drink?"

"An alcoholic drink?"

"Yessir. I'm not going anywhere."

The two detectives looked at one another. "Go ahead. But just one."

Josh went in the kitchen and poured himself several fingers of bourbon.

At one a.m., they carried the alleged perp out in a body bag.

CHAPTER FIFTY
ASHES TO ASHES

THEY PUT TAPE READING CRIME SCENE ACROSS the top of the basement stairs but allowed Josh back into his home. Ray held him as he wept over Fig. She thought about telling him he would get a new dog someday, but it didn't seem to be the right time. They lay in each other's arms through the night, Josh tossing fitfully, Ray unable to sleep.

Josh woke early and made coffee. He'd turned his phone off before going to bed but turned it back on now. Heinz Calloway had texted "call me." At nine, he could wait no longer. He called University Hospital. They would release Dolan when he arrived. He looked in the bedroom. Ray had finally fallen asleep. He wrote her a note. "Gone to hospital to get Dolan. Back soon."

He got his wheelbarrow out of the garage and took it in the backyard. Gathering Fig in his arms, he loaded her into the wheelbarrow, laid a tarp in the floor of the trunk and put her in the trunk.

As he drove into town, he realized that Fig's body

had lain outside. It was a sledgehammer to the gut.
Apart from Fig's namesake and Ray, he had never
loved a living thing so much. She had been getting on
but still had a lot of pep. The thought that his son
killed her murderer with a deer antler consoled him.
He hoped it had been painful.

He drove by First Unitarian where they were due
to be married in a week and parked in the University
Hospital lot. He went inside. There were three clerks
on duty. One, a young woman with red hair, looked up.

"Can I help you?"

"I'm looking for Dolan Pratt. He was admitted last
night."

"How do you know the patient?"

"I'm his father."

"Oh yes. He's in room 214. Take the elevator and
turn right."

"Thank you, ma'am."

"I'm so sorry this happened to you."

"Thank you."

Dolan was sitting up, wearing a hospital gown,
both arms bandaged, when Josh arrived. A nurse was
taking his pulse.

"Dad!"

Josh sat on the bed next to Dolan and put his arm
around him. "How's he doing?"

"Surprisingly well. It will be a while before he
should try to lift anything. We're sending him home
with some hydrocodone for the pain."

"Is he ready to check out?"

"He can as soon as we get a wheelchair up here."

"I don't need a wheelchair."

"It's hospital policy."

An orderly entered with a wheelchair. Josh helped

Dolan into the wheelchair. He seemed a little shaky. The orderly wheeled them in and out of the elevator up to the front desk. The orderly stood by.

A woman looked up. "Checking out?"

"Yes ma'am. Dolan Pratt, room 214."

She turned to her computer. "Your bill comes to twenty-seven hundred and fourteen dollars. How would you like to pay? Do you have insurance?"

"No, ma'am. I'll put it on my credit card."

"Neither of you has insurance?"

"No, ma'am."

"Well, I'm not going to tell you how to live your life, but you should have health insurance. Have you applied for Medicaid?"

"I don't think we qualify."

"You should look into it."

Josh handed her his credit card.

"How would you like your receipt? Printed or email?"

"Printed please."

She ran the card and handed him a printed receipt.

"Dolan, I'll get the car and pull around front. You stay in the chair." He looked at the orderly. "That okay?"

"Sure. I'll smoke a cigarette."

Josh stared at him to see if he was joking. The orderly had a poker face. Josh pointed.

"Almost had me."

He walked to the car and pulled around front. Dolan got out of the wheelchair and slid into the passenger seat.

"How are your arms?"

"They hurt when I move. The doctor said it may take up to six weeks for them to fully heal."

"Well damn. We'll have to postpone your driving test."

"Well let's just see how they are in a week."

They rode in silence until Josh turned onto Ptarmigan. Ray's car was gone.

"Motherfucker killed Fig," Dolan said. "I'm glad I killed him."

"I'm glad you killed him too."

When they got to the house Josh hovered as Dolan went inside. His legs were fine. "Why don't you stay upstairs while your arms heal."

"I will for a while. What are you going to do with Fig?"

"I'm taking her to the Bennett Funeral Home and have her cremated."

"Can you do that at a funeral home?"

"The owner owes me a favor. I have to do it now. Will you be all right for an hour?"

"I'll be fine."

Ray had left a note on the kitchen table. "Call me if you want anything. I'm going to leave you and Dolan alone for tonight. Will call in the morning. Love you."

Heinz called.

"Heinz."

"How you doin'?"

"As well as can be expected."

"Man, I am so sorry about Fig. How's your boy doin'?"

"Better than me I expect. He's a little cut up, but he'll be fine."

"Damn. The report didn't say how the intruder died."

"Dolan stabbed him with a broken deer antler."

"For real?"

"Yes."

"Where'd he get a broken deer antler?"

"Long story. I'll tell you next time I see you."

"Is the rehearsal dinner still on?"

"Yes."

"Well, I'll see you then, unless you want to meet me down on the terrace."

"See you Saturday?"

"Two p.m.?"

"Two p.m."

Josh was supposed to pick up his tux today. The tux wasn't going anywhere. Bennett Funeral Home was midtown, up the street from West High School, next to a cemetery. Josh drove over. There were only a couple cars in the parking lot. It was early. Although it was a bright and sunny day, the interior was appropriately funereal, with dark-blue velvet walls in a paisley pattern and wine-colored leather furniture. The front desk was suitable for an old European hotel. A young woman with a bob and cat-eye glasses sat reading a book. She looked up.

"Hello, sir. How can I help you?"

"I'd like to have my dog cremated."

"I'm sorry, sir. We don't do that. The Humane Society will do that."

"Is Perry Bennett in?"

"Yes."

"Would you tell him that Josh Pratt is here?"

She picked up a phone and relayed the message. A minute later, Perry Bennett appeared, a fiftyish man wearing a black suit, white shirt, navy-blue tie, white hair meticulously combed. He smiled and extended his hand,

"Josh. How are you?"

"Perry, did you see the news?"

"Yes, I read it in the *State Journal*. Josh, I'm so sorry. Thank God you and your son are okay. How's he doing?"

"He'll recover. Perry, the intruder killed my dog Fig. Until Dolan came along, she was my best friend. Would you consider cremating her for me?"

"Of course, Josh. Do you have her with you now?"

"She's in the car."

"Why don't you drive around to the back into the garage. I'll meet you there."

Bennett was waiting when Josh pulled into the garage. Josh popped the trunk and lifted the lid. Bennett stood next to him looking down at Fig's corpse.

"I'm so sorry, Josh. We'll take it from here."

"Where's the gurney? I'd like to lift her myself."

Bennett produced a hand cart and placed a blanket on it. Josh moved Fig to the blanket. Bennett gripped the handles. "I'll let you know when it's done. It will be this week. I assume you want the ashes."

"Yes please."

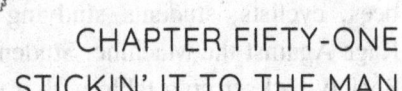

CHAPTER FIFTY-ONE
STICKIN' IT TO THE MAN

JOSH PICKED UP HIS TUX SATURDAY. HE TRIED IT ON. Briggs angled the mirror toward him. Josh posed like Jeff Bridges, turning slightly, thumb in lapel.

"This'll do."

"Excellent. I hope you don't mind, but was that you in that newsclip I've been watching all week? The one about the Milwaukee gang."

"I was there."

"How has that changed your life?"

Josh looked at him. "I would never have chosen tailor as your career."

Briggs shrugged. "I had an offer from Bluestone. That's a contractor operating out of Dubai. I'd rather sell clothes. This is my shop."

"Well to answer your question, it's brought a lot of unwelcome attention. I just want to be left alone."

"I know how you feel. There are two kinds of people in the world. Those who want to be left alone and those who won't leave them alone."

"Amen, brother."

Josh's phone had not stopped buzzing. Now Fox News was calling him. Timcast. CNN. He called Fleiss and left a message, then turned it off.

Josh parked in the Lake Street ramp and walked to the Union. The Library Mall was buzzing with Frisbees, cyclists, students studying their phones, and Rage Against the Machine. Students for a Democratic Society had set up a table with a picture of the President labeled LITERALLY HITLER and were signing up eager acolytes. A FREE PALESTINE booth was set up near the entrance. Josh glanced up Bascom Hill to check if the statue of Abe Lincoln was still there. Still there, though not for lack of trying. He walked through the Union, through the Rathskellar, out onto the terrace where Heinz had secured a table on the lower level near the lake. Dozens of white sails flitted around. Further out, power craft towed skiers. It was in the low eighties. Heinz was reading a Marc Olden novel.

"I'm buying," Josh said. "What are you having?"

"Brat and a beer. Two packets of mustard."

"Mustard?"

"I have seen the light."

Josh stood in line behind a skinny coed, her blonde hair fixed in a bun, aviator shades, wearing a Green Day tee. Josh got the brats and beers and returned to the table. Heinz put a marker in his book and set it aside.

"How you doing?"

"As well as can be expected."

"How's your boy?"

"He'll recover. He's tough. He wants to join the Marines."

"Holy shit. How old is he?"

"He's seventeen."

"That okay with you?"

Josh shrugged. "Hate to lose him, but it's not like I put in the hours. How's Ashley doing?"

"She's doing great. What about Fig?"

"Just left her at Bennett's Funeral Home. They're going to cremate her."

"How'd you swing that?"

"I did a favor for the owner years ago. His nephew was in Waupun. Having a hard time."

"What was he in for?"

"Check kiting. It's no place for a sensitive kid. I got in touch with a few people I know in there and asked them to look out for him. He got out two years ago. He's doing pretty well. He's an automobile mechanic."

"How is it you still have clout at Waupun twelve years after you got out?"

"Unfortunately, there are Bedouins who don't have powerful attorney friends. Weirdo and Fisher are in the final stretch of their twenty years. They expect to get out in the fall."

"You going on a honeymoon?"

"We're going to Hawaii."

"Beautiful place. Been there three times. You ever been?"

"First time. Dolan's going to hold down the fort."

"Tell him he can call on me anytime."

"I'll do that."

They sat in companionable silence staring out at the lake. Some long hairs started setting up on the raised stage facing the building. The Union hosted live music Saturday afternoons.

"What part of Hawaii?"

"The big island. It's got jungles, volcanoes, water-falls, beaches. You can even rent motorcycles."

They watched as the musicians checked their instruments. Guitar. Bass. Drums. Keyboard.

"Do you think we need a police presence at the wedding?"

"Hell no. I think they've had enough."

"You never did explain how Ray escaped."

"Ray perceived that the dumb thug holding her was superstitious. She played him like a fiddle. She threatened to put a curse on him."

"You're shitting me."

"Nope. And that other dumb thug who killed my dog? If they didn't get the message from the great departure, they must have it now."

"Well, I'm gonna suggest they do a drive-by just in case."

The band took the stage. Loquacious was written on the bass drum. The lead guitarist stepped up and strummed a chord. "Thank you all for coming out to hear us. We're Loquacious from Madison." He looked to his mates and nodded. The drummer hit the snare, and the band exploded like a downhill freight train, cannon bass, and aerial guitar.

"We're coming your way," the leader sang. "We'll stay and we'll stay...we'll smoke all your grass... you'll kick us out on our ass..."

Braxton looked at Heinz. They laughed.

"Well at least it's not political," Heinz said.

It was a fast, exhilarating two and a half minutes. Without pausing, they segued into "Launch Musk to Mars."

"I spoke too soon!" Heinz yelled to be heard over the music.

"I'm outta here!" Josh yelled.

"Me too!"

They pushed back, walked around the Union through the parking lot and headed for State Street. Heinz had parked in the Lake Street ramp too. They paused inside.

"See you in a couple of weeks," Heinz said.

"Okay, bud."

They embraced. Josh went up. Heinz went down. Josh had parked on the roof. He enjoyed looking out on Library Mall where students were stickin' it to the man, tossing Frisbees, and signing up acolytes for the Young Socialist Club. On the Union steps, some students were arguing with the Free Palestine table. One of the Free Palestine people, a knobby woman with a purple buzz cut, lunged from her chair and came out swinging. Her opponent looked like a frat boy. She struck him several times, trying to scratch his face before he slugged her back, putting her on her ass. The rest of the Free Palestine people screamed, swarmed, pulled cameras. One of them ran inside, no doubt looking for campus police.

Josh knew from experience campus police only showed up after a crime had been committed. Sometimes hours. Sometimes days. Shaking his head, he walked to his car. A white envelope beneath the windshield wiper. He pulled it out and opened it.

FIGHT THE POWER
FIGHT COLONIALISM
SUPPORT INDIGENOUS PEOPLES
RALLY JUNE 15 ON BASCOM HILL
MUSIC BY STICKIN' IT TO THE MAN

• • •

HE CRUSHED IT IN HIS HAND AND TOSSED IT IN A TRASH
can. Discarded fast food wrappers, plastic cups, crum-
pled paper, and flyers circled the trash can on the
concrete. Whoever dropped them wasn't just littering.
They were sending a message to The Man.

Josh stopped at the funeral home. The same receptionist was in.

"Oh, Mr. Pratt. Mr. Bennett isn't in, but he asked
me to give you something if you came by."

Josh sat in the front room. A walnut table held
magazines. *Madison*. *On Wisconsin*. *Sports Illustrated*.
American Funeral Director. *Mortuary Science*.

The receptionist returned holding a brass urn
shaped like Anubis, the ancient Egyptian god of the
afterlife, the brass lid in the shape of a hound. It was
beautifully made, heavy in his hands.

"Thank you."

When he got home, he set it on the fireplace
mantle.

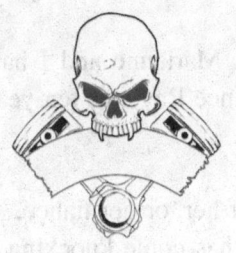

CHAPTER FIFTY-TWO
ENDORSEMENTS AND EVASIONS

DOLAN WAS WELL ENOUGH TO ATTEND THE REHEARSAL dinner. The private room at the Hoity Toity was just big enough to contain the party. Josh, Ray, the McRaneys, Heinz, Doreen, the Lowrys, Professors Martin and Lucrecia Eskew (the McRaneys' friends), Art Baker and his date Maureen, a slim redhead, Steve and his date Donna, a legal secretary, and Bobby Hines with a slim woman named Shannon. Hal sat at one end, Marianne at the other. Josh and Ray sat opposite each other with Marianne between them.

Fleiss took him aside. "Why don't you refer all these interview requests to me? I'll prepare a statement for you."

"That'd be great."

"I'll have something for you shortly."

Dolan sat next to Josh wearing a long-sleeved shirt to conceal his bandages. They were smaller now, and he could move his arms freely.

Two waiters served them. Drinks first. Conviviality

reigned. Twenty minutes in Hal started toasting. He stood, holding a martini.

"Thank you all for coming. Marianne and I have been waiting for this moment since Ray was ten years old."

Laughter.

"We could not be prouder of her, or her fiancé. As most of you know, Hollywood has come knocking at our daughter's door. With any luck, *Kung Fu Musical* will become a film. When we imagined a future husband, we always thought it would be some academic type. A liberal arts professor. Imagine our shock when she showed up with this hoodlum."

Laughter.

"Josh is not the son-in-law we imagined, but he is the son-in-law we hoped for. He's decent, honorable, and respectful. I don't have to tell you that he was single-handedly responsible for forcing a gang of foreign hoodlums out of Milwaukee."

"I had a lot of help, Hal."

"I know, and I don't mean to slight the brave souls who joined you, including our guest Art Baker who filmed the whole thing, which is why the whole world knows what happened. This may prove to be a model for how to persuade other criminal gangs to vacate the premises."

Heinz snorted. Josh was surprised his future father-in-law would say such a thing. Given Hal's politics, Josh had expected him to side with the gangs. Hal's exposure to Josh over the years must have given him a different perspective.

"To Ray and Josh!" Hal said.

"Hear, hear!"

"Bravo!"

Whistling.

Heinz clinked his glass and stood. "I'm Heinz Calloway. I was a police detective in Madison for twenty years. Were it not for the groom, my daughter would be enslaved to a monstrous cult or dead from drugs. Cops usually don't like bikers, but I make an exception for this guy and his lovely bride."

Huzzahs and whistles. And so it went until the appetizers arrived. Josh waited until the waitpersons withdrew before he clinked his glass and stood, all eyes on him.

"Did anyone order the mastodon steaks?"

People squinted, paused forks halfway to their mouths.

"Huh?"

Josh sat. "Okay. Just checking."

"Josh," Ray admonished.

"Just checking! Blackhawk doesn't have them either."

By the time dessert rolled around, Josh was ready to let Dolan drive. The restaurant had moved an upright piano into the room. While waiters took orders, Bobby sat and played "Jack the Bear."

After his third bourbon, Ray leaned over. "Why don't you ask the Lowrys if they'll drive Dolan home."

Josh turned to Lowry. "Dave, would you give Dolan a ride home?"

"Sure."

By nine, the last guest had left. Josh thanked the McRaneys. He and Ray split for the east side.

"I'm gonna walk around the back," Josh said. "Wait for me in the lobby."

"What for?"

"Just in case."

Ray grinned. "Oh, I think they got the message by now!"

Josh reached into the center console and pulled out a collapsed steel club, put it in his pocket.

"Be right back."

Josh circumnavigated the building staying in shadow. He clung to the shrubs delineating the property, leading down to the pier extending into Lake Monona. He stepped out of the shadows to walk out to the end of the pier. He turned and looked back. There was a light on in Ray's apartment. He tried the rear door. Locked. He went around to the front and entered. Ray sat on a bench staring at her phone.

"Did you leave a light on in your unit?"

"I always leave a light on."

"Okay. Let's go up."

They got off on the eighth floor.

"Give me your key," Josh said.

He unlocked the door and pushed it in. He paused in the doorway, club in hand, listening. Sid Vicious appeared and twined between his legs mewing. Josh rushed through the unit. It was clear.

"Come on in!"

Ray shut the door behind her laughing and twirled into his arms. "I knew there was a reason you sent Dolan home alone."

They went into the bedroom and closed the door on Sid.

They lay in each other's arms. "Sure is quiet in here," Josh said.

"Yeah. Too quiet."

Josh reached for his phone and turned it back on. He had fifty-four messages, including Fleiss.

"Check your email."

Josh Pratt is a private person. Sentenced to eighteen years in prison, he met a pastor who helped him turn his life around. Mr. Pratt was pardoned by Governor Knutson, who was made aware of his conversion and the mitigating circumstances of his upbringing. Mr. Pratt undertook the Departure Movement on behalf of elderly American military veterans, as well as ordinary Americans, who felt trapped. Some of these veterans have spoken.

Wayne Garretson: "Josh Pratt is an American hero who undertook, at great risk to himself, to rid our apartment building of foreign gangsters who had terrorized us and held us hostage for more than a year. I urge members of the press to respect his privacy."

Darryl Briggs: "Tren de Aragua drove out tenants who did not have the wherewithal to resist, took over their units, and used them to distribute fentanyl and traffic women, boys, and girls. Repeated requests to the Milwaukee Police Department went ignored. Members of the press should direct their inquiries to the Milwaukee Police Department, the Mayor, and the City Council."

Arthur Baker: "I met Mr. Pratt when he served me a summons. I was at a low point in my career. I am an independent filmmaker.

Plans I had made for my last movie fell through leaving me holding the bag. The few brave souls who had backed that movie had had enough. I don't blame them. They sued me. That's how we met. Mr. Pratt proved himself to be a man of honor. When he asked me to join him in his quest to remove foreign criminals from Milwaukee residences, I gladly agreed. It was my idea to document what happened. I would be happy to answer any questions for the press. You can contact me through my website, ArthurBaker.com."

Ray snatched his phone. "Gimme." She read it over. "Holy shit! This is just gonna make them more eager to talk to you!"

"Steve will hold them at bay."

"Now they'll want a movie starring Jason Statham!"

"I'll leave that to Arthur."

Dolan had called.

"What's up?"

"I scheduled a driver training class at 4 Lakes Driver Training on Tuesday. Can you take me?"

"Can it wait until I get back?"

"I could just ride my bike. An instructor rides with me."

"Okay. What's it cost?"

"Five hundred bucks."

"No prob. I'll write them a check. You sure you're okay to do this?"

"Yeah. My arms are working fine."

"What about a vehicle?"

"They supply the car."

"Can we request a manual transmission?"

"Daaaaaaaaad."

"Just kidding. That'll have to wait until Ray and I get back from Hawaii."

"I'll see you tomorrow."

CHAPTER FIFTY-THREE
THE PUBLICIST

The ceremony was held at the First Unitarian Church across the street from University Hospital. Josh and Dolan arrived at ten, Josh in tux, Dolan in a suit Josh had bought for him at Ross. There were already a dozen cars in the parking lot including the McRaneys' Rivian and Baker's beater. It was a beautiful sunny day. Mabel was waiting on a bench out front. When they arrived, she rose and kissed Dolan chastely on the cheek.

Josh, Dolan and Mabel entered through the narthex and entered the nave. The church was based on triangles. The church rose to a peak over the pulpit, the massive, multi-paned wall looking out on the trees and the hospital across the street. The auditorium was a triangle. Most of the angles were forty-five degrees. The pool was a triangle.

Inside the auditorium, early arrivers stood near the nave chatting. The McRaneys, the Lowrys, and Bobby Hines, arm resting on an upright piano, Shannon wearing a stunning blue dress. The pastor came out, a stout woman wearing a black robe with a blue tippet covered in palm prints. She smiled as Josh and Dolan approached. She took Josh's hand.

"Welcome to the First Unitarian. I'm Pastor Eugenia. Congratulations on your big day!"

"Thank you, Pastor. Is the bride here?"

"She's in my office. She won't appear until the ceremony begins."

The McRaneys and Lowrys approached. They had a lot in common. They all worked for the university. Both McRaneys were professors. Dave Lowry was an economics professor, and Louise was an administrator.

Lowry shook Josh's hand. "I never thought I'd see you in a tux."

"Me either."

"You're looking sharp, Dolan."

"Thank you, sir."

The Calloways arrived, and Steve Fleiss with Donna, wearing black slacks and a black sports coat over a light blue shirt.

"Josh, this is Donna."

"I remember!"

Donna laughed.

And so it went. Bobby pulled him aside.

"I'll play the 'Wedding March.' When the vows are over, I'm going to play 'On Green Dolphin Street.' That okay with you?"

"No bug music."

"I don't play that shit."

"You can cut loose at Blackhawk."

"I asked a couple brothers to sit in. Phil Morris on bass. Randy Cowan on drums. That okay?"

"You bet. Thanks, Bobby."

Idaho arrived wearing a red leather coat and a knit

cap with her date, a statuesque woman in a baggy blue suit named David Byrne. They took seats in the rear. Baker arrived camera in one hand Maureen in a summery blouse and creased slacks in the other. They headed toward Josh, who turned to greet them.

They embraced. "Josh, you know Maureen."

She offered her hand. "Hi. I've heard a lot about you."

"Thanks for coming, Juanita."

Baker hefted the camera. "You want me to record this?"

"Well, I don't, but the McRaneys probably do. Be discreet."

"Always."

Pastor Eugenia noticed Baker filming. She straightened up and assumed a more regal pose. Guests continued to filter in including Garretson and Briggs wearing suits with narrow lapels and skinny ties. Briggs carried a wrapped box. Dave Lowry said softly, "They want you to bring the gifts to Blackhawk."

"Oh. Oh right." Briggs left the church and returned without the gift.

The pastor spoke with Bobby. Bobby sat at the piano and played "All the Things You Are," soft but swinging. People shushed and took their seats. Josh found Dolan talking to Idaho. "We're up, bub."

"Where do I stand?"

"Behind me on the floor. When she asks if I have the ring, that's where you come in."

Dolan patted his jacket pocket to make sure it was still there. Bobby segued into "I've Got You Under My Skin," singing softly in a soulful baritone. Hal appeared from the back with Ray on his arm, stunning in a white dress that fell to mid-thigh. She was, after all, a dancer. Bobby switched to the "Wedding March."

They stood before the pastor. She said the words Josh had heard a thousand times in movies and TV shows. Dolan gave him the ring. He put it on Ray's finger. They recited the vows. They kissed. Ray whirled and threw her bridal bouquet directly at Idaho like Aaron Rogers. Josh half expected Idaho to tuck it under her arm and start knocking people over.

The rest was a blur of handshakes and congratulations until Ray took him by the arm and guided him to his car. Dolan and Mabel were already in the back seat. They drove to the Blackhawk Country Club, a tony golf course in Shorewood overlooking Lake Mendota. A parking spot in front had a sign reading, RESERVED FOR THE HAPPY COUPLE. Josh parked, and they went inside. The place was half full. Everyone from the rehearsal dinner plus some unexpected guests including Phil Bass, Paul, Terry, and Jerell. Some of Ray's theater pals, including several young women. Josh watched Dolan watching them.

The group broke into spontaneous applause when they entered the big room. A bartender in white shirt and black vest poured champagne as fast as he could. Hal and Marianne came up beaming, followed by a waiter carrying a tray filled with champagne glasses. Hal raised his glass.

"A toast!"

Ray handed Josh a glass. He raised it.

"Not only are we gaining a son-in-law, but a grandson-in-law, this young man Dolan, who courageously fought off a murderous home intruder!"

Cheers and applause rang out, except for Dolan who turned red and looked uncomfortable. The bandages had come off but the stitches remained. He wore a long-sleeved white shirt to conceal them.

Bobby cut through the crowd with a chord. Joined by Phil Morris on bass and Randy Cowan on drums, they broke into Horace Silver's "Nica's Dream." That segued into "Jack the Bear." Dave and Louise Lowry hit the dance floor. They looked like pros. Briggs led one of Ray's dancers onto the floor.

Josh had four glasses of champagne and remembered sitting on a sofa listening to the trio play the classics. At some point, Ray grabbed him.

"Let's go back to my place."

"I can't drive."

"I called an Uber."

"What about Dolan?"

"The Lowrys will take him home. You can leave your car here."

He let her lead him out front where some kind of electric car was waiting. He could tell it was electric by the smooth plastic grill. It whisked them silently across town. It was eleven when they stumbled into her condo. She led him to the sofa.

"Wait here."

That's the last thing he remembered until he woke in the morning still on the sofa, covered with a blanket. She'd somehow taken off his pants. His wallet and phone lay on the end table. He'd turned the phone off at noon yesterday. He turned it back on. He had thirteen phone calls, two from Katy Varner. He had thirty-three emails, some from major networks. It was ten thirty. The smell of coffee lured him to get up. He looked around for his pants. Instead of the tuxedo pants he'd worn, he found a pair of his jeans freshly laundered. He put them on and went into the kitchen where Ray sat at the table looking at her laptop.

"Sleeping Beauty!" she exclaimed.

"Sorry, babe. I'll make it up to you."

"I know you will. I was just watching Art's video. It's hilarious."

"Uh oh."

"Not you. My folks dancing. Two friends doing the limbo."

"What's the limbo?"

She gave him a funny look. "Are you kidding me? How low can you go."

"Huh?"

"Never mind. You need coffee."

She got up and fixed him a cup.

"What do I do about all these people howling for interviews?"

Ray flopped on the sofa. "You need a publicist."

"What the fuck. I just want to be left alone."

"I'll be your publicist."

"What does a publicist do?"

"I'll deal with all these calls. I'll explain that you're a very private person who just wants to be left alone and that you acted because it was the right thing to do. You don't intend to make a habit of it, but it does provide a road map for other beleaguered communities who may be suffering from a police staffing shortage."

"That's fuckin' bril. You just come up with that off the top of your head?"

"What can I say? I'm a genius. I'll prepare a statement for you."

"I knew there was a reason I married you."

CHAPTER FIFTY-FOUR
A TREE FOR FIG

DAVE LOWRY DROVE THEM TO THE AIRPORT. THEY went to Hawaii. Josh rented a Harley. They rode all over the Big Island, saw the lava fields, the rain forests, and the beach. A week later they returned. Dolan was working at UbreakIfix. They took an Uber to Josh's house. Josh's car was in the garage. Dolan had received his learner's permit and driven it home. The interior was immaculate. The lawn had been mowed. They drove to Woodman's and got steaks, beer, liquor, and broccoli.

When Dolan hadn't shown by five, Josh called him. "Hey, we're home! We cooked dinner!"

"Dad, I thought I'd clear out for the night and give you some space."

"Don't be silly. We're cooking dinner. Where are you?"

"I'm at Mabel's place. Her folks are in Chicago."

Josh almost asked him what he was doing at Mabel's place.

"You sure about this?"

"Yes."

"You being careful?"

"Super careful, Dad. I'll see you tomorrow."

"Okay. I'm not in any position to give advice."

"Yes, you are. I just don't need any advice on this."

"Okay."

He hung up. Ray looked at him quizzically. "What's going on?"

"He's staying at Mabel's place. Her folks are in Chicago."

"Ooooh."

"Yeah."

"Oh, don't worry about it. He's not doing anything you haven't done."

"Yeah. And he's the result."

"I have faith in that kid. He seems a lot smarter than anyone else his age I've met."

"He did say that if this were the eighteenth century, he'd be married with four kids working a plot of land."

When Josh entered his bedroom there was a wrapped box on the bed. He sat, slit it open with his pocketknife, and looked inside. Two books. *Finding Fish* and the *US Constitution* from US Comics.

Ray came in. "What's that?"

Josh held the books up. "They're from Dolan."

Ray took the books. She held up *Finding Fish*. "I've heard of this one."

"What about the other one?"

"I think I've heard of that too. May I borrow it?"

"Yeah. I'll read Antwone, and then we'll swap."

Wednesday morning, Josh woke to the smell of coffee and the voice of Ray talking in the living room. He pulled on a pair of pants and walked out. She looked up from her phone.

"He's up. I'll ask him."

She held the phone on her thigh. "Melvin Hyman wants to know if we can fly out to Los Angeles on Monday and stay for two days."

"What about the Aardvark?"

"We're not planning on opening until September. The Aardvark can wait."

"I guess. This is the guy who wants to film my life story?"

"That's right."

Josh held out his hand. "Let me talk to him."

Ray handed him the phone.

"Sir, this is Josh Pratt."

"Mr. Pratt. It's an honor. As Ray may have told you, we're interested in adapting her *Kung Fu Musical* into a movie. Now, of course, the entire country is aware of who you are. We'd just like to meet you and learn more about what brought you to your amazing feat. Getting a gang of hoodlums to voluntarily leave the building."

"Sir, I will accompany my wife, but I'm a very private person. I have never sought publicity, and I don't know. But I'm willing to hear what you have to say."

"Excellent."

"Here's Ray." He handed her the phone, went into the kitchen and poured himself coffee. He went out on the back deck. Fig's bowl still had water in it. It was a void Ray couldn't fill, nor should she. A woman was not a dog. Ray came out.

"I'm inviting Dolan and Mabel for dinner."

"Yes. Let's meet her."

Ray called Dolan. He was at UbreakIfix. Mabel

would meet him at the shop, and John would drive them home, with Dolan's bike in the back of the van.

Ray put a hand on Josh's shoulder. "What should I get?"

"Steak. Salad. Taters."

"Don't you ever get sick of steak?"

"No! Why would I? We haven't had steak in a week! I ate fish!"

"Anything else?"

"Yeah. Get some nuts. Almonds, cashews, pistachios. And a six-pack of Capital Pale Ale."

"I'm off."

Josh went into the house, grabbed the Antwone Fisher book, and went back out on the deck. By the time Ray returned, he'd read eighty pages. Antwone Fisher had endured a hellish childhood. Now he was a screenwriter in Hollywood. He had a compelling narrative voice. He wrote his story in the first person without affectation. It occurred to Josh that he too had an interesting life. Maybe he'd get AI to write his story. It reminded him of an old joke. A man walks up to an author.

"I have a great idea for a novel. I tell you, you write it, and we'll split the profits."

Ray came out. "What are you smiling about?"

"I was just thinking of getting artificial intelligence to write my life story."

"And how would they know your life story?"

"Well, I'd tell it to them."

"Why not just write it yourself?"

"I can't write."

"How do you know until you try?" She picked up the book. "Has this inspired you?"

"You might say that. I see why Dolan likes it. It's inspirational. My life too is inspirational."

"Well, you think about that. When we get to Hollywood, you can ask Mel."

"Who's Mel?"

"DUH! The producer we're meeting!"

"Right, right. Maybe I'll start making notes."

"I think that would be an excellent use of your time. Are you gonna grill these steaks?"

"Yes I am."

"Okay. I'll bake the potatoes and make the salad. You want to eat outside?"

Josh looked at the grass where Fig had died. It was still stained. "Let's eat inside."

Josh scraped the grill and put in the charcoal. He preferred charcoal to gas for the flavor. Ray had picked up two New York strips, total weight two pounds. He would wait until Dolan arrived to light the grill. They could sit on the deck and have a drink. He'd face the house. A light breeze held the mosquitoes to a minimum. He thought about offering Dolan and Mabel a drink. Josh had been drinking since he was fifteen. He decided against it. Just because he had done it didn't mean it was right for Dolan. Josh remembered wild drinking. Bad decisions, broken glass, hangovers.

He went into the kitchen. "Should I offer them beer?"

"Well, he's almost eighteen. One beer."

"How old were you when you started drinking?"

She smiled, hands on hips. "Sixteen."

"Should I offer her a beer?"

"What's good for the goose is good for the gander."

"Yes then?"

"One beer. Got any lite?"

"Hah!"

"That's what I thought."

Josh heard a vehicle pull into the driveway, slamming doors. He went out front. John was handing Dolan the bicycle.

"John, want to stay for dinner?"

"Some other time. Kathy's got fans."

"Thanks for giving these two a ride."

"Anytime."

Josh watched John back onto the road and head back to town. Mabel was radiant in a yellow sundress, no makeup. Natural red hair. No nose ring or tongue piercing. Dolan was a lucky boy.

"Let's go out back."

They sat on the deck. Josh had covered the spot where Fig had died with a tarp. He would plant a tree there. "Okay, you guys may have a beer. Would you like a beer?"

"Sure," Dolan said.

"I'll try one," Mabel said.

"Is this your first beer?"

"It's my first alcohol."

Ray stood. "I'll get her the three point two. Josh?"

"Bourbon."

Ray went inside. Josh lit the charcoal.

"I'm so sorry about your dog, Mr. Pratt."

"Thank you. You can call me Josh."

They ate the steaks. They drank the beer. Less than a week later, Dolan drove Josh and Ray to the airport.

"You can have Mabel over. Observe all protocols. Don't add to the population. Don't subtract from the population. Don't damage or destroy physical property. Stay out of the hospital, the newspaper, and jail."

"Got it."

Josh reached into his pocket. "Here's a knife." He handed Dolan the Kershaw.

Dolan took it and flipped it open. "Wow."

"Every lad needs a knife. Don't cut anyone."

"Don't worry, sir. I won't."

"Use the deer antler."

CHAPTER FIFTY-FIVE
JASON STATHAM

On Monday, June 30, they landed at the Burbank airport at two p.m. A liveried driver met them with a limousine at the front entrance. He drove them to Château Marmot where they were checked in to one of the private bungalows. Their chauffeur, whose name was Bernard, carried their bags in.

"Mr. Hyman will meet you at the restaurant outside at six p.m."

Ray threw herself down on the bed. "Wow! Hollywood, baby!"

"A festering sinkhole of drug abuse and pedophilia."

"Oh you! Get with it! We're here to have fun. Even if nothing comes of this, it's a free trip to Hollywood! You can't complain about that!"

"Awright. Awright. Imma throw myself in the pool. You with me?"

"I'm with you!"

At that hour, only a tanned couple, European from the cut of their tiny black jibs and George Hamilton tans, lounged by the circular pool. Josh and Ray threw themselves in, laughing and splashing. The tanned couple ordered more drinks.

"You want a drink? The studio's paying," Ray said.

"What studio?"

"Studio Giggly. That's what Mel calls it."

"So, it's Mel now."

"He loves me, baby!"

"I love you."

At six, they walked hand in hand toward the outdoor restaurant. Ray wore a strapless sapphire blue dress, three-inch black heels, and tiny pearl earrings, her hair an auburn mane. Diners surreptitiously stared. *Who is she? Is that Gal Gadot?* Josh wore creased tan khakis, a tan rough weave sports coat and a white shirt open at the collar, a portion of inked dragon tail visible.

Two men rose from a round table beneath the eave. One was a tanned, smiling, fit, fifty-something in a blue sports coat, gold chain around his neck, the other a fat guy with curly black hair wearing amber aviator glasses. The man with the gold chain came around to embrace Ray.

"Ray! I'm so glad to finally meet you!"

"Me too, Mel."

He let go and turned to Josh. "And this is the formidable Mr. Pratt." A warm, all-encompassing handshake. No attempt to establish dominance.

"Pleased to meet you, Mr. Hyman."

"Mel! And this is my associate and co-producer, Randall Bach."

"You have an amazing story," Bach said.

"You don't know the half of it," Ray said.

They sat. A waiter took their drink orders.

"First time to Los Angeles?" Bach said.

"It is for me," Ray said.

"Not me. I was here once before to interview Stefan Prouse."

"Jesus," Mel said. "You have led a colorful life. Why were you interviewing Stefan Prouse?"

"Wes Magnum's girlfriend Melissa hired me to prove that Wes had given her the rights to 'Marissa.'"

The waiter returned with their drinks. Hyman hoisted his martini. "To *Kung Fu Musical*."

They clinked. They drank.

Bach guarded his Manhattan with both hands. "Wasn't he the guy they found decapitated in his mansion?"

"He was," Josh said.

"When did you interview him?"

"The night before."

They stared.

"Holy shit," Bach said. "Did they ever find who did it?"

"No," Josh said, neglecting to mention that he had found the killer.

I shouldn't have answered that question.

Ray put her hand on Josh's arm. "Josh is a very private person. Let's talk about the musical."

"Well, we love it, of course, or you wouldn't be sitting here. It will need some additional work. It's a little short, and it could use a couple more songs. We would love to offer you a contract and bring you out here to work with us while you expand the script and write the songs. Do you have an agent?"

"HAH!"

"What about a lawyer?"

"She has a lawyer," Josh said.

"He's a criminal attorney!"

"Steve knows what he's doing, and he can also recommend an entertainment attorney."

"By all means, have your friend look over the contract. We're completely transparent and above board. Our production company, Ditz, has a solid track record of hits. You've heard of Art Camp, of course."

"Of course."

Hyman looked at Josh. Josh smiled. Ray patted his arm.

"Husband's only seen six movies. *Rebel Without a Cause*, *Easy Rider*, *The Bikeriders*, *Hells Angels on Wheels*, True Grit and *Wild Angels*."

Everyone laughed. While the producers put on the hard sell and showed Ray their talking points, Josh scrolled through his mail. He texted Dolan. He texted Fleiss. He texted Heinz.

"Very good," Hyman said. "We will send you the contract in a few days. Take your time. Have your lawyer look at it. Now let's turn to you, Josh."

Josh looked up. "What?"

"We did a deep dive into your background and could find very little other than court records and a few news stories. A man of your abilities and accomplishments usually has a lengthy resume. You can't hide from the internet. Except you did."

"I have a specialist who scrubs my name from the internet."

"Josh is a very modest, private person."

"What you did in Milwaukee is the stuff of legends. We watched the documentary and agree that it would make a compelling feature film."

"Guys, I really would rather just be left alone."

"The two are not mutually exclusive."

"I'm afraid they are. I'm not a public figure. What if you did it as fiction? You know. 'Based on' and all that shit."

"Not the same. Have you seen *Saving Mr. Banks*?"

"Josh has only seen five movies. *Rebel Without a Cause*…"

"Yes, yes, all those biker movies. Well, this is a biker movie too, in a way. In fact, Jason Statham has already expressed interest."

Josh and Ray laughed.

"Oil roight then!" Ray said.

"Ere's your 'at. Put it on your 'ead," Josh said.

Hyman and Bach laughed.

"He's very popular," Hyman said.

"Money in the bank," Bach said.

"We're prepared to make a very generous offer for the rights to your story," Hyman said.

"As technical adviser, you'd make a lot more," Bach said.

"Before you say no, Josh, let's think about it. What else you got to do?"

"What else indeed?"

The waiter returned. "Have you had an opportunity to look at the menu?"

They ordered. Josh had a cheeseburger.

After dinner Hyman and Bach took them to a jazz club. Jools Holland was playing. It was eleven by the time the limo returned them to the hotel. Josh was jazzed from the club and too buzzed to function. He fell asleep at once.

DOLAN PICKED THEM UP AT THE DANE COUNTY Airport at one p.m. They'd flown nonstop from Orange County. He got out of the car and helped Ray with her luggage. She had three bags. Josh had one.

"Would you like to drive, Pop?"

"You drive."

They headed toward the capitol.

"How was your flight?"

"About what I expected."

Ray swatted him playfully from the back seat. "Oh you! It was wonderful. They wined and dined us and showed us the sights. They're gung-ho on *Kung Fu Musical*! And they want to make a movie about Josh, or at least about the Great Departure."

"Jason Statham is eager to play me."

"Really?"

"Who knows. They spread the bullshit with a spatula. Jason Statham to star in Hamlet."

"Come on, Pop! It's the movies!"

"I thought you didn't like the movies."

"I love the movies. I'd layike to see more."

"Work your way through those biker movies."

They passed the capitol on the left and took Fish Hatchery to the Beltline. Dolan merged smoothly with west-bound traffic. "I got a library card and checked out *The Godfather*, *The Godfather II*, and *Godzilla Minus One*. We watched *The Godfather* last night. It's the greatest movie ever made. I still have the DVD for three more days if you want to watch it."

"Eh."

Ray put her hand on his shoulder. "You've never seen *The Godfather*?"

"Nope."

"Fine. We'll watch it tonight."

"All right. Got any food?"

"Mabel's cooking."

"Is Mabel staying the night?"

"If that's all right with you."

"What about her folks?"

"They're both university professors."

Josh laughed. "Of course! Why doesn't she have a nose ring?"

"She's rebelling. Listen. I'm not going to enlist right away. I'd like to live with you for another few months, see if I can get my own place. Mabel and I will live together, and I'll enlist in the spring."

"How you gonna get a place of your own?"

"John told Computer Doctors about me. I met the owner, Felix, and he wants to hire me full-time. Their office is on Odana near Whitney Way. I can ride my bike."

"You got your learner's permit?"

"Yes sir."

"I'll get you a car."

"Thank you! Can I get a five-liter Mustang?"

"Well let's look around first. Want a manual transmission?"

"No sir. I don't want to have to learn that on my own car."

"Smart boy. We'll look around next week."

"What's Mabel making?" Ray asked.

"Meatloaf. She found a pound of ground buffalo. I hope that's okay."

"My casa is su casa."

They turned onto Ptarmigan Road.

"Dolan, you ought to finish you senior year."

"I will."

"You gonna work a full-time job and go to high school?"

"Pop, it's simple. I don't go out for sports. Felix already told me that I can work after school and on weekends. He wants me to fix things, not deal with customers."

"Don't take on too much."

"Two hundred years ago I'd be married with three kids and a farm."

"I've heard that before."

"Mabel and I are getting married."

"Whoa whoa whoa."

"Oh Josh," Ray clucked. "Two hundred years ago he'd be married with three kids and a farm."

"Yeah, with a life expectancy of thirty-four."

"What are Mabel's plans?"

"She wants to go to veterinary school. Her parents will support her."

"What happens when they find out you and Mabel are living together?"

"Pop, they're college-educated Democrats. If it feels good, do it!"

"Are they okay with you?"

"They love me."

"Do they know about your part in the Great Departure?"

"They know all about it. Her parents may be college-educated Democrats, but they're not stupid. They don't support open borders."

"Good to know!"

"Mabel's got a dog."

"What kind of dog?"

Dolan pulled into Josh's driveway. A fusillade of barks exploded from inside.

"You'll meet him in a minute."

ABOUT THE AUTHOR

Mike Baron is the creator of *Nexus* (with artist Steve Rude) and *Badger*, two of the longest-lasting independent superhero comics.

He has won two Eisners and an Inkpot award and written *The Punisher, Flash, Deadman*, and *Star Wars*, among many other titles. He has also written for *The Boston Phoenix, Boston Globe, Oui, Fusion, Creem, Isthmus, Front Page Mag*, and *Ellery Queen's Mystery Magazine*.

Baron has published several novels that span a variety of topics. They have satanic rock bands, biker zombies, spontaneous human combustion, ghosts, and overall hard-boiled crimes.